PENGUIN BOOKS

YALPANAM

Shivani Sivagurunathan has been writing and publishing fiction and poetry for twenty years. Her writing has always been grounded in the Malaysian context and supported by a metaphysical foundation—it combines the local and concrete with the universal and abstract, reminiscent of the South American magical realist writers like Gabriel García Márquez and Mario Vargas Llosa.

In her first book *Wildlife on Coal Island* she created a fictional island as a means to explore the Malaysian context in ways that a non-fiction setting could not. The Indian writer Tabish Khair described the book as 'R.K. Narayan's Malgudi, turned into an island, meets Rudyard Kipling's *Jungle Book* in this highly readable collection of stories by a new and distinctive voice from Malaysia.' It was republished by Harper Collins India in 2012.

Her short stories and poems have appeared in numerous international journals and magazines including *Cha: An Asian Literary Magazine*, *Agenda*, *Construction Literary Magazine* and many others.

Yalpanam

A Novel

Shivani Sivagurunathan

PENGUIN BOOKS
An imprint of Penguin Random House

PENGUIN BOOKS

USA | Canada | UK | Ireland | Australia
New Zealand | India | South Africa | China | Southeast Asia

Penguin Books is part of the Penguin Random House group of companies whose addresses can be found at global.penguinrandomhouse.com

Published by Penguin Random House SEA Pte Ltd
9, Changi South Street 3, Level 08-01,
Singapore 486361

First published in Penguin Books by Penguin Random House SEA 2021

10 9 8 7 6 5 4

ISBN 9789814914116

Typeset in Adobe Caslon Pro by Manipal Technologies Limited, Manipal
Printed at Replika Press Pvt. Ltd, India

www.penguin.sg

To Achi, whose spirit guided the writing of this book.
To Maa Saraswathi, without whom this book
could not have been written.

1

Yalpanam, an old colonial affair, sits on the hill and sighs quietly within its walls, standing aloof, a vague member of a neighbourhood named after angels rumoured to have fled following years of neglect. The long, slow sighs rise and fall like waves soaring and gently passing away on the shore. Day after day, peaking at night, the house sighs to its oceanic beat. But for the house, and for the last remaining person in it, the actual sea—a part of the Straits of Malacca—is mere memory. Before the burgeoning of concrete, middle-class bungalows, the pale blue sea, turquoise in the maddening midday sun, could be seen from the garden of the house; not that the old lady (ancient, by contemporary standards, biblical) ever really looked up from her soil-caked hoe or plastic watering cans. The sea was always there, somewhere in the distance, water, waves, salt, over *there*. The sea coolly crashed on the crab-studded beach, unseen, unheard by her, permanently blocked by mustard-yellow, lime-green, turmeric-orange, whitewashed square blocks, plaster of Paris Roman pillars, and further down below, closest to the sea, the brand new rectangular body of the island's first mall. But the old lady wasn't looking, anyway. Her eyes had adapted to regarding the miniscule: earthworms and grit, pebbles and seeds, ants journeying through soil, lizard shit stuck between the rotting planks of her veranda.

Heard on one of those deadly still, full-black nights, when there is little indication that this island is hemmed in by the sea and its repertoire of breeze and wave-break, the sighs of the house sound like they originate from an ancient, ailing ghost. Low, long, and drawn out, as if from an unnameable core of an old, old heart and for the tragic-minded, eternal, carrying a flow of ineffable, weighted breath. Cool breath. Welcomed by the furred and feathered on hot, syrupy nights, it floats through the thick green windows of the house and into the little bodies of sunbirds that flit from pillar to pillar on the wooden veranda. Over time, a dim violet sheen has formed around the house, an auric light visible to animals, to the depressed, to the innocent, to the gifted. A ghostly sphere, it lures the birds again and again who are compelled by the light to be in the light; a light that is decades old but still new for the birds—time works differently for them. During the day, they see the orb's colour deepening, hints of gold within flecks of purple and blue. At night, the violet gleam morphs into an inky midnight-blue and when the moon glows bright enough to shed its silver beams on the vegetable garden that pulsates and flickers before the veranda, the globe of dark light leaks into the house through gaps beneath doors and holes formed over long years of decay, from the gnawing of insects and the comings and goings of people whose footsteps no longer give the house its voice. Deep in the night, when its sole inhabitant is asleep, the walls sigh their loudest, the floors creak, and a soft breeze of sighs blows in loose circles through the front hall, down the corridors, into the empty rooms.

There are yet shadows in this house and the ground on which the house stands that pine for rest. Between the shadows and the earth, the sighs heave, collapse into emptiness and rise—perpetual, patient, as constant as the lamentations of the restless dead.

When the house was first built, one hundred and thirty-eight years ago, nobody on the island thought much of it. It was just another establishment erected by a British planter among other establishments erected by British men who sought some semblance of home, hopelessly they soon learned, in a land that is a cornucopia of promiscuity: scorpions basking in the late afternoon light on the spine of Boswell's *Life of Johnson*, as one early inhabitant of the house discovered on his return from a jungle-clearing expedition; Indian coolies muttering Tamil-Chinese curses beneath their breath, the adopted half of those hybrid pejoratives picked up from opium dens and fish markets, a poignant outrage against their shared British masters; iguanas resting with wild dogs, perfectly at peace, in the shade of rain-trees. The man who built this house, under the circumstances in which the British found themselves, understandably longed for the dark silence of cathedrals, found also in his parish church back home. Divine darkness, so deeply quiet at dawn that the quiet turned into sound, 'divine darkness,' he used to say, 'spiced with the fragrance of wax and flame.' He yearned for stained glass windows that, as a boy, had enthralled him with their sweeps of colour and pictures of saints and angels and Jesus glowing against the dull winter light. Later, when talking to his lover about churches and windows, he explained, 'It is like being inside the soft glow of coloured light and knowing that the light has come from your own heart. That, my dear, is what love is. At its root, that is love.'

He added a single room on the topmost floor of the house with a stained glass window small enough to keep the room darker than the rest of the house, for in the exacting island sun, too exaggerated to be beautiful, he said, too glaring to be illuminating, the mystery that resides in darkened corners, in easily missed nooks, in the wholeness of darkness itself, is lost. To signal its difference from the rest of the house, a narrow spiral staircase, painted delphinium blue, snaked up to the smooth mahogany door of the room (causing several mild mishaps over the years), and completed the atmosphere of enigma and 'sacred spice' he believed was necessary in a place like Coal Island. When people still moved in and out of the room, eyes would land on the stained glass crimson roses that lined the window, the cream-coloured feet above it, the radiant violet-blue dress, tied at the waist with golden string, the benign, smiling face of the Virgin Mary looking down, arms outstretched, calling forth, ready to embrace, and one or two pairs of eyes would start tearing, other eyes would brighten or lower. Epiphany, in some form, was inevitable.

But, aside from this window, the house looked like any other colonial house. The most palpable difference—discounting its globe of light, its sighs, the whispering voices that sometimes sweep past the gable—is that unlike other colonial houses, the house is still here, luckily, magically, exempt from the local council's bulldozing agenda, in line with its motto: what's past is past; the future is here; modernize!

Tucked away on a slight hill, a small jungle behind it, sighing privately in its spectral sphere, the house stands apart from the rest of Coal Island.

On a morning overcast with dark amethyst clouds, a slim elegant plaque, copper and glistening, bearing the name "Eden's Eden", was hammered onto the front pillar of the house. A hyperbolic title, yes, but the man who designed the house, as is perhaps already evident, was a romantic, and romantics are given to exaggeration as well as, of course, to hypersensitivity and idealism. The Eden within Eden, he thought. An ultimate Eden, paradise regained, and secured in a protective Edenic layer, against tropical turmoil and the hotchpotch of island-elements—both human and otherwise. Interestingly, paradoxically, in its life as "Eden's Eden", the house saw and, for the most part, welcomed a significant range of visitors, and any neutral observer would say that the house became a microcosm of the island's multifariousness. Romantics tend to have open vulnerable hearts and Richard Miller, deeply open, deeply vulnerable, loved the stream of calling colonials and native clerks and menial workers who also took him up on his offers of 'an evening on the veranda'.

For many years, people simply called the house Eden, a term he eventually conceded to, until a new, bigger sign replaced the old one and the house became known as Yalpanam. By that point, Richard Miller was long dead and he, more than likely, approved of the name since the dead are vocal about their objections, and no ghostly voice was heard in connection to Yalpanam.

In its incarnation as Yalpanam, the house became very silent, as silent as an empty cathedral but without the romance of divine darkness, and it grew used to the buzzing of flies, to the soft tapping of spiders' legs, to the chit-chitting of lizards, and to the gently thumping feet of the woman who lived there. She spent the minutes, hours, days, years, decades, letting the house be, easily forgetting the Eden she'd once known. She swept its floors when her sneezing worsened and wiped surfaces with a sarong scrap only when she could draw stick-people on the windowpanes and on the sole remaining table in the house positioned between two ragged wicker chairs in the front hall. She never laid a finger on the cobwebs, on the trails of ants, or on the generations of rats that lived underneath a rotting wooden panel in the kitchen. Idealists—yes, romantics like her predecessor—may have labelled her a pacifist, a pantheist, a lover of all life. But the truth, known by the walls and the insects, and deep, very deep within, by her own self, was that she was lazy. What lies beneath that laziness—well, that is a much deeper thing, more evasive, hardly ever seen. She allowed the holes and cracks in the walls and windows and floor planks to be as they were, pristine in their decline, undisturbed by human will, surrendered to the life force of the universe. No one watched, and by the time the house began its sighing—sometime in the middle of the twentieth century—she was already older than she should have been, older than the sum total of the years the British had spent on the island, older than the jacaranda tree opposite the house that had witnessed groups of Dutchmen surveying the land, and as she grew in age and in solitude, she could forget mere walls and windows and ceilings and furniture and crockery—she'd lived too long to wander among objects, to wonder about them.

Not only objects—there was the past too. Complex, as all pasts are, but more so for her, close to two centuries old and, on occasion, she indulged in a surreptitious suspicion of her deathlessness, her 'I' immortal, a placeless, timeless mass of something, she used to say aloud to the walls. So many selves had lived within her, forgotten, never truly seen before they seemingly passed away into the placeless, timeless mass of something. In recent times, however, the most ordinary of human worries has crept in. Mortality, rather than immortality. Fittingly so, even though her substance and stature had, in the past, been placed in a category not far off from the gods. Sibyl, some called her; Banyan Woman also, as she sat peering at the sky with eyes fashioned in mysticism, at the land, at the many men, hopeless, frightened, despondent, before her. But that was so long ago. At least three generations of islanders had been birthed since then. What was there to remember? Why remember? What's past is past; the future is here. It is much simpler with objects. Forgetting them is much simpler; new objects arrive and easefully cancel out the old, and if austerity slowly creeps in, unrealized, unintended, attention is easily diverted, as in the old woman's case, to her thriving vegetable patch.

So, she forgot about the dazzling chandelier that used to hang from the ceiling in the hall and how hundreds of eyes sparkled in its golden orange glow; she forgot about the brass doorknobs and how each one was embossed in the middle with a tropical flower; she forgot about the purple paint like freshly steamed yams that had once pleased the walls of the room where butterflies lived and how ten, twenty, red, yellow, turquoise, black-spotted green wings fluttered against the purple walls and mesmerized hearts; she forgot about the piano in the corner of the hall and how thousands of songs had been played on it and people sang and danced and laughed.

There was no need for Pushpanayagi to remember. Every morning, she sat on a mat in the hall and closed her eyes for hours. Later, she sat in the garden all day. True life was lived with eyes shut, or else outdoors. Hoe in hand, earth between her toes and luxuriant vegetables, fertile, forever surrounding her, she could smile and feel that her obeisance to the departing sun was earned. Soil to sun and sun to soil. The house was where she went to sleep, to chop vegetables, to drink water, to tend to the practicalities of her overlarge and demanding human body. Sometimes, she flipped the pages of the *Ramayana*, the only book in a house that had once nursed a library of books alphabetically arranged on rows and rows of floor-to-ceiling shelves. Mostly, she yawned as she sat in the hall and turned the pages and soon, she gradually waddled her way to her bedroom where she lay on a mat and eventually fell asleep, forgetting also the lace-curtained four-poster bed that, many years ago, had stood like a majestic creature in the centre of the room.

Why would she remember?

She'd walked on this earth for more years than she'd cared to mention. Behind her, no footsteps marked the soil. Behind her, the air absorbed her tears and laughter, her thoughts and memories. Ahead, no brothers, sisters, friends or lovers would whisper her name in their souls. Ahead, no children would continue for her.

Why would she remember?

There was no one to listen to remembrances. She'd stopped talking to the walls and floors decades ago. Now, she simply went on, and she let the house be. When the mild winds blew this way and that through the house and the whispering voices floated between walls, or when shadows coasted down corridors and lurked in the corners of rooms, Pushpanayagi gave no sign of having heard or seen anything. If she was awake when such forces moved through the house, she chewed her meal of vegetables in silence and gazed at the bowl on her lap through half-closed eyes.

The twentieth century came and went and the twenty-first century took over and Pushpanayagi lived on, harvesting vegetables and fruits, bathing from the well behind the house, gliding through inner waves of peace, alone. From time to time, she sits in the garden and tells her vegetables of the deathless realm, of her never ending life, of the bitter loneliness of living forever, and when she says, 'How long must I wait to be released?', the doors of the house rattle and the shadows within stir. But mostly, when she has finished her work in the garden, she sits on the earth and gazes at the sky, at ants crawling through the grass, at birds swooping high and low, at clouds forming and breaking and at cats or dogs sauntering past the gate. When dusk descends, she thanks the Universe and slowly makes her way into the house. Preparing for her return, the house stops sighing and expands its walls, warms the air, welcomes the last rays of the orange sun into its courtyard and calls out to the birds that gather in small flocks in the open-air centre of the house. As darkness slithers in and clambers through nooks and gaps, the house sighs and the slow oceanic rhythm seeps back in. Pushpanayagi switches off the lights, lies down on a mat and closes her eyes.

*

'In KL, there'll be none of this bullshit,' Maxim muttered to herself, waving a fly away. Or maybe it was some other insect; who would know in this heat! Everything felt the same. Icky, sticky, burning, bothering, noon attack of the sun. She stepped back from the gate. "NO.42" shone in gold against the brown plate grilled above the gate-bell. Mother's house . . . no, it was her own house too. Still. Her fingers twitched inside her shorts pockets. No, for the hundredth time, the house keys were not in there. Nowhere inside her backpack. Not in the back pocket of her shorts. Not in her tiny sling bag that only ever had her mobile phone anyway. That's it. That's *it*. One, two, three, and Mother will emerge out of her precious palace and start the ear-rape. Heart-rape, she'd thought at college today.

She sighed, turned around and walked toward the giant clump of wild, unbending yellow bamboo a few steps away, on the public land next to NO.42's fence. *Good energy bamboo! Good energy bamboo! Why want to cut?* But all the other wild stuff, like the Flame tree and the aloe vera and the papaya tree, Mother had got Muthu to chop down.

She sighed again and walked further along past the bamboo clump to the edge of the street where the jet-black road, smelling of very dark coffee and tar, sloped up in a straight incline towards Yalpanam. The house was partially hidden by the blackish green leaves from a tree Uncle Colonel had planted without permission, one of those dense tropical trees she didn't know the name of. It never fruited, had no flowers, and according to Kak Isma, a spirit called Nunu lived inside its trunk, which made sense since the way the tree's branches curved away from its roots and up towards the old lady's house, it looked like it wanted to grow in Yalpanam. Trees like that knew where to go to belong, like with like, weird and weirder. The triangular tip of the house, it was called something, the gable, peeked above the foliage. A black thing stood there, possibly a crow. A *crow.* Of course, a crow. She was a witch. An ancient witch, everyone said, and crows loved witches. Not that she'd ever seen her. The old witch was a legend, a myth, a cuckoo priestess of the underworld. Coal Island underworld . . . if ever . . . full of white-whiskered parrots, one-eyed cats, all the cobras, and Mother.

The midday light soaked through everything on the street. The roofs glittered brown and red, brown and red. The glare bouncing off Uncle Colonel's aluminium roof created big red spots each time she blinked. Quickly, she looked away from it and back at the jet-black road leading up to Yalpanam, newly tarred by Daddy's Party, Daddy's buttering-up Party. Elections coming. Make people smile. She spat on the ground, glanced back at Uncle Colonel's roof and blinked away the red spots.

Sweat dripped down her neck. She swung her backpack forward and jerked the zip open. *Using old things like poor people! Zip already break still want to use!* She snatched a brochure she'd picked up at the Uni fair at college that day, slung the bag back over her shoulder, unzipped, and began fanning herself. She could just ring the doorbell instead of standing around like a daytime cockroach waiting to be smacked with a slipper, so available under the midday sun, the perfect target for people like her mother and Mrs Teng who was probably already pressing her moonface against her front gate, trying to see what-what was happening to Little Girl Maxim, stranded near the monsoon drain outside her own house.

Something softly knocked on the ground behind. Tick-tock, tick-tock, loud, louder, loudest, close, closer, closest. The tick-tocking stopped. She turned around. Mother, in hot pink sweats, jacket included, stood inches away to her left, pointing a long metal walking stick at her. On her head, pushing her perm down, a hot pink visor looked like a child's make-believe crown. She big-walked her way up, hips swaying like the shemales in town, face crumpled, the small, thin mouth tightened, the lower earlobes already bright red, peeking out from tufts of blonde highlights. 'Oi! Doing what in the hot sun?' Mother attempted to whisper. But her voice was enough to send some birds on the ground flying.

'I left—'

'Ya, I know what you do. Forever forget this, forget that. Kak Isma found your key on the floor near the dustbin. Where your head, ah?'

'I'm sorry, Mummy,' she said, looking at the bamboo clump behind Mother. *Ear-rape*. One, two . . .

'Eighteen years already but still behave like baby! Who go and stand in hot sun? You want become black like Indian, ah? Shame only! You got hear about responsibility, ah? You know the problem or not? We spoil, spoil, spoil you until no good already.'

She tapped Maxim's shoulder with the metal stick. The Sign that it was time to go back into the house, away from The Glare. Neighbours could see them. Grabbing her hand, Mother hurried back into their compound, the metal stick tock-ticking as the hips swayed. Mother clicked the auto gates shut, pulled her toward the front door and stared at her with beady, birdy eyes, waiting for a reaction.

'Ya, that's why. Cannot speak now. Why? Because you know Mummy is right. Forever dreaming about this thing, that thing.' She swung the metal cane and landed it at Maxim's feet. 'I have too many thing to do,' she continued, 'why I have to worry about you? Hah!' She snorted and shook her head. 'I got my walking club now but you see you make me late.'

The black and white porch tiles twinkled, scrubbed like mad by Kak Isma yesterday, Mother (green-tattooed eyebrows raised and stiff) watching by the door, screaming, 'harder, harder', until Kak Isma went for it, putting all her hatred into the sponge.

'Dumb already isssit? Wait and see. Your Daddy got something big to tell you! But he going to be late. Your Daddy having some problem now with the Party. Seem like Hamzah trying to bring him down in the next election. You think somebody your friend and then . . .'

Mother looked up at the porch ceiling, probably scanning for dust. The silence was nice. Two or three birds sang.

'May I go inside please?'

Wordlessly, Mother stepped away from the front door, eyes still glued to the ceiling. She waved the metal wand in the air and began rambling on about useless girls and the Internet which she did when she felt guilty, no doubt, about dreaming of dirt when, really, she should have been obsessing about her daughter's problems.

She sped towards the half-open front door, quietly kicked it open and without bothering to shut it, ran—almost leapt—up the stairs to her bedroom. She panted as she hurriedly twisted the doorknob, let herself in, and locked the door behind her. Her panting turned into sighs of relief. She chucked her backpack on the floor and crashed into a beanbag. She opened her legs wide, finally resting her back, erect for too long. She gazed at the brochure she'd used earlier to fan herself. Mother hadn't even asked what it was, clutched in her hand the whole time. Universiti Malaya in KL offered a three-year Environmental Science Undergrad programme. She ran her fingers across the smooth cool surface of the brochure and sighed.

Through the window, up on the hill, the old lady's underworld house stood like a location for a movie. A Thing. Sturdy. The thin frame of its red roof, the not quite-white that made up its outer walls, visible at this hour but at night the whole house vanished into jet black darkness. The black thing, the crow, was still perched on the gable. But that was all. Nothing else seemed alive in the old lady's house. The darkish non-automated gates were shut as per usual and no one came out or went in, except on Tuesdays and Thursdays when the Malay guy, the guy who sold vegetables at Market Square, let himself in and reappeared, sometimes hours later, with two or three pink plastic bags loaded with stuff. Then he putted down on his motorbike, on the jet black road close enough to NO.42 for her to see him better, one golden brown arm hanging by the side of his body, the other loosely clutching the steering handle, cigarette hanging out of his mouth like a gangster, too handsome to be a vegetable seller.

She looked away from the window. Yalpanam had always been there, would always be there, day after day, a perennial building with murky, drooping eyes that watched her life move in meandering snail steps. She glanced at the brochure. Thick black words ran across the pages; in between chunks of passages, photographs of young multiracial people with Colgate smiles, some fake-reading books, so psyched to be filling their heads with knowledge.

The main point was this: it took approximately two hours and forty-five minutes to get from the Coal Island jetty to the twin towers in KL, the only place her parents had taken her to in KL, twice, because relatives from Hong Kong were visiting. Even the poorer kids at college had gone to KL umpteenth—*for the umpteenth time, get the crane driver etc. etc.,* as Daddy would say—umpteenth times more than she had. There's a buzz, there's a buzz, they kept saying, so pleased with themselves that she, the richest (but, in their heads probably the poorest) kid had never been to Central Market, Petaling Street, Little India, the Planetarium, Merdeka Square. They screeched, laughing like Pontianaks, that she'd been to England, Greece, Turkey, Germany, America, Canada, Japan, but didn't know her own backyard. KL had tonnes of lok-lok trucks, eighty not ten billboards advertising not refrigerators but movies, Chris Hemsworth in your face, malls *everywhere*, Baskin Robbins ice-cream and actual cinemas, not an old town hall converted by a pork-seller called Uncle Ah Fatt into a 'movie theatre' that showed five-year old action flicks and epic Cantonese dramas under humungous creaking ceiling fans. So what? Paris had everything. Ah, but you had to *fly* there. KL was *here*, a Malaysian's birth-right, they said.

She flung the brochure at a wall. In less than a year, she'd be there, eating every speck of KL, coming home only for Chinese New Year if The Parents insisted.

She fished her phone out of her sling bag hanging off her shoulder and unlocked it. Nothing flashed. No new emails. No new messages. She clicked on FootsyTootsie24's webpage. He was coming at the world, he said, with laser eyes. Why's the sky blue? Thought about the Universe, lately? Is a chair a chair, or only particles our brain *thinks* are a chair?

Below the main blog on the homepage, a new post had been put up, 'Jupiter's Coming, Yo!', published two hours and fifteen minutes ago. Stupendously, incredibly, Jupiter was arriving in our skies. Footsy wanted to celebrate. A competition. 2000 words on uncertainty, the miraculous. Winner gets 'cool stuff.' At the bottom of the post, Stephen Hawking's words: '*THE UNIVERSE DOES NOT BEHAVE ACCORDING TO OUR PRE-CONCEIVED IDEAS. IT CONTINUES TO SURPRISE US.*'

She stretched her back and sank deeper into the beanbag. Her fingers loosened, the phone slowly slipping out of her grip. She let it fall gently onto the carpet and closed her eyes. On the bus home, she'd read a few pages of *A Brief History of Time*. Hawking insisted that the universe was not held up by a stack of tortoises. He asked questions, pushed people to think about Origins, what was before what is. Footsy didn't mention the tortoises. Green-shelled creatures with sleepy eyes holding up the cosmos. Tortoises holding up the world, the *cosmos*. Pretty like Footsy. He sounded pretty. Blonde with blue eyes, probably. Wrote like someone with hard muscular arms, a surfer, a surfer-singer, fit and sensitive. One day, maybe, she'd write to him and tell him that Hawking was Special, that he and Footsy both, Hawking-Footsy, did things to her mind. The delayed universe. Who would have thought? Delayed: *Late*. Belated: *After the fact*. The stars that blink every night died millions of years ago. Sunlight is eight minutes late. We're not seeing what we think we're seeing. And Mother dared to talk nonsense about house keys and too much salt in porridge as though people like Hawking-Footsy didn't exist. Mother, too stupid to care about the stars and the planets and the expanding universe.

Where did the universe come from, and where is it going? What is the nature of time? Will it ever come to an end?

No, Mother would never understand. Daddy could, maybe, get why someone would ask such questions. But he was too busy building shop houses and housing areas and now Coal Island's first mall, D'Place, named by his board and *allowed* by him even though he knew it was the stupidest name on the planet. D'Place of what? D'Place where? Anyway, wormholes weren't going to add millions to his millions. D'Place would. Wormholes weren't going to win him the election. His eye-bags would. Wormholes, worm food.

She opened her eyes. A red-eyed blackbird pecked at the window. It stopped tapping and gazed at its reflection on the glass. It twittered madly, flapping its wings, screaming at itself, not knowing that there was nothing to be scared of, it was only its own self flopping around like a poor, sad psycho. She pulled herself up from the beanbag and went to the window.

'Shoo, shoo,' she said, flicking a fingernail on the glass. The bird froze and glared at her finger. It looked cute, tilting its head, trying to figure out what was going on. If birds didn't get scared so easily, she'd open the window and let it come in. Mother would go bonkers. *Wait for your Daddy! He going to deal with you!* Whatever Daddy's news was, they could all go to hell for all she cared. That's all they ever did—scare the living daylights out of everyone they met. The bird pecked at the window again, tick, tick, ticking, then pulling away to gape at itself. If the news was that Daddy was going to pull out of the election and live quietly developing his properties, what had that got to do with her? No, it was something else, something involving her. The bird sang a short staccato song, calling for somebody, another bird: its mother, its father? Had they found out from some island snoop that she'd smoked a cigarette in the girls' toilet? But she'd only had two puffs, three at most, and she'd hated it, it was like drinking traffic fumes, but that didn't matter. The Parents would flip out and lock her up in her room for a week; maybe two weeks? The bird flapped its wings and flew away. She sighed and looked up at the house on the hill. At least the old woman was trapped in her house because she'd *wanted* it like that. No friends, no family, as old as . . . well, no one really knew. She'd always been there, practising her black magic or whatever it was Kak Isma said the old woman did. Part human, part unknown. If children were bad, the old witch would come down the hill. She never did. But at eight every night, when she shut the blinds of her bedroom windows, she saw the light go off at Yalpanam; every night for twelve years, it was the same.

She dragged herself back to the beanbag and dropped into it. It would be hours before Daddy came home. She picked up her phone from the floor, clicked on her Touching Bones page and began scrolling through her friends' latest updates.

*

The damp hoe fell from her grip. Pushpanayagi gasped and patted her chest. 'Not now,' she whispered and reached for the hoe. She lifted it, her back creaking as she rose. Clumps of earth softened with water clung to the hoe's edges. A stream of ants poured out from a crack in the dirt on the hoe. No, death won't come, not like this when gardening without slippers had been going and going for decades, not suddenly like this.

She waited for the ants to reach the tip of the hoe's handle. When they had safely arrived, she blew on them until her breath was too strong and they fell off. She gasped for breath, head spinning, heat rising like big flames in her blood. No, death won't come, not on a morning like this, with two toads sitting under the tomato plant looking so peaceful. Not when the toads– the toads . . . the toads were deep in bliss. No, death cannot come. Their ancestors were good, like them, helping, cleaning the well with their urine. One or two even came into the house and slept on the mat.

She squeezed the hoe, slowly lowered her body, and sat on the dirt. Never like this, the wheezing, the coughing, the big fire inside the body. In her head, her death had been different, had to be. Death was supposed to be one final slip into nothingness. Before it came, behind her eyes, in the blackness, she'd see the thatched roof hut in her mother's village. Above the hut, clouds of mist and in front, grass glowing with cool morning dew and frogs croaking by the well. Then slowly, slowly, she'd sink deeper into the picture until breath left the body and the hut disappeared.

She stroked her burning neck. Why was it so terrible now? She pressed her palm against the earth and closed her eyes. Om Shanti, Shanti, Shanti, Om. In peace, I come. Yalpanam, old warm land of Mother, Yalpanam, dark sea of Shakti's womb.

Her body was failing. All of a sudden. Almost two centuries and nothing. Never had a doctor touched her body; never had a cough disturbed her throat; never had she needed anything from anyone. And now, her body screaming, sore, melting into the end, she wanted to wail for the boy. He would come, he should come. She opened her eyes. Her heart beat hard and fast, her flesh slowly turning yellow. Would she go like this, against the current? To have lived so long and still fight the waves; after years of silence, of peace, of sitting inside God's heart and still clutching to the earth. What was wrong with her?

She lay flat on the ground, the hoe beside her.

Something in her had lived, was still here. Lived her life well so well. It brought her to the earth every day, and she kissed the dirt. It opened her mouth and she talked to the plants and vegetables. It moved her arms and she held pumpkins, piles of bright bean-purple brinjals, carrots, sun-coloured tomatoes, rocking them gently, her heart bursting open. It knew when she had to lift worms and place them away from the hoe. When rats stopped in the kitchen and stayed for days, she prayed to Lord Ganesha, asking him what he was trying to tell her by sending his rats down to her house.

She surrendered to the sun. She surrendered to the soil. She surrendered to the insects and to the birds and to the angels. She surrendered to her own silence. She surrendered to It. What more did God want?

In the end, everyone is alone. She sighed and felt the pulse at her neck with a finger. It flickered fast, slowed down, and flickered fast again.

Ok, let death come. If Death wanted to come and take everything, let it come! If it thought she was frightened, it could think again. She was the daughter of Ma Kali.

Kali kills Death. Kali is Darkness itself.

She placed a hand on her chest and took a deep breath. Fire scorched her blood. A tear rolled down her cheek.

Again and again, the Universe had told her, 'Deeper than me and you is an untouched spot that gives birth to everything, including me and you. It does not know death.' Year after year, she looked for the spot until one day, under the mango tree in the garden, she found it. The unbroken spot warm with peace and even when the mango fell on her head, the spot did not feel it.

She closed her eyes. Ee oh. Oh oh. Ee oh. Oh oh. Mynah bird, Mynahkutty. The wind rustled leaves. She pushed past the pain and pulsations of her body and with all the life force she had, whispered, 'Rama, Rama, take me home. Take me to the unborn spot before death comes.' She dropped into Lord Rama's name, fell deep into the word. A quiet blackness washed over her and a slow hum quivered deep within.

'What is death anyway?' a voice said.

'Even in the last second before death, there is still life,' another voice said.

She gradually rose and brushed the dirt and small stones off her elbows and arms. A new energy throbbed within. She hobbled past her vegetables and stopped by the gate of her house. The thin, grey, tail-less dog that sometimes came to see her limped past. It paused by the gates and stared at her. Yellow phlegm-like mucus filled the corners of its sad, glistening eyes; its fur damp, its ears wilted. It whined at her, asking, whether for food or for something else she didn't know. Unholy dog. Scars, scratches, wounds, glaring at her. It was too close to the earth, struggling without a bark, bones poking out, ready to slip into a hole and lie there. Only its bones could say that it had also had a life, once upon a time. A tear rolled down her cheek. She went to the mango tree, plucked a fruit, and waddled towards the front gate. 'Bless you, bless you, my baby dog,' she said as she reached out through the bars of the gate and placed the fruit in the dog's mouth.

2

The thing a person uses to move forward and backward—the rocks do not know it; nor the plants and trees; even the animals do not know it. The thing germinates before the person is born, in the cells of their ancestors, and of their ancestors before those ancestors, and so on and so forth. The thing, well, perhaps it would best be referred to as an impulse, yes, the impulse, mostly, they take for granted. It is so embedded in their structure, so much an invisible force, an underground noise heard only by underground things, that it goes unnoticed. Sometimes, others looking deep enough at them will see and hear it. And they themselves may have felt it when they watch a sibling rip a letter into a hundred pieces, or their mother devotedly place beautiful lacquered showpieces on a polished display table in the living room. Something makes the actions happen. Life-force, life-principle, yes, but these are impossible to fathom. There is something else, more visceral, more available in the eyes. A nostalgia, a prophecy.

The glaze in the old lady's eyes, for example. It forms a glittering layer that, if looked at carefully, is filled with uncountable pixels of light, each pixel a unit of time. Like a fly's eye, one may say, but less functional and more a collection—a *coagulation*—of periods of time. Even if mirrors still existed in the house, she would not have seen it. Indeed, when all the other inhabitants of the house had died, and the old lady still kept the heavy oblong mirror in the small room next to the master bedroom (the modest room once before lived in by her when her compulsion was to give others the best, in this case the master bedroom, so as to avoid the guilt of enjoying what was rightfully hers), she would walk past the mirror in hurried steps, hardly ever stopping to glance at her form, let alone at the glaze in her eyes. Perhaps because it was a temptation, a few days after the nation of Malaya was born—and perhaps, this was her symbolic gesture of acknowledging her own birth of sorts—she unhooked the mirror from its place on the wall and abandoned it in the drain outside the house. Perhaps, perhaps: herein lies the thing that moves a person, the old lady of the house, forward and backward.

The trees within the compound and the trees in the jungle behind the house move differently, very differently. The rocks jutting out into the sea down the road form lines in union with the elements. The sea plays in alliance with the moon. The worms, the millipedes, they travel in rhythms always in association—with the soil, with specks of food, with the temperature. Beneath the glaze of the old lady's eyes, communion lives deep, deep beneath. The thing that moves, that impulse—it could be called time—is burrowing its way into her heart and vivifying her fingers, her tongue, her legs in unique ligatures. Today, it is *prestissimo* and fills her body with fear; tomorrow, *adagio*, slow, casual, empty, and the day after, *accelerando*: she is throttled by a time already finished, lost and found again as though it had never really left. It moves, it would seem, on a whim. But, really, how could she see something as dark and as mysterious as the lifeline of the Universe? Behind time, behind bondage is the Universal and universal freedom, like air, and radiating with infinite light.

Time, the shape-shifter, opens its wings.

*

Maxim's left foot tingled and sent showers of stars through her leg. She looked up from her phone, her feet now disappearing from having sat cross-legged for too long, like Indians at the temple, *like Indian so dirty-dirty always sit on floor, eat on banana leaf as though no money buy plate.* She slipped her phone into her shorts pocket, pushed herself up from the beanbag, and made her way to the window. It was almost eight at night and Daddy had not returned.

The dim light of the moon lit up parts of the clouded sky. Folds of ice-blue cloud bled into patches of twilight blue sky. No stars out, only moonlight and birds squawking after the azan at dusk. She'd left the window open, thinking the dumb bird would take her invitation to a brand-new life but it hadn't.

She stuck her head out of the window. A warm, rose-scented breeze floated past. On the tiny and only patch of grass, Muthu's gardening shears glinted in its wheelbarrow. Mother's rose bed had been pruned and spruced up, just in time for the Ladies' Club meeting tomorrow which meant that she'd have to plug in her headphones, listen to a new podcast, maybe the one on Kismet that Footsy had recommended last week, and block everything out, all the screeching and howling from the pack of manicured *ladies*.

She shut the window and waited for the lights to go off at Yalpanam. Down below, in the wet kitchen, pots and pans clinked and clanked. It was already eight, it felt like eight anyway, with the pots and pans and Mother's silence brought on by 'Heaven's Pleasure' blaring away in the locked TV room. No food after eight, no chocolate, no sweet drinks, only Chinese tea, and eight was when Kak Isma showed her loyalty to Mother's House Rule (among other displays like, once, throwing out all the yellow things in the house because Mother had decided that yellow blocked *chi*), washing everything up, putting it all away until the next day when the pots, the pans, the plates, came out again and the whole ceremony was repeated. Kak Isma, as patient as a snail, as kind as a saint, as foolish as a saintly servant. The maniacal pan-washing and 8 p.m. food ban were small inconveniences, really, compared to the Yellow Fever Period, and the Frog Craze when brass frogs, gold frogs, silver frogs, and even plastic frogs filled the house, flooded the staircase, the rooms, the hall, the kitchen, and made every part look like a cartoon dream. Frogs brought money, that was the logic. But they already *had* money. Still.

She looked up at the hill. Darkness swallowed the old lady's house except for a dull yellow light blinking through the front windows that, at any moment, would disappear. The old lady was never late, as if she'd programmed her bedtime to sync with when Kak Isma turned the tap on to start The Wash. But Kak Isma was already minutes into her nightly grind and Auntie Pushpanayagi must be, well, what did she actually do?

She dragged one of the two stools from under the study table beside the window. She sat on it and stared at Yalpanam's light. Her toes grew cold. Something in her belly darted here and there like a teeny tadpole or anchovy dashing around, trying to settle somewhere. Slowly, her fingers also turned cold. The pulse in her neck throbbed, a feeling of wind rose from her belly up to her throat, and she jerked forward but no puke came, only a humongous burp. The taste of kaya played in her mouth. Her belly filled up with a sharp vinegary slush. The bread with kaya Kak Isma had sneaked up had tasted fine, delicious even, and more than enough. She'd not wanted the full-blown rice, soup, pork and mushroom dinner and Mother had shouted from the kitchen that sickness would come to her, ungrateful child, god give, you must say thank you, thank you, not be rudeness like devil. And now, the curse had come true. Listen to Mother, listen to Mother.

She placed a palm on her belly, its warmth soothing to the touch, suddenly making her body limp and weak. A tear rolled down her cheek, then another fell swiftly, and another until tears streamed down her face, endlessly, and she was sobbing. She covered her mouth with her hands, afraid to scream. She couldn't say why she was crying, had no reason to really, but the more the tears formed and ran, sprinkling her thighs with warm liquid dots, the lighter her belly felt. She wiped her eyes and nose with her T-shirt, blowing lightly into it. She looked up at her bedroom lights reflected on the windowpane. In front of the lights, she saw herself, sitting slouched, gaping like the bird that had gaped at its own reflection. She looked past herself and up at the hill. The lights were still on at the old lady's house.

She yanked her phone out of her pocket and clicked back onto Footsy's website. Of course, he wouldn't want a story about a neighbour's lights not going off at the usual time, but how would she explain what that meant? She blew more snot on to her T-shirt. Her eyes were hot, her sight fuzzy, but her arms and fingers felt strong as if a new pulse or a strange kind of lightning had been dropped into her body by an alien, maybe god if such a thing existed. Not so much about the fact that the light was still on at 8.37 p.m. but that it had never happened. She sighed, her shoulders sagging again. As quickly as the pulsating lightning had come, it disappeared.

She clicked onto her Touching Bones page, her belly normal again, the tears slowly drying up as though she'd never cried. She scrolled up and down the phone, searching for something that would take the strange taste of rust out of her mouth. But she kept bumping into Bobo Chan's mental dumps. It had only been ten or twenty minutes but he was back moaning about 'GROSS INJUSTICE IN MALAYSIA'S POLITICAL SPHERE'. His brain ran on an overcharged motor, churning sentence after sentence about chucking out all the guns in the United States, about how China's ethical system (or lack of one) would be the downfall of the world and how Malaysia, dear, sweet, dying Malaysia, was drowning in a sewage hole of corruption. Day in, day out, Bobo wrote chunks, whole essays, for his fans who told him how clever he was, how right he was, how he should become a political analyst or write for the *New Yorker* and put Malaysia on the map. Several times she *almost—very nearly almost—* commented with 'Fuck This Shit', or 'Shut The Fuck Up', but she'd never said anything on anyone's posts and it would be too weird if she screamed at Bobo, out of the deepest, darkest blue, as though suddenly she had something important to say. People like Bobo loved the spotlight on their faces, pockmarked and all. Nobody was looking at the scars from his acute high school acne, anyway. Too clever to condescend to frivolous things like beauty, his mouth was big enough for others to agree that people like him were exempt from a lot of common, ordinary things since they were *gifted* and went to sleep every night buzzed on their brilliance, knowing absolutely that one day they'd self-propel to the moon purely on brain-energy and the special inbuilt light shining out of their asses. If he hated Malaysia so much, with its bullshit and life-threatening corruption, then why doesn't he just jump on a plane and get out of here once and for all? She scrolled and scrolled, and let herself be taken in by all the things that people were saying so freely as though they were really that free.

Heat rose through her neck and cheeks. She glanced at the clock on her phone. It was nearly 10 p.m. already. She looked up. The light at Yalpanam was still as yellow as ever. Maybe the old lady was fed up of doing the same thing every damn day and, finally, after four hundred years or however many it was, she said to herself, enough is enough, I'm going to sleep at 10 p.m. today.

New posts kept emerging on the page. Update after update and yet, she herself hardly wrote on her own page. What was there to say? Only people who couldn't keep their mouths shut wrote like they were purging all the dinners they ever ate. Or people who were desperate for compliments about how great they looked in their photoshopped pics. Or people who needed other people to see how happy they were eating lunch, driving a car, walking their dogs. In any case, everything was already being done. How would Touching Bones benefit from her adding junk to all the junk that piled up every day, second after second?

Minah Dain was doing her obligatory mass-posting of self-help articles. '10 WAYS TO LOVE YOURSELF'. 'EAT

YOUR WAY TO FREEDOM'. '5 STEPS TO IMPROVE SELF-ESTEEM'. '25 SIGNS YOU ARE IN A TOXIC RELATIONSHIP'. How Minah applied this knowledge was a total mystery. She didn't talk to anyone except Titi who never looked anyone in the eye and seemed happy to be failing every subject. The duo, joined at the hip Siamese twins, didn't, *couldn't* leave each other's sides, ate from the same plate, sipped lime juice from the same cup, laughed at the same jokes. But once in a while, Minah said 'Hello. How are you?' to Maxim when they were waiting to enter the General Studies classroom, half a step towards improving self-esteem. Half of five was quite bad.

She scrolled down, past Saras Devi's ramblings on yoga and inner peace, Mindy D'Cruz's holiday pictures, mainly of a roof and the signboard of a resort on the east coast, Desmond Poh's inappropriate thoughts about his mother, 'a truly special lady I've been thinking about lately', until she reached TinkerbellAng's 1001 selfies, mandarin-orange lips, pout after pout after pout, fake eyelashes, blood-coloured blusher, *caked*, eyes trying to open wider than they could. Look at me! Look at me! Well, she looked cheap.

She clicked out of Touching Bones. Enough was enough. People like Tinkerbell Ang needed to get a life. Who wanted to see her stupid moonface hour after hour?

She chucked her phone on the floor and sat up straight. The essay on *The Catcher in the Rye* was due next week and she hadn't even started doing the research. No chance of that happening tonight. The articles Ms Dolores got them to read were for people like Bobo, full of ugly words like 'homogenise' and 'liminal', and each time she tried to even look at a page, her head tightened as though someone was pushing bricks through her skull. The front gate screeched, the auto gate wheels whirring until the screeching stopped and an engine's hum grew louder. She bent down and checked the time on her phone. The engine continued to drone even as a door opened and closed. Perhaps Daddy had brought home a friend, one of those fast-talking, noodle-slurping guys from the office. At 10 p.m., it was possible for him to arrive with company. Otherwise, why would Daddy be home so early? He never came home before midnight, unless there were people with him.

She stood up and went to her study desk. A stack of library books played coaster to a mug of old tea she should have taken down to the kitchen ages ago. Books on planets, the universe, time and space covered the rest of the table. She pulled out the remaining stool from underneath her desk, sat down and opened up *The Myth of Time.*

The relativity of time presupposes that time, as an absolute and objective entity, is a misperception. It would seem that because we use calendars and clocks and, in the past, sundials, water clocks and hourglasses, to mark the passing of time, that Time as a substantial quantifiable object exists. But in fact.

She looked up from the book, feeling in her bones that Daddy was limping his way up to talk to her, to reveal whatever it was Mother had told her was coming.

A light knock on the door.

'Maxim,' Daddy said like a man talking to himself.

He didn't bother to knock again as if he knew she'd heard him.

She left the book open and tip-toed to the door, her heart thumping, her fingers cold. The Big News was seconds, minutes away. The last Big News was when they'd picked Tanah Merah International College for her to study A-Levels at, after years of public-school education which Daddy criticized *all* the time, but his fear of Mother's fear of Little Girl Maxim on the mainland was too strong to send her to a good school in KL.

The doorknob twisted. She dashed a few steps back and found her bed, but she saw her phone on the floor and quickly darted forward. She snatched it off the floor, rushed back to her bed and fell onto it. She punched at the phone and pretended to read from it.

Daddy walked in, hands in pockets, face lowered.

'Maxim,' he said to the floor.

She feigned surprise. 'Daddy, didn't hear you. How come you're back so early?'

He dragged his feet to her bed, and looked at her as though *she* had arranged this meeting. Cheeks pulled inward, fat eye-bags under each eye. If it wasn't for his golden Rolex, the salmon-pink Gucci shirt, and the beige Gucci pants purchased by Mother, he could have passed off as one of his construction workers.

He reached for the remote on her bed and clicked the air-con on. He let out a long, heavy sigh and sat next to her. 'Ahmad is here. We have work to do tonight.' He dropped the remote onto the bed and placed his hands on his knees protectively. 'I don't think I'll be sleeping tonight,' he continued, 'we have so much work to do, I think we might not even finish by tomorrow afternoon.'

She nodded.

'There are a lot of things you don't understand, girl.' He looked around for evidence Mother most likely instructed him to find. 'And there may be more difficult things to understand in the future.'

'Have you eaten today, Daddy?'

His eyes softened and, slowly, a half-smile appeared on his face. 'Yes, yes. We had lunch. How was dinner?'

She studied her toes. 'It was ok.'

'Good, good'. He paused. The air-con burred.

'It's going to be very busy until the election, right, Daddy?'

He nodded abruptly. 'Listen, girl, I don't have much time tonight. Trying to get everything done, haiiiiih . . .' He glanced at his Rolex. 'But you don't need to hear about all that, girl. Another time, when you're older, if you like, we can . . . but never mind, anything you want later is fine. Now is different, you understand?'

No, of course she didn't, he was talking nonsense like his wife but with better English. She nodded to be polite. No boat needed to be rocked tonight, whatever the Big News was.

'Mummy and I have talked and we both decided it's time for you to leave the country.' He turned to face her. He tried looking into her eyes but she couldn't bring herself to look at him. She blinked at her lap and waited.

'If you want to develop, go to a developed country. The situation here is getting from bad to worse. This country is so backward, I cannot tell you how much I feel like we're all drowning in so much rubbish . . . haiiiiih . . . girl, you all don't see what I see.' He placed his hand on hers. She carried on blinking at her lap, and slowly pulled away. A sudden blast of air-con air brushed against her arm and sent a wave of goosebumps down to her wrist.

His cough echoed through the cold, dry air. 'That's right, you all don't see what I see. Behind the scenes, girl, the story is different. I won't go into the details. You don't need to know all of that. But trust your Daddy when I say that the country is standing on quicksand.' He leaned forward, elbows on his lap, but quickly straightened his back. He shook his head as though a tiny spring held up his neck.

'Out of love,' he said, his voice quivering slightly, 'we are sending you away from this mess.'

'Okay', 'I see', 'Thank you' were all that came to her, but her voice had gone back to that black space inside where everything got stuck. Her tongue dry, her chest hot, she felt sick.

'I've made special arrangements so you don't have to worry about anything, ok, girl?' He waited for her response.

'Never mind. I know this is big news but we're only doing this for you. The college in Australia will take into consideration the subjects you've studied here and put you on a foundation program to prepare you for a first degree. Don't worry, girl, no money or time has been wasted, ok? You've not lost anything . . . and Mummy will stay with you for a few months.'

He glanced at his Rolex and shot up. 'It's getting late. Daddy really has to go now.' He held the knee he'd twisted running down the stairs at the office months ago, and limped as fast as he could towards the open door. He stood there, kneading the knee, needing no medication, no rest, only hard work to make darker, fatter eye-bags. He turned around to look at her.

'Ahmad booked your flight yesterday. You have two more months, so don't worry, okay, girl? A lot of time to pack and all that.' He turned around swiftly and hobbled away, calling out, 'Isma, make tea for the office room.'

And that was that. He was gone. Didn't even bother to close the door. She stretched her body out on the bed and stared at the whirring air-con. If she closed her eyes and tried hard enough, she could make its whirr the whirr of Jupiter's gases, twisting and spinning around in the deep silence of outer space. But she couldn't make it that far. Over and over, she knew too clearly that it was only the air-con and she was only in her bedroom, waiting for her legs to carry her to the door to lock it shut, so that she could lounge around in peace again.

*

Pushpanayagi gripped the clay jug of water she kept on a stack of old empty boxes by the meat-safe in the kitchen. Something in her arm—a dark heavy feeling above her elbow—fought with her thirst but she pulled her arm up in one quick tug and poured the water into her mouth. It spilled down her neck, her breasts, wetting her sarong close to the navel. She'd never felt this kind of wild thirst; this kind of thirst coming when the morning hadn't even started. She lowered her head. Through the kitchen window, the black sky was empty except for a crescent moon, its tip hiding behind cloud, glowing in dull, flat yellow beside a lonely silver star. Where the jambu tree stood at the back of her garden, was pitch-black night-morning. The other morning, sun-morning, was far away. Now and again, the outline of its leaves glimmered ghostly white, the only clue the tree was still there. She placed the jug back on the boxes and trudged towards the hall, her throat dry again as though water had not touched it. It felt like sea-wind, cold and salty, was blowing between the walls of her neck, sucking up all the moisture. Once in a while, suddenly, the illness pretended to leave. Then the body started pounding, her legs felt like air, and she knew the demon was only fooling her. It hadn't gone anywhere and it wasn't planning to go anywhere until it finished with her body for good.

She entered the hall and sat on a wicker chair. Her chest rose and fell; the breath did not come and go as breaths should come and go, easily, nicely. She groaned each time the lungs tried to get air, too painful to be done in silence. The pulse at her wrist was going berserk, as berserk as the vein in her neck, and the dry wind in her throat kept beating like a wild monsoon storm. Would the boy come soon? How many more leaves had grown from the tomato shoot since he last came? A few, at least she could remember that, a few. Maybe when the sun was up, he'd come. It was time to leave, to prepare.

Nod goodbye now to everything that had come into her life—coldness churned in her stomach and rushed to her heart—everything, one by one, karma complete. Millipedes, spiders, bees, sunbirds, rats, all the moons, every sun, dark, indigo, storm clouds. Water gliding down the throat, teeth cutting vegetables, soap making bubbles on the skin. Eyes opening after sleep. Mud between toes. And people, no, they had all disappeared. Goodbye to the boy. Would she be able to look into his eyes when she bid him farewell?

She tilted her head back, silently screamed, 'Ramaaaaaaaa', and closed her eyes. Nothing bumped or treaded in the hall. No sounds escaped from the outside into the house. Deep in her ears, a dull creak like bamboo bending rose in the silence. It slithered from ear to ear. She pursued it as it slipped down her throat, into her heart, down to her navel. It lay there, and creaked louder. She fell into the loud low creak like bamboo bending and her body melted, oozing out into the thick deep silence behind the creak.

When she opened her eyes, the front hall was bright. The sunbirds chirped from their nest on the veranda. Through a green window by the front door, one bird floated in mid-air. Its wings fluttered rapidly, krrr-krrr-krrr, KRRR-KRRR-KRRR. The sound grew in her ears, lifted louder, then the bird dipped low and dove down and everything was quiet.

She stood up. The light in the hall was still on from the night before. She raised a foot. Something along her spine cracked. Maybe it was an air-bubble bursting. A good thing, at last. The thirst and its sea-wind had vanished, another good thing. But where the wind had been, there was a slowly rising heat that spread through her chest and collected at the edge of her stomach. She pushed her body forward, her limbs stiff and sore, burning like the taste of pounded chilies.

She reached the steps of the veranda, and the heat—the fire—gushed down her arms, burned the tips of her fingers, threatened to surge out of her body. She clutched a pillar, grabbed the railing with her other hand and inched her way down into the garden.

The sky was empty, the sun big and pale, alone, not even a dot of cloud to keep it company. Swallows flew low and glided past the garden. Higher up, the small yellow birds flitted in the air, looking, before plunging towards the hibiscus bushes next to the rose bed.

She stopped, caught her breath and sat on the ground. The grass needed weeding, but the boy would do it when he came. When would he come? She pressed her palms on the soil and slowly, gently, lay down. Behind her, the house stood on its low columns, white paint flaking off the walls by the front door.

The wide veranda, two or three of its dark wooden planks missing, had been left empty for the sunbirds who had returned to build their hanging nest on one of the veranda's thick vertical beams. Spun out of twigs, bark, strips of newspaper, pink and yellow plastic bags, shards of eggshell, and old sarong cloth she had cut up into confetti for them along with a lock of her hair, the nest hung from the beam, still empty. Soon, the birds would be back with eggs and there would be chicks again to chirp, until they also flew off and returned with their own eggs. Their ancestors had built nests out of bark and twigs, dead flowers and bits of wood, but the new generation was very modern. They liked human things. They took fibres from household brooms and rubber from old Japanese slippers. They liked the thin gold chain she'd left out for them. Years ago, it glistened between twigs and bark. Then she'd put out a gold ring, a pair of sapphire earrings, copper bracelets, a jade necklace, one day at a time, until she had nothing left to give them.

'Radha Krishna, oh ho,' she whispered, half to herself, half to her vegetables. The sawi swayed, listening.

'All the days are coming to an end,' a voice inside her said.

She positioned a hand on her chest, ready to beat it, to start howling the heat out of her body, but she could not find the thing she needed to do it. As much as she wanted to stand up and migrate to the rose bed on the other end of the garden, she could only lie next to her vegetables, tears rising as quickly as the fire in her body. She loosened her sarong and slowly removed it. The yellow on her flesh had deepened.

'But what? But what?' another voice said, 'What is all this?'

She closed her eyes. A man with milk-white skin waved. 'Hey, hey,' he screamed. 'You left me like that,' he said. The fire dropped below her belly, spread down her thighs.

'Rama, Rama,' she finally said, 'let the boy come soon'.

When he came, she would tell him where the money was. No need for a funeral, there was no one to attend it. Buy the cheapest coffin and the rest of the money he could keep. Everything else he could burn. All the sarongs and what else was there? Hardly anything. He could keep whatever he wanted. And the garden? What would happen to her garden? Who would make sure the tomatoes turned from green to the colour of the sun at dusk? Or that the leaves were dark enough for the worms to come? The boy didn't know. He helped to dig the soil sometimes. His arms were strong but he couldn't speak to the vegetables. They would wilt and cry into the earth, their hearts broken. If God could see—tears gushed down her face—what love had come out of her hands and out of the ground. He knew. He must see! Rama, Rama!

She opened her eyes.

Yes, she had to leave the house to the boy. There was no one else. The vegetables, they would be taken back into the earth. The house the boy could use to raise a family. Maybe he will keep chickens in the garden. Maybe this is the last of the sunbirds. Maybe the birds had only come to keep her company.

'Keep me alive until he comes,' she said. But it was no use. She could feel life slowly fading away into darkness.

'Soon it will all be ash,' the voice within said.

'And it will all be nothing,' the other voice said.

She closed her eyes. Another pale man emerged, faceless. He waved as though he was being bitten by an animal. Up and down he jumped. 'Where did you go?' he said, again and again. But she could not speak. She could feel him as someone she'd known a long, long time ago, a person in a dream, unknown but somehow known.

'From nothing we come, into nothing we go,' the first voice said.

Then silence. The pale man disappeared. She fell into the unmoving spot, into its deep silence, until she found the creak like bamboo bending and then there was nothing.

3

All day, all night long, on certain days, for over seven decades, the bones by the jungle behind the house—indeed, what could it be called, the expression of these bones? No longer holding up bodies. No longer acknowledged as belonging to anyone. Unlooked upon. Unheard. Bereft of sculptured headstones to mark them, to state to whom the bones belonged. Insolence! Yet, in whatever cavern or pit a life-object is flung—flung out of shame or hatred, the conduits of pain—be it a human body, a carcass, the trunks of massacred trees, something watches, nods in ethereality, corporeality, or both, and marks the neglect, marks the span, however short or long, of the life-object in the cavern, pit. So it happened, sometime after the Japanese left the island in 1945, that four stones extruded out from the ground, centimetres apart from each other—a nod from the earth, one may say, and also from the ghosts that hovered above the bones—a decent and honourable confession that lives once associated with the house were not far away.

Stir, yes, the bones *stir*, amid ordinary life. Like little fish wriggling in the sea. Like a thousand bees departing the hive.

Every day, the earthworms inch their way through grit and soil; termites and ants faithfully, diligently, construct their long kingdoms in the belly of the earth, warm, damp host of the secretive; and the young beetles try out their existence here, before they are called by the air, by the magnetism of sunlight, to rise. These are normal, everyday, every-year, every-decade, and century occurrences. What moves in the ground is an approximate mirror of what moves above. Life—what else?

Rich, hot, life. Bountiful, bombastic, wild, inexorable.

And the dead. What? Life is impossible without one eye fixed on the corpse of a centipede coiled around a small stone. Yesterday, for example, a person clapped his hands and sang a slow ode to the woodpigeons; he boasted about his steady pulse—straight back from the doctor's well-visited clinic—and he spoke about cruising on boats around the Indonesian islands, climbing Mount Kinabalu before dawn. His friends know so well the elasticity of his dark pink lips, the limpid brown eyes carrying sparks of intention, excitement, and the nose twitching at the mildest scent of food. Yet, today, following his fatal accident with a lorry carrying mounds of oil-palm, he is covered in white cloth, his face exposed so his friends may gaze at it and ask: what is no longer there? What has happened to the sheen in his eyes, bubbling with globe-trotting fever? Where is his *animation*?

But would they? Would they open their hearts as wide as the galaxy and wonder what on earth is going on? What on earth, on this earth, is going on?

If a person observes a water-lily in a pond, for instance, not to identify its genus, or its inclinations in the tropical climate of the island, but to see nothing except the water-lily, as it is, they might get close to this mystery. Or perhaps they'll feel it when they watch ants kiss as they pass each other on their eternal trek up and down a wall. Their own teeth, the colours of this world.

There, where the bones stir, life and death meet, twins of different moods. When one is faraway, the other pines for its return.

The old woman, unfortunately, too often looked with the eyes of the neglected twin, death; the twin so deep within that its presence is like a tree that has been in the garden for years and years, the eyes no longer see it. How else could she have summoned a group of labourers up the hill, into Yalpanam's compound, and pointed with an unwavering finger at the Banyan tree opposite the house, on land not belonging to her, and told them, her voice clear and deep, 'Chop that tree. Only that tree. The rest, leave alone.' And when a coffee plantation coolie, eternally seeking work beyond the estate, said, 'Ma'am, too much bad luck to cut Banyan. In India, Banyan God's tree. Lord Krishna tree,' Pushpanayagi, perhaps reeling from the grief of her lover's death, perhaps filled with the inhuman clarity of the betrayed, replied, 'You coolies from India have, honest to God, developed arrogance not suited to your station. Eh oh, Thambikutty, go back to India if you don't want to live properly in the new land. I am paying you, correct? You want to eat gruel again tonight? Or do you want to eat fresh fish from the sea? Keep your coolie ideas to yourself and cut the tree!'

The tree was chopped, cleared and gone in a week, ten days after the unexpected death of her lover—in truth, her *ex*-lover at the time of his fateful voyage back to England—nine days after she learned of her inheritance from him ('Bless his heart,' she'd said, 'love isn't real, but at least now I know there's such a thing as *caring*') of the house he'd built on the island, and a significant sum of money that would free her of obligations and worry for the remaining six years of the nineteenth century, and a good half of the twentieth. She was comfortable, attached to the house like an oyster to its shell, and lucky, she knew, a home-owner in a century when and in a society where women like her didn't even think of things like property and ownership, only propriety, procreation and tropical pests; attached like an oyster that inevitably yields to the heat of boiling water, but in the old woman's case, she'd boiled the water herself and welcomed not a literal death, but death of another, subtler kind.

And still—no—it really must be said, she has created a beautiful garden for herself: hoards of pumpkins, tomatoes, tall stalks of leafy vegetables, cabbages, cucumbers, two neat rows of red roses, a thick, tall mango tree. It is beautiful, oh yes! Beautiful and glossed with routine. Beautiful but glossed with routine. It is only *one* Banyan tree, a person desperate for answers may say. There are billions of trees on this planet. One tree does not matter. One, two, three hundred trees do not matter. And, besides, she has more than made up for it by nurturing and nourishing her lavish garden. The banyan tree does not mean much.

Where do her eyes land? Far into a different kind of mystery. A mystery she does not yet know she is seeing.

A thin, but firm, electric current courses up the hill and jolts her heart awake. The bones stir.

*

Eyes burning, head throbbing. Better to lie in bed a bit longer, at least until the throbbing calmed down. She hauled the fleece blanket over her shoulders. Sleep had passed, the normal time had passed. Let Mother think what she wanted. Knocking on the door like a psycho, screaming at her to get up. *Sleep, sleep, sleep until become old lady! Young people these days so lazy!* Staying up all night staring at Yalpanam was *not* lazy. The opposite. Could Mother do something like that? *Would* she? Never in the lifetime of Jupiter. The Parents didn't know what self-sacrifice was. They had no clue that self-sacrifice was actually sitting patiently by a window, waiting to see if an old woman who lived by herself was OK.

Of course, she wanted the lights to go off, that was why she'd kept herself pumped by eating all the imported M&S sweets from Mother's Thank You hamper to one of the Botox Aunties. Who wanted bad things to happen to people they didn't know? If the lights never got switched off, well, there was a whole medley of stuff that could have gone on up there in the house of a witch, bomoh lady, human dinosaur, she-devil, to keep the lights going all night. When the white-yellow morning sun rose, it looked as though the lights had been switched off, but it was probably just the sunlight. *Of course,* she didn't wish anything bad on the old lady, whoever, *whatever* she was. If anything had happened, the vegetable man would eventually find out. Would it be too late? No, of course she didn't want bad things to happen to the old woman. Suicide? Hung herself with a fat rope in the front hall. The rope, thick and rough, like the kind they used to pull oxen in shows set in 14th, 15th or whatever century it was.

She curled deeper into the blanket, leaving her nose uncovered so she could breathe in peace. The soft, furry blanket felt so warm, like a nice little cocoon spun around her forever. She nestled into it again, feeling like a bird in its nest or a bunny in a velvety patch of grass.

Maybe the old woman had been murdered? But who would want her dead? *You think can trust people, ah? Choiiii. Don't be so stupid. The world full of bad people always wait to get you.* Mother was right. Daddy was right. Stuff happened every day around the world, grim, random stuff. People closest to you could turn around and stab you in the back, spitting at you as you die. It was in the news. People talked about things like this all the time. On *Devil Beside You*, a teenage boy hacked his parents to death with a kitchen knife the mother had been using to chop vegetables for dinner. The police found a half-cut carrot on the kitchen floor, coated in the mother's blood. They'd shown photos of the crime scene, bodies slashed, faces disfigured, blood smeared on their hands and feet and on the floral wallpaper. The son called 911, his voice trembling, saying intruders had taken his folks away from him, 'taken his folks away from him', that's exactly how he put it. But all the evidence pointed at *him*, the small wimpy boy with innocent blue eyes, crying for the parents he'd just killed. Had the vegetable man bludgeoned Auntie Pushpanayagi to death? Handsome guys did bad things too. Would the police be up on the hill any time now? Busting the mildewed doors open, pointing their guns around in case the killer was hiding behind a cupboard.

In a corner of the kitchen, most probably underneath the sink, the old lady's body would be coiled up like a millipede, mouth open, eyes half-closed, in a pool of sparkling blood.

That would just be *awful.* Taman Bidadari would be swarming with reporters, TV people, trying to get the scoop on the mysterious old woman who had lived for centuries. Mrs Teng would have a field day, putting on her best ugliest samfu, blotching her face with over-white powder and smiling like a creepy wooden doll as she looked directly at the camera and told her lame joke that the neighbourhood was named Bidadari because it was full of angels like her. Evil angels, perhaps. And Uncle Colonel would be parading shirtless around the women reporters, sticking his chest out, waiting for one of them to comment on his grey jungle of chest hair. As if he didn't know he was gross. And then winking, always winking while smoke puffed out of his pipe.

She threw the blanket off and sat up. She couldn't just lie around in her room, waiting for the worst to happen. The worst could already have happened and there she was rolling around in bed like the goat-babies that sometimes lazed on the wild bamboo land. What did people call it? Moral obligation or moral conscience? *Dream, dream, dream! Every day also dream!* No, it wasn't that she wanted the limelight—*not* Bobo's tacky spotlight—of being the first one to discover the body, or of being the first one to walk up the hill and dare to enter Yalpanam. The Parents would freak out if they knew she was going up the road, by herself, all alone. *You want become like Auntie Bonnie? Live in condo by herself, paint donno what picture, then tell me she one artist. Artist, artist is what, you tell me? Smoking cigarette, drink whiskey like she born a man. Where got woman like that? Crazy, ah?* At least Auntie Bonnie knew how to smile. At least she brought cool books to read and handcrafted bags of mochi when she was allowed to visit, which was hardly ever. Auntie Bonnie would go up the hill. She wouldn't even think about it. Just zoom up the slope and ring the geriatric bell.

She rushed to her en suite bathroom, splashed water on her face and neck, and quickly considered a shower. No, a shower would take too much time. She splashed more water on her face, and rinsed her mouth with her favourite green-tea flavoured mouthwash, then headed back into the room, collected her phone and sling bag from her bedside table and squeezed the phone into the bag. She scanned the room. Dark purple fleece blanket bundled up in the top right corner of her bed, books scattered on her chocolate-brown study table, thick Ribena-red carpet, lime-green Puma backpack lying open underneath the violet-sheeted bed. But there was nothing to carry up the hill. Naked without her backpack like one of Hawking's tortoises that had lost its shell. But, really, there was no need for the backpack. It would just be a quick pop-in. Hi, glad you're not dead, Bye. And if the old woman had hung herself or got herself murdered, it would be accidental fame. Then absolutely, definitely, she'd win Footsy's competition. But, really, she wasn't going up the hill to win a competition. That would just be wrong. Tasteless. Nobody, except maybe Mother, could use tragedy to win a free book and other stuff. It didn't matter how cool the stuff was—iPhone; hardcover set of Hawking's Complete Works; a T-shirt with Footsy's surfer-tanned face on it—the point was that the story would be a side-thing to whatever was happening or had happened to the witch.

She surveyed her room again, as if for the last time. Too many times she'd done nonsense like this, thinking something humungous was going to happen and she had to prepare for it by memorizing things like hotel rooms, the inside of someone's car, the way the sea danced through the splotchy window of the Coal Island Ultimate Ferry, the island growing smaller and smaller as the ferry glided away. Nothing ever really happened. Every single time, she found herself back in her bedroom, unchanged. No matter how far the family went, Paris, Dublin, Tokyo, when she walked back into NO.42's living room, she felt as though she'd come back from down the road. But she couldn't stop memorizing places and objects to keep with her in case the plane crashed, The Parents screamed each other into a divorce, or she was snatched by an alcoholic tramp, raped and dumped for dead. Pigeon-grey fan blades in a small B&B run by a fish-smelling grandmother in Brittany, eggy blue custard at every breakfast at the Vienna Hilton, slabs of cured meat lit by brilliant yellow lights at the Paris Christmas Market.

The same old coldness spread through her chest and down her arms, making her want to pee but the urge to pee was fake. She was clever enough by now, too used to the havoc this feeling created, to know what was what; this feeling was like opening a door and stepping, without looking, into really dark space. *Why want to feel like that? Cry, cry, cry, and then? Scare, scare, scare, and then?*

She shut the door behind her and hurried down the stairs.

*

Turquoise and lilac, jade-green and topaz-yellow spun in circles of light. They rushed up, down, left to right, right to left, and exploded into darkness. Pushpanayagi opened her eyes. Pumpkins hung like lanterns above. The deep yellow sunlight felt much older than when she last awakened. That time the sky was without birds and the toads were burping after drinking dew all night. Then, the kailan unfolded its leaves and said that the sun was still new, so she closed her eyes, feeling that she'd never wake up again. But now her eyelids flickered and her fingers vibrated and the old merciless thirst was back. How she had moved from the central garden to the pumpkin patch, she didn't know. She could barely walk without wheezing, without her whole body breaking into a long slow ache. Even her bones quivered in the flames that leapt from her stomach to her heart and charged down her arms. And yet, God is great, she'd managed to pick up her sarong and walk, crawl, stumble to the pumpkin patch.

She'd been far, far away or long, long ago, somewhere unknown, a new place not of this earth. A place without things to touch and smell and taste. But she'd seen something. Faces, voices, old songs, legs and arms moving to a rhythm she'd known, like images and sequences in dreams. The more she tried to pick them up from deep within, the more they hid in their secret corners. Like evil magicians. All she had now was a feeling. A feeling that she had been talking and laughing and shouting and crying and watching, like she had touched someone, maybe even hugged them, and something good had been said. A place deep in the well of Time. A place made of air and darkness. Had there been a big orange balloon in the sky? And a balloon holding up the basket? And blue-yellow flames sparking between the great orange head and the people waving beneath? She had seen someone ancient, too ancient; she tried to turn her body but the ground clung to her, clung so hard as though it had fingers.

Either death had come or when she closed her eyes again, the moving pictures stopped. Why did they come if she couldn't remember them? And here she was, trying to grab them, empty pictures. Had she not let all of this go? The clutching, clinging, keeping: dust in the mist! She'd blown them back into the thick clouds that kept the world murmuring in sleep. If people wanted to drown in illusions, that was God's problem. Her fate was to dig deep into the pit of God's dream and dwell in the centre where reality was.

So, one by one, she had let them all go, the desire for beautiful paintings and books, even scriptures, ornaments, tailored dresses, face powder, machines to wash clothes, to store food, to suck up dirt, to entertain, fame, love, friends, honour, the living and the dead, the lost voices of the people who had inhabited her head, one by one, she had let them all go.

She purged and purified, danced and bathed in Shiva's holy fire, the ashes of her filth rising into heaps, and at last blown away by Shiva's breath.

Day and night she worked for God, got herself ready for when He came. She listened to the still, small voices within, and to the soft, silent spaces within and to the messages in Rama's book and to her memory of Lord Krishna's book. *Perform work in this world, Arjuna, as a man established within himself—without selfish attachments and alike in success and defeat.* And that was what she did. She worked with the soil and the plants and the creatures and she loved them with the full power of her heart.

Had God abandoned her? The heat in her face seemed to burst into flames. But it did not feel like Shiva's fire. This was the body burning to its death. 'Let the sleep be empty or bring Yama to me,' she whispered and closed her eyes. In the darkness, groups of men dressed in suits and shiny shoes talked and laughed, their voices buzzing. 'Yes, I went there tomorrow,' one said and another said, 'And did you find her, my man?' and another said, 'She is a difficult block of ice.'

She gasped for breath, and tried to open her eyes but her eyelids were glued tight. The men drifted in groups up and down a brilliantly lit room. Some smoked pipes, others drank from small twinkling glasses filled with dark purple liquid.

They laughed loudly and sang, 'Dear, dear Sibyl is a merry old soul, and a merry old soul was she! Where is she now that the party has come? Or has she gone back to tomorrow and some?'

They cheered and joined their glasses in a wave of tinkling and clinking and all at once, they evaporated. A row of them reappeared; Chinese, White, Indian, Malay men standing in a straight line, their arms touching, looking straight ahead. Together, they said, 'Why have you left us here all alone?' One of them stepped forward and bowed, then lifted his face. Tears poured down his cheeks. 'Madam Deborah,' he said, his eyes lowered to the ground, 'I am a doll without legs.' His legs disappeared and the rest of his body floated up and away. 'And I,' another said but none of the mouths were moving, 'have lost my heart.'

Something cold foamed in her chest. She tried to open her eyes again but the force within lugged her in deeper. The men's screams echoed through her bones and slowly waned. Silence, darkness. She lingered in the soft peace that gently, gently, washed away the last traces of voices and pictures that had clotted in the smooth sea of silence.

She opened her eyes. The day was still bright, brighter than before the men appeared in the darkness inside her. Drops of sweat dribbled down the sides of her face. Her neck felt too damp, too sticky. The jar of water she'd brought from the kitchen rested against her arm. Her tongue was dry, powdery, and her throat ached for water but she had no strength to sit up and drink. She couldn't even move her toes. Her eyes shut again.

A long thick plait, tied at the bottom with frayed red string, flashed in the darkness and vanished. It slowly re-emerged. A head turned. 'Pushpa? Pushpa?' it said. A wide mouth began to distort above the chin; above the mouth, a flat brown surface. A large dark eye arose, a nose, another eye. 'Pushpa? What are you doing there?' the woman said. The mouth broke out into a smile. 'You are such a naughty one! Looks like I have three grownup babies in this house,' the woman laughed. The rest of her body floundered into life. Behind the woman, colours frolicked in long spiralling sweeps. Powder blue oozed into scarlet, butter-yellow into emerald green, pale orange into violet, and a wall appeared, a pot, steam climbing high and fast, a stove, a sink with a copper tap, water dripping, tok, tok, tok, a stack of tins beside the sink, a bold golden cross on the label and the words 'Blue Cross'.

Savitri twirled a ladle. 'Well, Pushpa? Are you just going to stand there and watch me?' Savitri laughed and laughed and laughed. Her dark brown eyes twinkled; her cheeks reddened. A soft white light formed an aureole around her. 'I figured as much,' she said, waving the ladle, 'you, Abu, and Charles want to talk in your little group, isn't it? You want to discuss your luck, isn't it? Even the Japanese won't come near the three of you. They rather leave Yalpanam alone than have to penetrate the three of you!' She laughed and stared ahead, the dark brown eyes still glimmering as though stars had dropped into them. 'What is that, Pushpa? No words yet? All right then, my sweetheart. It's better if you go into the hall and sit with Charles. He's being a grumpy humpty dumpty! Let me get on with the cooking. We better hope the bombs are quiet today.' She stood motionless. 'Ah, ah, Pushpa, if the soldiers come, you better transform into Deborah!' She turned around and skipped towards the boiling pot. The thick black plait bounced in her aureolic light.

From a distance, voices called out, 'Tuan!' 'Careful!' 'Shut up!' Echoes, dream voices, they floated towards the kitchen.

'Oh, would you shut up, Abu?'

'Dirty Communist pig!'

'He needs to be helped!'

'Not always, Tuan.'

'Would you stop spouting nonsense, please?'

'Dirty Communist pig!'

A cool wave spread across Pushpanayagi's face. Water seeped into her eyes and nostrils. She gasped for air and opened her eyes. Drops of water leaked into her mouth. Above, looking down at her, a young girl stood with the clay jug of water in her hand, watching, frightened.

4

When Maxim Cheah arrived at Yalpanam, the gate was locked. One of the front doors of the house was flung inward, the other outward towards the veranda. She stood wide-eyed before the gate, then leaned forward, and tugged at the lock once more. She looked to her right at the ivy-covered pillar bearing the plaque that had 'Yalpanam' etched in faded black cursive, at the stone tiger sitting on top of the pillar, a bird's nest in its mouth, open mid-roar, and she grunted, defeated.

Through its open shutters, the house sighed to the sky and the sky listened. The sky listened to the muffled trill that drifted through the wooden planks of the aged veranda walls. It listened to the soft murmurs that breathed out of the stained glass window in the solitary room on the top floor and it listened to the susurration of voices floating, tarrying, over Yalpanam's gable.

The young girl stood on the horizontal shaft supporting the bars of the gate, and peered into the compound. The violet sphere of light around the house brightened, but the girl could not see it. Her eyes fell instead on what they could see: a congregation of five twittering wrens on the edge of the dirt path that separated two halves of the garden, powerfully lit by the amber light of the morning sun. She gazed for a long moment, first at the long sheaves of grass and stalks of leaves overflowing in an intricate network of green on the left; then at rows of immaculately pruned roses glistening in voluptuous shades of ruby-red and vermillion on the right. Her face knitted into a frown. She shook the bars of the gate and tried to push herself up, the frown crumpling into a pained scowl, her face getting ruddier and ruddier the harder she pushed. But her palms slipped off the rods. She glared at the house and sighed. Hearing another sigh—a sigh finally from a human body—the house sighed the loudest, longest sigh it had sighed in decades. The girl gripped the bars again, lifted herself as far as she could go, grabbed the top of the gate for support, lunged over, and landed on the dirt path. She got up and as if she knew exactly where she was going and what she needed to do, sprinted towards the house, up the steps of the veranda, and into the front hall.

She stood in the middle of the large, empty hall. Sunlight cascaded in through the green-glass windows from the courtyard adjacent to the hall. She studied the two wicker chairs facing each other on the rattan mat, the single light bulb—still on—that hung low near an open room to the right of the hall, its door no longer there, only the hinges remaining. She crept towards the open room, and peered at it, hesitantly, from outside. The narrow rectangular room was empty, except for a large cobweb spread across a corner between two walls, a fat black spider in its centre. It sighed when she walked past it.

She clutched the small bag slung over her chest, patted it several times as though checking it was still there, then jerked out her mobile phone, and fitted it back into the bag. She hurried to the front door and stepped onto the veranda. She stared at the rotting floor planks, at the gaps between them large enough for a whole foot as small as hers to slip through. She hopped over them and stood by the veranda steps, gazing out.

The sprawling garden shimmered and waved in the gentle breeze; bees, sunbirds, and other winged life hovering over shoots, stems and branches. Tucked away in the furthest corner of the vegetable garden, almost hidden by the long grasses, pumpkins hung from a trestle covered in vines and leaves. On the ground beneath, an object too misshapen to be a wheelbarrow, too large to be a domesticated animal, lay in shades of umber amid a sea of gold-flecked green.

The girl ripped the phone out of its bag, stepped down, then changing her mind, turned back to face the veranda, and changing her mind again, slipped the phone into her shorts pocket, slowly turned around, tip-toed down, very carefully, almost too carefully, as though afraid to disturb the littlest life living in the apertures between the planks. She crept in the direction of the pumpkin patch like a frightened animal, hands in her pockets, her movement slowing down, as though now she finally had reason to believe that the ground was too undetermined to cradle her feet.

Pushpanayagi's naked body lay inert inside the pumpkin patch, near its entrance. Plump black ants crawled in a single, purposeful line over her navel and up her chest where two large breasts drooped like dried-up papayas to the sides of her body. The clay jug, its handle missing, tilted against an armpit; the hand that had left it there, open, a beetle resting in the middle of the palm.

The girl hurried over to the other side of the body. A faded blue sarong lay in a crumpled heap near the old woman's feet. She closed her eyes and in one swift motion, smoothed out the fabric and lowered the sarong to cover the body, chest down to the knees. She reached for the jar nestled in the old lady's armpit, closed her eyes and tossed the water, aiming for Pushpanayagi's face.

Silence permeated the pumpkin patch. The air deadened. Maxim opened her eyes and glimpsed at the old woman. A rasping groan pierced the silence. Pushpanayagi's mouth opened, a yellowed snag tooth releasing its grip of her lower lip. The air softened into a mellow breeze, the mellow breeze whirled into a gust, the gust swelled into a wind, and the wind rattled the posts holding up the trestle. The old woman's long white hair whipped the air, blowing violently this way and that, and the girl's small, feeble body swayed like a dangerously weak plant, nearly lifting off. She clasped her shorts pockets for support, but the wind, too intent on ripping the plant from its paltry hold on the ground, slapped one of the girl's cheek, then the other cheek, and she ran, against the wind, out of the patch.

'Savitri?'

The young girl jumped. She reached out as if to grab something solid, but all around her were leaves and plants, and she was not close enough to the pumpkin patch to lean against one of the structure's poles. She pinched the insides of her pockets, locking her knees.

Pushpanayagi wheezed in and out. She raised her upper body very slowly and attempted to sit up. Her arms quivered each time she tried to press her palms against the ground, the folds of flesh around her stomach wobbling the more she pressed. She paused and breathed as deeply as the wheezing would allow.

'I am very thirsty,' she said, licking the water drops on her lips.

Maxim slowly turned around and stepped forward. She took another step, and another, gripping the sides of her shorts as she moved, inch by inch, towards the pumpkin patch.

Pushpanayagi crouched over and held her arms out. They wavered in the air and landed back by the sides of her body, unable to reach her knees. She shook her head. 'Come and help me, child. I want to sit properly.'

The girl stood outside the patch, watching the old woman gather her long white hair into a single bunch and place it over her shoulder. The winds in the pumpkin patch rose and whirled, shaking the dark green fruits like buoys on a rough sea. The sarong blew away and out of the patch, shimmying towards the vegetable garden. It landed on a tomato plant and hung there quietly where the wind did not stir.

Pushpanayagi coughed and the cough resounded through the universe. The young girl rushed forward and grabbed the old woman's arm, looking up at the pumpkins as she seized the flesh with one hand and grasped Pushpanayagi's stiff crooked fingers with the other. The old woman coughed again.

'Better I get you some water, Auntie.' She released her grip on the old woman's body and Pushpanayagi slowly sank to the ground.

Maxim picked up the clay jar and ran out through the garden, up the veranda steps, and disappeared into the mouth of the house.

The winds simmered down. Pushpanayagi tilted her head and examined the pumpkins, this pumpkin, that one, the pumpkin further down the line.

'Oh hoho,' she said, attempting to wag an arthritic finger, 'stay up there, babies. Down here the land is cold. You're hearing?'

She lazily shifted her gaze to her feet. 'One toe, two, three, four toes. Look at that poor family bending down to pick up coins from the road. Am I right, Charlie? You see how those Japanese are throwing banana money in the drain?' She clicked her tongue and shook her head. 'They don't want those fellas anymore, Charlie. Those fellas cut heads, you know. You see the heads? There, over there, five in one row stuck on the fence. Bye-bye, Charlie. How is death? Can you still play with butterflies?'

She closed her eyes and moved her arms up and down on the ground. Bits of gravel collected in the furrows of her flesh. 'I don't mind,' she said, 'if you sit on the floor and cry. But you must at least try to forget. Abu, Abu, what did you do? Why do you want to worry so much? Everything comes and goes, doesn't it?'

A single tear streamed down the side of her face. Another small tear followed, its journey ending at the base of a deep eye socket.

The young girl returned with the clay jug filled to the brim with water. 'I think you better sit up, Auntie.' She paused and looked around as though there were other people in the patch. 'Otherwise difficult to drink,' she continued as she held the jug out in her shaky hand.

The old lady squinted, her forehead wrinkling, her eyes suddenly like slits, her whole face a frown. 'Who are you, actually?' she asked, her voice pitched high.

A splash of water from the jug fell onto Pushpanayagi's arm, but her face remained unchanged.

'I am . . .' the girl replied, pinching vigorously at her pockets, her eyes darting around the ground surrounding the old woman's body, 'I am from down the road.'

Pushpanayagi stared at the frail figure hovering above her. Rather than adding bulk to the girl's frame, the billowing T-shirt accentuated her thinness. The overgrown fringe nearly shielded the girl's eyes. When she moved, a shiny tremor threatened to expose the forehead.

Pushpanayagi's frown transmuted into mild shock. 'What is down the road? They have something down there? Circus? Pasar malam? Why they sent you?'

Maxim held the jug out. 'Shouldn't you drink, Auntie?'

'Drink? Oh ho, drink. Acha, acha.'

The girl helped Pushpanayagi up and held the jug as she guzzled the water noisily. She drank without stopping. When the jug was empty, she looked up sleepily at the girl and burped.

'Yes, thank you very much, child. Now I am the ocean again.'

'I think,' the girl said, looking at the vines curling around the shafts ahead, 'it's better if you go inside. You're sick, right?'

Pushpanayagi burped again and smiled, satisfied. 'I am feeling,' she said, the smile fading, 'it's the sickness for very old bodies.'

'Is your doctor also Doctor Ipe Gomez?'

The old lady shook her head.

'Doctor Aziz, is it?'

A soft breeze blew over the pumpkin patch. Two or three wrens flew in through the gaps at the top of the trestle. They pecked at the grass and chirped quietly as they listened to the voices in the patch.

'If not, then it must be Doctor Lim? He's the oldest doctor, but everyone says he's not so good anymore.'

'No doctors. I have never used a doctor'.

She stared at the old woman as though something indecent had been said. A few magpies added caws to the wrens' cheeping. Finally, she said, 'I don't have Doctor Ipe's number but I think, I think . . . my Daddy has, so I better ask him.'

Pushpanayagi cleared her throat fussily. 'No need, child. Doctors don't need to come here. I must rest.'

The phone in Maxim's shorts pocket buzzed, paused, and buzzed again. It vibrated once more and stopped.

'Oh ho,' the old woman said, 'now I have to go again? They hummed for me to come?'

The phone whirred again, and again, and again.

'Are they coming? Now? Time has come?' Pushpanayagi slowly lifted herself up.

The phone vibrated again. Maxim wrenched it out from her pocket and answered.

'Hello, Mummy.'

'Yes, Mummy.'

'I was in class.'

Pushpanayagi stared at the young girl, mouth open, as if the call had something to do with her.

'Replacement class. Teacher was sick last week.'

Pushpanayagi smiled and nodded knowingly.

'I sat in the library when the teacher didn't come.'

Silence.

Pushpanayagi brushed strands of long, white hair away from her shoulders and leaned forward to touch the girl's foot.

'Soon, Mummy.'

'Ok, Mu—'

Maxim clicked the phone off and slid it back into her shorts pocket.

'Yes, you're right, child,' Pushpanayagi said, attempting to rise, 'it's better to sit inside the house than outside. Come and help me.'

Maxim told the old lady to hold on. She rushed to the tomato plant and retrieved the sarong. When the old lady received it with a blank look on her face, Maxim suggested that a clothed body was better prepared for whatever was coming.

'Coming where?' Pushpanayagi asked as she lifted her arms and allowed the girl to drop the sarong over her head. She tied a knot on the fabric above the old woman's breasts, then held Pushpanayagi's arm. 'I'm going to take you in now,' she said and pulled hard. 'Let's go, Auntie,' she said as Pushpanayagi grunted and groaned and slowly rose.

When they entered the house, Pushpanayagi pointed at the corridor to the left of the hall and instructed Maxim to lead her down to her room. She talked about butterflies fluttering from wall to wall, old man Abu—now with no teeth, and the roasted-peanut seller's bell that tinkled through the skies over oceans wide enough to make families forget. Maxim kept silent as the old woman spoke.

'Hear that or not, child? I think so he's coming.'

They plodded down the corridor, past rooms on either side, and finally entered the last room. Maxim lay Pushpanayagi down on a mat and gently placed her head on a pile of sarongs that functioned as a pillow.

'Rest now, Auntie. Close your eyes and sleep.'

She watched as the old woman's eyelids drooped and opened, drooped and opened. When at last they closed, a profuse peace spread across her face as though the peace had been on the verge of spilling forth, patiently standing by for its cue.

On her way out, Maxim stopped outside a room along the corridor. Like most of the house, it was empty apart from a large cardboard box sitting in a corner close to the windows that opened out onto the courtyard. On the box, printed in red block letters, were the words 'F & N Orange'. The box was full, so full that it looked like it was about to split open at the sides.

She went into the room and knelt by the box. She started taking out the items and began placing them on the floor. One by one, the objects that had been buried for so long stretched and yawned. Copper candelabras breathed and opened their eyes, dusty blotches of red wax like frozen tears beneath their rims. A tattered map of Ceylon fluttered and belched its memories of the eyes that had looked upon it centuries ago. The silver flowers on a torn, coral-red sari winked, their petals straightening to glow brighter. She reached for a pair of leather sandals, the toe straps on both sides still attached to the soles by two or three slivers of thread. As she pulled the sandals out, a slim wad of letters fell to the floor. Bound by brown string, its fibres fraying, the first and last letters in the pile had inherited the imprint of the string. She untied the string and unfolded the first letter, dated 8th May 1880.

Dearest Penelope,

I do sincerely hope you have not suffered further injuries to your dignity since we last departed. Why won't you accept that I do not wish to enslave you but only to liberate you? You are indeed a special breed, my dear Penelope, but is it not enough for you to know this, the man who adores you by your side, and not a swarm of indiscriminate men trailing behind you like bees their Queen?

I beg you to receive my gift and not look upon it as a token of charity. It is more an acknowledgment of your value and a plea that you exercise other faculties which, I am certain, you can rule over and flourish from. Since you have rejected the first, more important offering of my heart, you must, if I am to believe you respect me, honour me by accepting my second. But if you change your mind and see me as a suitable partner for life, then my first offering remains true.

It is my sincerest wish that you reconsider it. What is the use of life if it is devoid of love? You cannot deny that it was love which we had in those months on Coal Island. Surely, my love, you cannot have forgotten those delicious feelings of wonderment and delight at the sight of each other's faces upon awakening in the morning. Surely, you still remember how our hands felt intertwined. If you wish not to make a man suffer for the rest of his life, then marry me.

Herewith I enclose a sum of twenty-four shillings. Please do not return it like the last time.

Ever yours,
Richard

Maxim unfolded and read the second letter, the third and fourth letters, until she reached the fifteenth and last letter and began digging through the box again. A neatly folded piece of paper lay between a Huntley & Palmers biscuit tin, its paint chipped, and a leather-bound notebook. She placed the paper on the floor and opened the notebook. She flicked through empty pages of yellowed paper, until she reached the middle. Three dead butterflies, perfectly preserved and loosely stuck to the page, threatened to slip onto her lap. The smallest one was mainly black with little orange spots scattered on each wing. Another, black with a splash of green in the middle of its wing. The biggest butterfly was pure red. She gently placed the notebook on the floor and picked up the paper. Her fingers trembled as she unfolded it and began to read.

August, 1943

My dear Pushpa,

It has come to this, hasn't it? I have to write you letters like a poor fool in her own house! Not my house, I understand this much. *Your* house. I know it is yours, and Charles and I are your guests. Long term guests but guests nevertheless. Although, as the years pass, I don't think of myself as a guest to you, only as a sister. Please know that I am ever so grateful for our sisterhood. Orphans like me feel blessed when we find the siblings we have wanted all our lives. I know the nuns at the convent (my beloved mothers, each one) would be so happy to know about you.

Therefore, I sigh long and hard as I write this, my dear one. I can't seem to bring myself to talk to you in person about this. As I sit here in our underground room, our little 'Den of Peace', you are in the hall playing songs for Charlie on the piano, trying to make this whole business of war that much lighter, that much nicer for all of us.

And that is who you are, my sweet, sweet Angel. You have lightened all of us with your magic.

But even with your light, these are dark days. Ever since that Communist, that poor sweet soul, died in our 'Den of Peace', I have not rested. I feel him here in my bones, Pushpa. He haunts my nights, he agitates my days. He tells me to send him away from this house. Oh, my darling one, I have prayed! I know Charlie doesn't like me going up to the Top Room, but I went and sat in front of Our Lady of Sorrows and wept.

That poor, sweet man wasn't anyone I knew, but to watch a man wail and cry as death took over his body! And his regrets! Oh, Pushpa, his regrets! He moans and screams now in death.

I hear them whispering, Pushpa. This house is full of voices. I wish you would tell me about the past. What has happened here? I do not mean this as an attack, my sweet sister, but why do you never speak of yourself? Why do you, Charlie, and Abu keep your friendship to yourselves? I have tried so hard to ease my way into your bond, but I always fail.

I don't know what I am asking of you. I feel a terrible darkness descending. It is already covering the whole island. It is all over Malaya. It is deep inside this house. I wish you would speak to me, Pushpa. Perhaps that is what I am asking of you. I simply wish to hear your sweet, sweet voice telling me what lies deep in your soul. I want us all to breathe again.

All my love, your sister,
Savitri

5

The gibbons in the jungle awakened. The one-eyed dog beneath the jacaranda tree opened its eye and peered at the dew-kissed swifts flying low. By the well behind the house, the frogs awakened and the sole toad lifted its heavy eyelids, their tongues darting for insects slowly emerging in the rose pink morning, the sun a new sun. A baked disc, fresh arrival, still kind to naked eyes, indiscriminate mother of the earth: blackbirds sang loudly, mad about the new glittering rays streaming onto grass, pebbles, flowers, water, worms, the old lady's finger perched on the veranda railing, blindly pointing in the direction of the cabbages. Her eyes—did they register the morning morphing from pink to orange? She gazed far out in the distance, past the land opposite her house, perhaps at the clear wide sky, perhaps at the sepulchral bushes surrounding the land.

The illness had momentarily lifted. A girl had come—brand new like the morning sun—and had walked the old lady; hand in hand, forgetting her fear, into the house. Could it have been believed that the rats in the kitchen—starved of food but loyal to the history of rats in Yalpanam's kitchen—the noses of these rats, could it have been believed, twitched and twitched as though sniffing the change of air? Believed or rejected, it was in fact what happened. And the walls, for brief moments throughout the day and night, stopped sighing. The spider in the rectangular room finally left its web and inched its way out through the front door.

But the old lady, still wishing and breathing in sync with the clock of her own making, looked steadfastly at her precious vegetable patch and sighed as if to compensate for the house. Once before, years and years ago, she stood at the very same spot on the veranda and gazed out into the garden, her hands dripping not with water from gardening but with juice from a coconut she'd drunk straight from the unhusked shell after which, delighted, refreshed, she proclaimed to the magpies that had come to steal the little butterfly collecting tools left out on a table, 'How good is life! How good is life!' It would be unfair to dismiss this declaration as a feverish exaggeration brought on by the coconut juice consumed with gusto on a dazzling silvery morning. There were, indeed, very good things happening in and around the house, and certainly, in the lives of those who lived in it. The old woman—not yet astonishingly old then, but not entirely young either, a mature middle-age—had new guests in her home, guests who soon turned into comfortable residents who embarked on an unlikely life with her. Unlikely because colonial society on the island was not privy to what it considered to be bizarre assemblies or camaraderie of any kind, be it servant-master intimacy, Malay-Chinese riverside banter while poaching fish, or mongrel families that sometimes formed, quite spontaneously, across the island, all defying classification. Ironically, the head guest Pushpanayagi invited into her home had a passion that matched, and sometimes even surpassed, the colonial love of order. He was a butterfly man, a lepidopterist with sharp blue eyes for minutiae, and he spent most of his spare time catching butterflies, breeding them in a room in the house, studying them under large, imported-from-England magnifying glasses, giving his beloved winged creatures long, elaborate Latin names, dipping them in formaldehyde and pressing them neatly between sheets of rice paper. The day over, he would materialize from his butterfly room, accomplished, in the highest of spirits, ready for the feast his servant-cook had laid out on the long, mahogany table in the dining area beside the front hall. And Pushpanayagi, already a lady of inheritance and therefore of leisure, would sit across from her guest at the dinner table, delicately cut her food with a fork and knife while glancing at her guest from time to time, asking him agreeable questions about butterflies and about the plantation he managed. The guest's wife, by this point a self-professed invalid, too 'unimaginably melancholic' to eat, would be upstairs in her room, counting jasmine petals from a bunch the servant-cook brought her once every two days, out of, as he told Pushpanayagi, 'something burning in my heart.'

Perhaps those who had been allowed to visit the wife (there were none) would have concluded: this is *not* a good life and it certainly does not warrant gulping down fresh coconut water and exclaiming to a deaf world that life is good. But those phantom onlookers would have been people attracted to veneers, to swift, easy conclusions. Mary Tanner, transported by her desperate husband to the house of the mystical Sybil, was, in the minds of Charles Tanner and Sybil herself, lucky.

It had happened like this: failing to find a cure for Mary's mysterious ailment, Charles, in an uncharacteristic fit of something, sought the help of the woman who had inherited his second cousin's house; not for that reason, but for the glaring fact that people, colonials and natives both, talked about her supernatural connection to the land, of her past as the Mystic under the Banyan Tree, of her ability to commune with devils and unseen entities that swarmed the island, stealthily entered homes and possessed the living. For, he one day concluded, Mary, cherub-faced, merry cherry-eater and meadow-skipper in England, transformed backwards, from butterfly to caterpillar, not immediately upon stepping foot on the island, but gradually, over three or four years, so that, he further concluded, he had no other choice but to believe his cook-servant, Abu, when he whispered to his master, 'Is Syaitan, Tuan. Mem got Devil inside.'

At least, the house-owner and the head guest agreed the few times they broached the subject at dinner that upstairs she was safe from spirits. Sorrow, they said, was a normal human feeling. It had nothing to do with devils. And so it went on, these peaceful dinners, and this unlikely co-existence colonial society believed was 'incredible', 'remarkably strange', 'improper—Husband, Wife, Servant, and . . . ?' Even then, Pushpanayagi, whether consciously or not, defied the kind of categorization favoured by her head guest. Interestingly, he did not seem to mind—in fact, he enjoyed the murkiness about her, which he decided was the mark of all good mystics. The plump, audacious Blavatsky was awakening something in the English world with her occult ideas and esoteric eyes. Mediums, ladies with swirling eyes, were channelling spirits and souls, piquing the interest of men and women of genius, poets, artists and intellectuals: not ordinary folk, not the mediocre, but those with *vision*. Darwin (Charles Tanner was secretly flattered that he shared the great scientist's name) had burst biblical bubbles, and those new rock-men, studying the earth, silts and sedimentations, boldly revealed that the Earth was not six-thousand years old, as the Bible said, but older, much older. There was Charles Tanner, in the midst of this dichotomy between hard facts and spiritual unravelling, between a new physicality—a new earth was, after all, being discovered—and a new ethereality, a man proud of the Victorian age that, luckily for him, was still alive and flourishing, a man of Empire, a man of science, make no mistake, but subject nevertheless to rupturing notions of reality, thousands of miles away from his original centre of gravity, on an island not generally known by ordinary British men and women. Life was good! An Indian Blavatsky (in his head alone; no one else made the connection) by his side, articles on tropical butterfly and moth life in entomology journals, Charles Tanner saw himself as a New Man, modern, very much in the eye of the zeitgeist storm.

And the Blavatsky of his making (the names Blavatsky and Sybil were soon dropped by Charles and replaced with the more modest 'Deborah'), ignorant of her Russian precedent, assumed her role as she had assumed her previous role as Banyan Woman: charmingly, and without question. She gave counsel with silence and eye-gazing, successful techniques for Charles who was less interested in being helped than in believing he had, after fifteen years on the island, adapted to its eccentricities.

Thus it proceeded until the end, Charles's bones given to the land he could not, for whatever reason, bring himself to leave. Stirring, yes, some of those bones behind the house are his, stirring without the old woman's knowledge.

But—those are ancient stories—too ancient, some may say—for a rich tangerine morning when every creature that should have awakened had awakened, and the air smelled of fresh, new life. The old woman, finished with her gazing, turned around and coughing between sighs, moseyed back into the house, yearning for sleep, too tired, unlike the rest of the awakened world, to remain with eyes open.

*

She sat by her bedroom window, phone in her hands, waiting for Footsy's reply. Up on the hill, the gate she had climbed over in a fit of madness looked strange. *Falling* into the compound like a thief. Now the house felt far, far away, as though it lived on a different land entirely, its wooden walls translucent, exposing the hall with the two chairs weirdly facing each other, the ground-floor rooms starved of objects, of paintings (not even a tiny statue of a god), the room with the dubious box, and the last room where the old lady slept on a mat: no bed, no chairs, no dressing table, only a pile of musty sarongs and a huge hardback copy of *The Ramayana*.

No, Yalpanam wasn't flickering. What did they call it? Optical something. Or she was going mad. Or the old lady had somehow put a curse on her. Pretending to be sick while she played voodoo on her? Kak Isma talked nonsense sometimes, but maybe Little

Girl Maxim had been too skeptical to hear the warnings properly. *That old lady there, she's a witch. If you don't eat, I call her to come.* All this while, Kak Isma could have been telling the truth. Illusion, yes that was it, an optical illusion.

No lights blinked on her phone. She'd found the courage *four whole hours ago*. Why hadn't Footsy written back? She unlocked her phone screen, clicked into her email account and brought up the message she'd sent him at 13.21.

Was it too desperate? But there was no one else to go to. He may suggest calling a doctor for the old lady or he may tell her to let the whole story go and find a new one. If he told her to forget about it, shouldn't she still go back to Yalpanam and see if Auntie P was ok? And if she was really dying, would Daddy allow her to ring Dr Ipe to ask for help? Maybe he wouldn't mind, now that he was packing her off to Australia. But going up the hill once more felt like a dream. How could she do it all over again?

She flung the phone on the carpet and fished in her pocket for the letter she had taken from the old lady's box of things. The old lady was like one of those statues in the Indian temple by the sea. She didn't exactly look like the luminous dolls dressed in tacky saris, with powdery pottus on their bronze phosphorescent foreheads, their faces sometimes flat with no features. It was more the way the woman seemed to her, or was it the way she moved and spoke? Something temple-like.

She unfolded the letter, so thin and fragile in her hands, grainy but soft, a small, expanding rip right smack in the centre. She lifted it to her nose and breathed in deeply. All old things had the same smell, a mixture of antique table drawers and cockroach.

The letter was a *small* theft. There were, what was it, twenty, twenty-five letters? One almost-torn letter missing from the box wasn't going to cause a hurricane. And clearly, the old lady had forgotten that the box even existed. What was she doing with letters addressed to prissy English women anyway? Catherine, Deborah, Penelope. All sounded like they needed a tight slap.

Written on this very island, some over a whole century ago. Was the old lady really that old? Or was the old lady a thief like her, keeping letters that weren't hers to keep?

She breathed in the stale smell of the letter. A tingling wave spread through her body. The paper felt alien in her hands as though it didn't belong there, as though she was holding one of those chunky gold necklaces hanging like an albatross around Mother's neck when she returned from trips to KL. Something about the letter she stole was different; more desperate, more pumped with darkness, more real than the others, the only one written by a woman. Like the other letters, this one licked the dirt on Auntie's feet, oh, you sweet, sweet Angel, you have lightened all of us with your magic! But Savitri was no idiot. She'd seen Mother do the exact same thing. *Wah, Mrs Lim, so pretty today. So nice lah you. Your bank transfer still no come through.* Except Savitri was more elegant. Savitri's suffering wasn't like the plastic tears and moans and groans that Mother churned out when things weren't going her way. Kong ah, Kong ah, Kong ah, and Daddy would call his men in to replace all the lights in the house. Or whatever it was she wanted. Savitri wanted Pushpa to tell the truth. Stop bullshitting and tell the goddamn truth!

Savitri could not *rest*. The poor sweet Communist had died in her—no, Auntie P's—house and his ghost was haunting her *bones*. Could a Communist really be sweet? The history books at school said they were evil killers who tried to take the country down. Savitri watched an actual Communist die and look at her suffering. What did the people who wrote history books know anyway? Did a Communist die in *their* arms?

The faded, blue squiggles on the thin paper were neat, beautiful, the letters curling and curving into one another like a gently flowing stream. Hard to read at first, but once she cracked the code of how Savitri's pen moved, it was easy. No one ever wrote words like a gently flowing stream anymore. No one ever wrote on paper.

This house is full of voices. Why do you never speak of yourself?

She fingered the letter, her heart thrashing about in her chest, her throat heavy. She leapt from her seat and paced up and down the room, folded the letter into her pocket and stomped out of the room. She waited at the top of the staircase, then rushed back into her room to check her phone. No message from Footsy, but a purple light blinked which meant a new post had been uploaded on Footsy's website. She clicked open the new post. 'In an infinite universe, every point can be regarded as the centre because every point has an infinite number of stars on each side of it.'

She stood by the window, unable to move.

'Maxim, ah, Maxim!'

Thumping footsteps up the staircase.

'Maxim!'

Mother stood by the door, hands on hips, hair freshly permed.

'Girl, ah! Why never answer? Calling, calling, my voice also koyak!'

Mother smiled and sauntered in, swaying her hips, obviously in a good mood.

'Come downstair, girl. All the aunties be coming five, ten minute already.'

Her eyes travelled from Maxim's feet to her chest and down again. The smile dwindled away.

'Eh, I say to get ready by six o'clock! This stupid Batu Ferringi T-shirt ah, I going to tell Kak Isma throw away already. You eighteen year already, must start behave like lady. Cannot wear this kind of T-shirt and short pant. When you go Australia, you think can walk around like tomboy, ah? Cannot! You must be woman lah, girl. Faster go change. Inside your cupboard got so many dress.'

Mother twirled around and left the room, not waiting, weirdly enough, for Maxim to nod or grunt some kind of response. Mother seemed so pleased about the whole thing. The ladies from the Ladies' Club coming was one excitement, but the other more important golden nugget was Maxim's disappearance into the wilds of Australia. Perhaps not the *wilds*,but Australia was far away enough, a whole different continent where people dragged vowels out and had kangaroos as roadkill.

'Mummy!' she called out.

She ran to the entrance of her room. Mother stopped by the second flight of stairs, looked up and silently mouthed, 'What?'

Maxim sprinted down the stairs. Any moment now, the doorbell would be whining "Fur Elise", starting over as each lady arrived.

'Should we buy a new suitcase for when I leave, Mummy?'

Mother laughed. 'You, ah! Mummy already buy for you.'

'How about sweaters, scarves, stuff like that?'

Mother made the tut-tut sound she made when she wanted to show regret or superiority. 'Of course, lah. Mummy already buy. Your suitcase in the storeroom. Every day, Kak Isma pack one two thing.'

Mother waved her hand, gesturing that Maxim was taking up too much precious time. The tinny sound of 'Fur Elise' resounded through the house. Mother bounded down the stairs, checked her lips and teeth in the hall mirror, fussed with her perm, then raced to the door.

'Ah, Kimberly! Come, come, come.'

Maxim ran down the stairs and paused where the two women were air-kissing each other.

'Oh, you see my girl, hahaha,' Mother shrieked, 'never got time to change. Say hello to Auntie Kimberly, girl.'

'Hello, Auntie Kimberly.'

The woman smiled and touched her earrings as if she wanted to draw attention to them. 'Maxim should come over one day,' Auntie Kimberly said through her smile, 'she and Christopher will have a lot to talk about. He's studying in KL right now, but he comes home once a month.'

Mother shrieked again. 'Of course, of course,' she said, leading the lady into the hall where trays of biscuits had been arranged on the coffee table.

Maxim slipped out the front door. She ran towards the open gate and looked left, right, left. She jogged out and dashed past the bamboo clump, then turned off up the road leading to Yalpanam. A motorbike was parked outside the slightly ajar gate. She pushed past the gate and headed for the front doors.

The garden felt strangely silent. Nothing moved. The plants glowed in shocking bright green and the red roses stood like beautiful soldiers ready to kill with their allure. The birds that had hopped and twittered that morning were gone. Only the breath of a soft, nearly non-existent breeze.

She braved the hall and looked around. A man stood at the entrance of the corridor, his arms folded, his face in shadow. He hoisted a hand as if asking her what she wanted. But her voice had gone back into the black space within. His shadow clung to the wall by the corridor. Suddenly, it moved and she almost fell back. He jerked his head, asking her what she was doing there. She froze. A deep groan echoed through the silence in the hall. The man turned around, nearly vacating his guarding spot. She darted forward. The groan grew louder and louder, then stopped. He rushed down the corridor and into the old lady's bedroom. She also ran. She stood by the bedroom door and glanced inside. The man dabbed sweat off the old lady's forehead with a cloth. The sarong she had tied around Auntie P earlier that day was still intact. The man raised his head. The shadows from his face lifted. He looked different from when he rode down the hill on his motorbike, his face sharper, more handsome. The old lady opened and closed her eyes and opened them again. She looked at Maxim and nodded. 'Come, come,' she croaked. A weak smile appeared and disappeared on her wrinkled yellowish face.

*

Better rest, they said, and then they left. They wanted to shut the door but Pushpanayagi insisted no, no, it was already too dark and hot in her room. The air felt heavy, low, as though it could strangle and choke. She coughed and spat into the little tin the boy had placed on the floor 'for emergencies.' Like a frightened rat, the girl had watched the boy refolding the sarongs for the pillow-pile. Death around her, no wonder the poor child shivered.

Down the corridor, they were talking about something. Hadi nicely-nicely raising his voice and the girl so quiet, almost unheard, but now and again, something sharp shot out of her mouth and into the bedroom. Maybe they were arguing. Hard to know. She'd only seen Hadi talking to her and always his voice was soft like wet soil. Every time he came to see her, he sat with her, or helped in the garden, made sure she had everything she needed, that she was happy and healthy and only then he left.

He sounded angry with the girl. He was asking her something in the same tone, over and over again. Why, why . . . what was he saying? Why are you here? He wanted to know what she was doing there, all of a sudden. And something else. He mentioned 'My Auntie'.

She closed her eyes. A cold dark feeling swept through her body. The feeling leapt high, dipped low, swayed from side to side. It rose from her belly and out beyond her body, overflowing into the room, merging with the air. It rose higher, and wider, and fused with the entire space of the house, the garden, the road outside the gate.

Voices echoed through her.

'I wanted to see if Auntie was ok.'

'Why all of a sudden? I have seen you at Market Square. All these years, you never asked about my Auntie even once.'

'I cannot explain. I just wanted to come back.'

Pushpanayagi's body disappeared into the dark cold feeling. She grew and grew, and leaked into gaps and corners, into the space between leaves, into the airstreams of tree trunks. A burst of warmth charged through the feeling and the feeling expanded into the sky.

'Come back, come back.'

'That's what I said. I had to come back to check.'

The feeling sizzled through Pushpanayagi's body and swelled out beyond the sky, beyond the planet, into dark empty space. Stars quivered. Spots of light flashed through the darkness. They sprung in coils and orbited Pushpanayagi, spinning wildly as meteors and comets darted through her and she fell deeper and deeper into the black silent air until all the stars, all the helixes of light and meteors, and comets vanished and there was nothing. Nothing flickered, nothing seen, nothing heard. Black. Motionless. Peace.

She opened her eyes.

Steam billows in whorls and clouds from a pot on the stove, the water bubbling, spitting, giving away little of what is being cooked, only a vague scent of boiling plants. Open tins with spoons sticking out stand between blackened hobs. A woman in a pink maxi housedress is chopping tapioca at the counter beside the stove, her head bent. A tiny rat sniffs at the sooty cement floor and scurries forward. It pauses when something rustles in the kitchen, when something solid hits a surface. It scampers towards a mountain of vegetable peelings on the floor and buries itself between two thick shavings of tapioca skin.

The woman turns around. 'Oh my darling Pushpa, why are you just standing there?'

Savitri laughs and stirs the pot. She lifts the ladle and blows on it, then licks it and pirouettes around. 'You know, if I have to say it myself, I will!' she says, mock-boasting, 'I am a damned good cook!' She throws her head back. Her bony shoulders heave and tremulous laughter reverberates through the kitchen.

Pushpanayagi waits by the entrance of the kitchen, hands folded at her back, one foot already touching the pavement opposite the courtyard.

'Do you know I have managed to make the most superior soup, my own, sweet, Pushpa? If the Japanese think they can murder creativity too, they are as mad as their Emperor! Am I right, sweetheart?'

Laughter rises through the kitchen like steel cups clashing. It peters out, stops. Birds twitter and chirp in the courtyard. The pot on the stove bubbles louder and louder.

'Have you lost your voice, Pushpa?'

Savitri throws the ladle into the pot and dusts her hands as though she'd been touching soil. Her face flags. A small frown emerges, her eyes hollow, her thinness so pronounced it has spread to her forehead and cheeks, more bone than flesh. She looks at Pushpanayagi for a long while. Finally, she says, 'I suppose you are waiting to take something out to the boys?'

Pushpa nods.

'All right, all right.' Savitri looks around the kitchen, searching, then heads for the other end of the kitchen. She reaches for a plate stacked with golden-brown slices. 'Perhaps they will like these tapioca chips,' she says, peering beneath the plate. 'All clean and good,' she nods, 'I have worked magic for this birthday, my darling.'

Steam from the pot suffuses the kitchen, heating up walls, cheeks, armpits. A robust smell of boiling vegetables finally rises. It is the everyday smell of boiling water, of the same vegetables meeting fire and heat: tapioca, sweet potato; tapioca, sweet potato; mashed, fried, boiled, steamed; the habitual, now-familiar smell floats through the nostrils and into the cells of the body.

'How did you manage to get so much tapioca and sweet potato, Savi?'

Savitri winks and smiles as though she has been waiting to reveal a secret. 'I begged the boy Zafar to find *anything* he could find for your birthday. He searched high and low, that clever boy!'

Pushpa blinks slowly at her. 'What were you expecting to do during a war, Savi?'

'It isn't enough, is it?'

Pushpanayagi remains stoic, statuesque.

'I am doing the best I can.' Savitri's voice trembles. 'I sat down and planned your birthday menu. Specially. I went to the den and I wrote on a piece of paper. Dish-ends soup. Roasted snails. Mashed sweet potato. Tapioca chips. Papaya leaf curry. Tapioca balls. I am working hard to make everything normal again. Can they see that? I really do wonder sometimes whether people can see all that I do.' She stares at a spot on the wall, then quickly looks back at Pushpa and says, 'Then sweet Zafar, feeling guilty he only managed to bring me vegetables, went *out of his way* and brought me a whole fish at dawn this morning. I couldn't believe my luck. Look over there.' She gestures towards the space between the sink and the stove. The bloodied carcass of a long grey fish lies filleted in half, a knife glistening between the two pink-red halves. 'Now I can also do a baked fish with basil from the garden.' Her eyebrows narrow down. She glares at Pushpa with dark, retreating eyes.

'More than enough, Savitri. Birthdays are not that important. You should rest.'

Savitri places the plate of tapioca chips back on the wooden counter. She skips towards Pushpanayagi and rubs her eyes, exaggerates her blinking. 'Am I talking to Pushpanayagi? The very same Pushpa who combs my hair and makes new patterns in my braids? Sister from the Continent?' She laughs and shakes her head. 'The very same Pushpa who sings 'Goodnight, Ladies' at the piano as bombs blast away in the skies? The Pushpa who grows chillies in secret and who has fooled Japanese soldiers with her pretend madness?'

'What do you mean, Savitri?'

'When difficulty comes our way, we carry on anyway. That's what I mean. You sound so defeated.' She steps forward and studies Pushpa's face. 'Has Abu's gloom infected you? Or have you been listening too much to Charlie's ramblings?'

'Neither.'

Savitri shrugs. 'I don't believe you. Please, listen to me. If your spirit goes too, I don't know what I'll do. It's not in our blood to give up. We're sisters from different lands, remember? But united in this new land. Don't lose heart, sweet sister.'

She drifts back to the wooden counter and brings the plate over to Pushpa. 'Take this to the grumpy twins, ok? Tell them some sweet, soothing stories before lunch. All I want is for us to have a nice, decent, normal celebration. With or without bombs.'

Pushpanayagi takes the plate from her and turns away from the kitchen's entrance. She lurks by the corner of the window closest to the entrance, and tilts her head slightly. Through the partially open window, she watches Savitri skip towards the stove and pause as if contemplating whether to carry on cooking. Her skeletal frame, poorly disguised by the long, loose dress, reveals what cannot be hidden, the effects of the times they are living in. Savitri stares at plumes of steam, finger in her mouth, waiting for something to happen. Then, she lurches forward and grabs the ladle from the pot and begins stirring madly. 'For she's a jolly good fellow, for she's a jolly good fellow,' she sings, arm on her hip, head nodding to the beat of her song. She spins around once, twice. Liquid from the ladle drips onto the floor. The rat bolts forward, licks the drops and scurries back to its home beneath the mound of tapioca skin. 'For she's a jolly good fellow, and nobody can deny!' Savitri tastes from the ladle and clicks her tongue. 'I dare say, Mrs Tanner, you are a marvellous cook,' she says, dipping the ladle into the pot and tasting more of her dish, 'absolutely spectacular! Even if no one in this house or the universe sees how special you are, rest assured this soup knows!'

Pushpanayagi cowers away from the window. She hurries on tiptoe towards the passageway opposite the courtyard. The neatly stacked tapioca chips threaten to collapse. She stops to allow the chips to settle back in place and takes a deep breath and then another, and turns towards the windows facing the courtyard. Behind the green glass, silhouettes of plants close in on a shadowy block in the middle. Birds flit above the block like little black creatures descending on prey. The shadows seem to bend and slither. They seem to be growing bigger and bigger. Pushpanayagi gasps, flings a window open and pushes her head out for air. A light breeze blows in circles but the plants do not stir. They loom over the broken water fountain, waiting to consume it. The stone cherub at the top of the fountain tips a waterless jug, its smile lost in moss, its eyes blinded by dark spots of fungus. Between its arms, palm leaves fight for space. Above, they spread out freely and lick waves of stony cherub hair, sending long pointed shadows down the bulging stone belly.

Wind blasts through the courtyard. The open window flings violently towards Pushpanayagi. She pulls back and ducks down.

A soft hum rises in the wind. It grows louder and morphs as the wind twists and turns. The hum spins into a buzz and the buzz swirls into a soft, low voice. 'To see at night, we turn on the light,' it whispers through the soaring wind.

The wind dies down. Silence ripples through the corridor.

'You have to try, Tuan, try!'

A deep, long grunt.

'Turn the wheel like that!'

The grunt grows deeper, shorter.

'You will fall lah, Tuan! Ya Allah . . .'

Pushpanayagi gets up and sidles towards the voices, holding out the plate of chips like a peace offering as she enters the hall.

Beams of sunlight spill in through the open front doors. Charles sits slumped on a wheelchair, pointing a dark wooden cane at Abu who stands hunching in front of him. Abu's mouth turns slowly, chewing, like a cow savouring grass. His hands hang limp by his sides. 'If you don't turn the wheel, Tuan, you can't move,' he says. The cane comes down in one swift drop and lands in a thump on the floor, quivering in Charles's hand.

'You infernal fool!' Charles says, his head mildly bobbing. 'Why in the world would I want to spin about like a desperate child at a fairground? Who has brought this beast into our house? Not I! Certainly not I.' He strikes the floor with the cane, inches away from Abu's feet.

Abu regards Charles half-amusedly, then trudges towards him as though his feet have taken on a sudden weight, grabs the handles of the wheelchair, and spins it around, his eyes landing on Pushpanayagi. A crooked smile unfurls on his face. Two or three blood-red teeth flash through his dark cavernous mouth.

Pushpanayagi hurries over and settles the plate on a side-table by the loud floral armchair beside Charles' wheelchair. Abu glares at the plate as though plotting an attack on the tapioca chips. 'How many time I tell Ms Savi already, no hard food for Tuan. Why she don't listen to me?'

'A fool remains a fool for life,' Charles says, tapping his cane on the floor, 'I will eat whatever damned well pleases me and you better damned well leave me alone.'

Abu grins and grabs Charles by the armpits. 'One, two, three and we go, ok, Tuan?'

'Get away from me! Go and sit in your chair, Abu.'

Abu releases his grip on Charles. He hovers over his old master, watching, waiting, but Charles's eyes are drooping into sleep and the hand holding the cane trembles softly like the wings of a butterfly, and slowly the cane loosens from the unsteady grasp, but Abu, whose eyes are rarely averted from his master, catches the cane, sacrifices his balance for it, and attempting but failing to rise, resorts to whimpering. 'Ai, Pushpa! Come and help me. Ya Allah,' he says, one hand supported by the wheelchair, the other holding the cane.

Pushpanayagi scurries over to Abu and pulls him up. 'At your age, Abu, you should be sitting down more.'

'Your age, Pushpa? What your age? You never tell!' Abu breathes out loudly like a large, tired animal. He tips his head towards Charles and glances at his old master through the corner of his eye. A soft gleam floods his face and soon hardens. 'You think Ms Savi can take care of her husband like me?' he says, shaking his head mournfully. He reaches for a metal bowl on the floor beside the wheelchair and spits into it.

'She don't know,' he continues, 'she don't know Tuan properly. She here twenty years only. How long I have been here?'

He stares at Pushpa, waiting for an answer. His eyes, violet with age, permanently watery, look as though they had been made for tears. Pushpa peers into the bowl. Meat-red splotches and splashes on the walls of the bowl look like flesh has been beaten to a pulp. She looks away and rests her eyes on Charles who is slowly waking up.

'You've been here a long time, Abu. Yes, I know. I have also been here a long time,' she says, almost whispering.

'Life so long.' Abu spits into the bowl.

Charles raises his head as though he has been awake all this time, eavesdropping. He looks out the front doors. He covers his eyes with his hand, recoiling from the glare of the sun. 'Why does it always have to be so bright?'

'This not because of age, Tuan. You always scare of the sun.'

'Scared? You must be joking. There's nothing in the tropics that scares me. I practically built this island. Why would it scare me?' He pretends to laugh and peeks at Abu from under the shade of his hand.

'This island not built by you,' Abu says, 'before all your people come and all the Europeans—'

'Came, my ancestors were already living in houses here. They had religion, families, songs, stories, life, Tuan, they had a real life before it was taken from them.' Deep pink blossoms across Charles's cheeks and forehead, a slanted smile motionless on his face. 'Yes, yes, Abu, we've heard it all before. You're a broken record playing the same dreary music day in, day out. You seem to think that the British were gods with total power. Well, let me tell you what I've been telling you for years—'

A bomb goes off in the sky. Its blast is mild, soft even.

Charles hits at the armrests of the wheelchair. 'Take me away. God damn this place and take me away,' he screams.

'Only other side of island, Tuan. They don't come this side.'

'You think I'm bloody scared of the Japs? They can rot in hell for all I care. They don't know the island.' He tries to turn his head around to face Pushpanayagi. 'There, her,' he continues, 'our dear Deborah knows what I'm talking about. She's the salt of the earth. From day one, I've said she's a strange sort of goddess. She doesn't meddle. You hear, Abu? Meddling gets you into trouble!'

From down the corridor, Savitri shouts, 'Pushpa, Pushpa.' She rushes into the hall. She pants, waves her hands, calls for attention. Chunks of her hair have come loose from the tie; big frizzy waves stand static, shocked, close to her eyes, over her ears. 'You must come with me, Pushpa,' she says, 'Ah Ching has just been through the back. A man is injured. They have nowhere to let him rest. We can take him to the den. Come with me, Pushpa. We have to get the den ready. God knows how we're going to prepare for an injured man!'

Abu spits into the bowl and says, 'You bring Communist into our house?'

Charles grunts. 'In this house, any enemy of the Japs is a friend to us.'

'You think so, Tuan, Japanese don't want freedom for us? They good—'

'Please, please,' Savitri says, her voice panicked, high-pitched, 'we don't have time to waste. Ah Ching is coming with him soon. A man is a man, be he Jap or Commie.'

A dark swirl of air descends into the house. It curves and dances and bursts into a golden white light. The light spins through the hall, darts through Pushpanayagi. She gasps for breath. The light grows brighter, brighter, and combusts into darkness.

Pushpanayagi opened her eyes. Bluish silver moonbeams lit the walls of her bedroom. The ceiling fan creaked as it turned in slow, laboured sweeps. Beside her on the floor, the young girl lay curled like a foetus, a bundle of sarongs in her arms.

6

Long dark whorls of the night stretch and melt. They spill into Yalpanam's front hall, slip through cracks, and leak into its locked rooms; they rise like great dark waves along the corridor and collapse in the old lady's bedroom into pools of moonlight-flecked liquid tar; the dark tide floods the room where the young girl encountered her first scent of the past, and splashes across the room beside it where insects live and sleep, in honour of the butterflies that had once surged out of cocoons, over a century ago, from boxes and cupboards.

Maxim and Pushpanayagi sleep deeply and dreamlessly. The young girl reposes foetus-like on the floor, head propped on her hands, peacefully, facing the old lady whose mouth is open in abandon. Both drift in the black void of the dream-state, unaware of each other and of two slow-gliding shadows that travel in and out of the bedroom, stealing glances at the two creatures. Once in a while the shadows irradiate when the old lady snores or when the young girl's head shifts a little. But mostly, they remain dark with silver light periodically flashing through them. They roam the corridor and float through rooms.

As the two shadows move, a moderate chill entombs the house. The insects huddle deeper into their wings. The front doors chatter, 'Come in, come in.' The green-glass windows all the around the house whisper, 'Open, open,' and the coolness soaks into the wicker chairs in the hall as they bask in a dark silence. The shadows coast into the hall and levitate over the chairs. They move in circles and chase each other. One dives close to the floor, the other lingers above, then lunges down and clashes into the other. A single shadow forms, large, tumescent. It pulsates and trembles like a black, airy cocoon about to rupture. It drifts on the floor, in strained inches, towards Pushpanayagi's bedroom. It writhes and trembles, struggling to break itself open.

The shadow sails down the corridor, back towards the hall. It slips through the hall windows and climbs over the stone bench in the courtyard.

The pebbles in the courtyard shiver.

The frogs, their heads long embalmed in moonlight, croak.

And the snails, submerged deep in their shells, sink deeper in.

The shadow loops around the dying hibiscus bush behind the stone bench. It slinks between the crinkled leaves and the still supple leaves and shakes the bush from within. It gushes up and out and bifurcates. One shadow speeds to the kitchen opposite the courtyard and the other follows.

The first light of the day slowly illuminates the courtyard in deep shades of blue. The whistling thrushes begin to sing. The shadows circle the kitchen, then slip back to the underground room between the kitchen and the corridor that leads to the hall. They rise again when the deep blues of the courtyard turn golden and the birdsong maddens worms into a dark subterranean dance.

They drift through the house like perennial clouds and watch.

They watch Pushpanayagi's long, slow, solitary days. They watch her sigh and close her eyes and chant, 'Guru Brahma, Guru Vishnu, Guru Devo Maheshwara', peace eventually trickling down her face like drops of water from a patient, leaky faucet. They watch her dig her teeth with a finger and laugh to herself and suddenly sulk at a crawling centipede or beetle on the floor and say, 'where are you going? Where are you going?' Then a sombre look engulfs her face and she nods off.

The shadows lurk close to the ceiling and follow her like her own shadow into the kitchen, into the courtyard, into her bedroom. When she is asleep, they roam the rest of the house, the parts unvisited by her, untouched, covered in calcified dust.

When she goes out into the garden, they bide their time on the veranda. As she probes the soil with a hoe, prunes leaves, plucks weeds, waters the plants, vociferates to the vegetables, pats the pumpkins, and pecks the mangoes with flaccid lips, the shadows pace up and down the veranda until dusk descends and they are free to pursue her back into the house.

They watch as Maxim rouses, stunned at the sight of Pushpanayagi who lies listless as though dead, eyes fully open. They move to the floor and circle the girl as she pokes the old woman with a diffident finger and the old lady gasps, 'What is it? What happened?' And the girl rushes out and back again with a jug in her hands and the old lady drinks and drinks and wipes her lips and drinks.

They watch as day turns into twilight and twilight turns into early night and early night turns into deep night and deep night turns into twilight and twilight turns into dawn and dawn turns into early morning and the mornings fall into more mornings luxuriant with birdsong and the hum of bees and the nights fall into more nights rich with screeching crickets and the plaintive hoot of owls and the long moony wails of rhinoceros beetles.

Days and nights pass and the shadows balloon. They spill out into the hall as the days come and go, come and go. They watch Maxim patrol the corridor as though anticipating the arrival of an intruder on her first two days at Yalpanam. She chews her fingernails distractedly, sucks on her fingers as though she has found a new peculiar function for them, hardly speaks to Pushpanayagi, never to the young vegetable seller. She flits from room to room, glaring, peering, sniffing the walls, the box of Pushpanayagi's mementos, like an animal acquainting itself with a potentially hostile space. They watch as she holds her nose and gingerly steps into the outdoor toilet and reappears, tears streaming down her face. They watch as she sits on the stone bench in the courtyard, eating cubed mangoes, and glances at her mobile phone after every other bite. On the third day, she feeds the old lady pieces of mango and cucumber and when the feeding is over, she charges out the front door and sits in the pumpkin patch and returns, her face ashen, her eyes pickled with shock. She collapses on the floor of the old lady's bedroom and sleeps.

On the fourth day, Pushpanayagi emerges from her bedroom and invites the girl into the garden. Together, they water the plants and the girl plucks weeds and yellowed leaves. For two days, the old lady's strength persists and the shadows observe from the roof of the house as Pushpanayagi teaches the girl how to use the well and the girl takes her first bath at Yalpanam, a baptism of sorts, and enters the house again, wearing one of the old lady's sarongs. The shadows drift along the veranda and watch as Pushpanayagi talks to the girl about how long it takes to grow tomatoes and cabbages, about the hazards of using pesticides. When the vegetable seller comes, he stays until nightfall and when he returns on the seventh day, he finds Maxim sitting alone in the hall. The old lady is in the deepest sleep and cannot be woken up.

On the seventh day, the shadows do not leave Pushpanayagi's bedroom. They orbit her like moons around a planet. Slowly, they inflate and fill the entire bedroom. They push against her body and a deep murmur rises, louder and louder, until the walls begin to tremble mildly.

*

Maxim wrung a wet scrap of sarong over the kitchen sink. She stared intently at the wall in front of her, blackened with dots, dashes, distorted commas, long dark strokes; the strokes streaked up to the ceiling and melded with splotches of dirt into shadow-like cauliflower shapes. The kitchen exuded an undecided odour, a mixture of old floor, animal droppings, wood repeatedly dampened.

She leaned over the sink and wiped the wall with the wet scrap, then pushed herself onto the counter, folded her legs and worked sitting down. She rubbed the lower half of the wall, her hands going over the old, dark curlicues close to the copper tap in slow gentle arcs again and again. She rinsed the cloth, squeezed it, and wiped the same markings, then rubbed harder. One arm moved fiercely, the other's palm pressed against the counter. She scrubbed and scrubbed, gasped and stopped. The black markings had only faded slightly.

Sweat rained down her face and neck. She tossed the sarong scrap into the sink, spun around, unfolded her legs and shrugged. A lizard clicked from behind the meat-safe. She hopped down and walked languidly to the other end of the kitchen where a steel tray lay near the edge of the wooden counter. On it, a mammoth cucumber curved around two robust tomatoes, a chipped ceramic bowl beside them with a copper teaspoon slanting inside. She picked up a knife next to the tray and began slicing the cucumber.

'Looking for what?' Hadi tapped the kitchen door.

She jerked back and the knife fell to the floor. 'You scared me,' she said, turning towards him.

'Oh, sorry, ya.' He slipped into a pair of Japanese slippers by the door and entered the kitchen. A large yellow plastic bag in his hand bounced and rustled against his knee.

She grabbed the knife and stood up, the knife loosely pointed in his direction.

'Careful. All sorts of accidents can happen.' He set the bag down next to the chopped cucumber on the counter.

The knife jittering in her grasp, she watched him remove objects wrapped in newspaper and arrange them close to the tray. Then, forks, spoons, plastic chopsticks, scattered across the counter, and last of all, a family-sized bottle of gaudy pink detergent thumped down heavily in a corner behind the tray. A slice of cucumber rolled to the floor.

'Please,' she said almost to herself.

'You said something?'

The open shutters swung and flapped into each other. A low blowing breeze thrummed quietly through the kitchen.

'No, no. What did you buy?'

He pointed his nose at the counter. 'There. All bought already. Four glasses and two plates. You can unwrap?'

They looked at each other for a short moment.

'Don't worry,' he said, 'I will leave you to make Auntie's tray ready.' He smiled. Deep dimples formed, one on either cheek. He blew at his thick curling hair. 'This kitchen is hard to clean.'

'The dirt has been here . . .' She looked around as if to confirm the existence of the dirt. 'It's been here for too long—'

'You need that rough type of scourer. Silver in colour.'

'You bought?'

'No. Next time. Maybe the dirt will come off then.'

'Yes, maybe,' she said optimistically.

'Never did I think that something like this would happen . . . but . . .' He lowered his eyes and glanced sheepishly at her. 'But, maybe it is a good thing that you want to help Auntie.'

She glowered at the floor as though her communication was happening with it rather than with him.

'That's all,' he said.

The soft, secretive breeze retreated back outdoors. Inside, the air was still, warm, infused with the smells of the old kitchen, of its objects and of the effects of ageing; not yet—as the breeze hoped and as the walls of the kitchen hoped—of food. The afternoon light was luminous, but little of its radiance entered the kitchen, blocked by the shade of the jambu tree.

He looked at her hesitantly.

'Sorry, ya,' he finally said, 'I know you don't like to talk much. But . . . I thought I should ask you.' He tried to meet her eyes.

'Max?'

Slowly, cautiously, she looked at him.

'I thought you couldn't hear,' he said, trying to laugh.

Silence seeped into the kitchen. It entered the tap, the cracks on the walls, and the striations on the wire mesh of the meat-safe. It spilled deep into Maxim's bones and waded through Hadi's blood.

'Okay,' he finally said. He lumbered towards the entrance of the kitchen and stopped. With his back turned to her, he said, 'Another thing. I know we're not old friends, but I feel it is my duty to tell you that . . .'

He spun around. 'At Market Square, I just wanted you to know, at Market Square there are posters.' He took a few reluctant steps in her direction. 'Already nine days you've been here, and down there, your parents are looking for you.'

'Actually,' he continued, his tone bolder, 'the posters are also in town. And your mother . . .'

'What happened to my mother?'

'Nothing. She comes to Market Square. She talks to the sellers, asking if we've seen you—

'And what did you say?'

'Nothing. Nothing.'

'There's nothing to say—'

'I know. I only wanted you to know—'

'Thank you.'

'Sorry, if I offended you.'

'You didn't *offend* me.'

'No, that's not what I meant. It's only that . . .'

'What are the people saying?'

'Island nonsense.'

'What are they *saying*?'

'You really want to know?'

She glared at him.

'Some are saying you ran away from home. Others are saying you found a boy and went with him. Some other people say you were kidnapped. Some say murdered.'

'Okay.'

'Okay?'

She nodded and headed for the sink. She picked up the wet scrap and began wiping the counter. Then, she turned the tap on and left the water to run on the scrap in her cupped palms.

'Max,' he called out. But she watched the water and did not turn around.

He walked up to her. 'Max.'

She turned the tap off. 'Yes?'

Silence soaked through the kitchen. Slowly, her upper body shuddered. He inched closer to her, but quickly pulled away and stepped back.

'I need to finish cleaning,' she said.

He reached out for her again, but promptly brought his hands down to his pockets. 'Yes, the kitchen is very dirty.'

'Very dirty. You can go now.'

He gazed at her back, a forlorn look on his face, then slowly turned around and strode to the kitchen's entrance. 'Another thing,' he said as he slipped out of the Japanese slippers, 'Inside the plastic bag, there's another plastic bag. Hope you like mee goreng. You will soon disappear if you don't eat normal food. Only Auntie can eat like Auntie.'

A thin smile flickered on her face and abruptly disappeared. 'Thank you,' she said. Once he left, a fuller smile appeared, her cheeks reddened, and her fingers danced with greater dexterity as they worked the scrap and attempted to scrub the walls clean of their obtuse black markings.

*

The girl sat on the floor, a small steel tray in her jittering hands. Pushpanayagi yawned and slowly lay down on the mat again. Night would be coming soon, but she had already slept for many long hours. She patted her stomach, massaged it as though it carried a secret, a child. Her arms had lost their jaundiced yellow; her feet too, now soft brown once more.

A sharp high-pitched wail like a banshee's penetrated the silence. The girl jumped and the tray nearly fell to the floor.

'Tut tut,' Pushpanayagi said. She attempted to shake her head but the sarong pillow-pile was too snug around her ears and neck. 'Put the tray down, child. Nothing to be scared of. That's only a beetle.'

'Never heard before,' the girl placed the tray on the floor.

'Acha. This one is a special beetle.' Her eyes widened as though she'd stumbled on a revelation. She tried to get up in a quick instant, but the girl rushed forward, held her arm and settled her back down.

'Oh ho,' the old lady said, 'you must help me. When Hadi comes, you must help pick the correct vegetables to give him for the market.' On the tray was a ceramic bowl, one of the items bought by the boy, now filled with chopped tomatoes and mangoes. 'But, Auntie, I don't know how to do that.'

'Chit, chit. I showed you the other day. Just put your ear to the vegetables and ask if they are ready to go. They will tell you when they know you are listening. Hadi is a good boy but he doesn't wait long enough. Always he is rushing to go on his motorbike. The vegetables know, you see. They know he is waiting to go.'

The old lady closed her eyes and smiled furtively.

'All right, Auntie, I'll try. I'll let you sleep now. I'm going to dust the walls.' She tottered towards the door, paused, and opened her mouth as though she had something to say but nothing emerged.

'The vegetables will talk to you,' Pushpanayagi muttered, 'they will talk, but you must be there to listen.'

A black swell of silence surged through Pushpanayagi's body. It scaled through the room, pushed out into the rest of the house, the garden, the island, the planet, the universe. A storm of stars pelted down through her, through the dark bloat of silence. The stars fell and fell, and whirred in a pool of luminous saffron light.

The luminous saffron light swirled upwards and exploded into sharp white light and the sharp white light receded into warm black peace.

Pushpanayagi opens her eyes.

The flames from four stout candles glow dusky orange against a dark wall. The candles stand in a row, inches apart, held up by their own wax on a narrow strip of cardboard. Coils and twists of vapour hang in the dark, moribund air, lazing, lagging, hardly disappearing. A thick, musty smell like frying nuts spools around the cellar, its womb. It expands as Abu sucks on his pipe. He suspends the pipe over the burning oil lamp, his body like a fallen leaf lying limp, almost flat on a wooden slat—and sucks again. His eyes close momentarily. He is perfectly still. A smile glimmers on his face, a sleepy, almost regal smile. Slowly, very slowly, he lowers the pipe again and opens his eyes. They glisten, glazed with liquid, with kept secrets.

'Pushpa, forever we wait for time to come,' he says, his words stretched, ponderous like the sweet musty smell of opium, like its spirals of vapour.

Pushpanayagi leans back, gently presses her palms against the floor and watches him take another drag from the pipe. Beside the lamp, a tray sparkles with metal objects. They twinkle like fallen stars; a pair of scissors, a long needle, a blackened scraper.

'I tell Tuan already he must do something.' He smiles and adjusts the pipe until its little knob of a bowl meets the lamp's flame. He lowers his head and sucks.

'For what?' Pushpanayagi asks.

Abu lays the pipe down. He rests his head against his hand and gazes at her through indifferent eyes. Mechanically, he says, 'For Mem. White woman like that cannot live here.'

'Abu. Tell the truth. You didn't talk to Tuan Charles.'

He chuckles. 'Push, Push, Pushpi. Why I don't work for you? This your house, sister. You bring white people here, you say nice-nice, "Charles, we take care of you. Come sit in Yalpanam."

White people like that, sister. You give them one spoon, they take whole kitchen.'

He hums a low, tuneless melody, taken from the birds, from the pots and pans of his long days serving his master, from the snakes he hears when he uses the scythe to hack off stubborn high-growing weeds behind the house. He stops humming and sucks on the pipe. Tendrils of thick vapour bloom in the air. His mouth lingers close to the tip of the pipe, ready for the next drag. 'I talk already, Pushpa. I tell him his wife talk with ghost. He got to send her back England.'

'And when you told him that, did you also tell him about this place?'

He stares above, unblinking. 'This place my business, sister. You yourself say to me, Abu, use this place for rest. For play and own self thing. Please, sister, you only see what is my life. Ever I ask you for money? Ever I ask you for big-big thing?' He sniffs and gently turns his head towards the pipe. He sucks hard, holds the vapour within and exhales loudly.

'If Charles finds out about this cellar and what you do here, what will happen to you, Abu?'

'Sister, sister, please. This cellar small thing. Inside here, Abu is free man. The big-big thing up there.' He wiggles a finger, vaguely indicating the upper level of the house. 'I think so I hear Tuan say Mem got to go. She too much frighten here.'

'Abu, you talk like this only when you are here. In your opium den, suddenly your mouth is so big. You haven't talked to Tuan. But it's okay. Better you go to sleep. Too many black thoughts in your head.'

'Not black thoughts, sister. We talking about freedom. Every day I am working. You think who I am working for? Not Tuan. Tuan, he is talking with big-big men in the office. At home, he pushing out butterfly, putting them inside big-big book. Always he is catching butterfly, putting them inside the book. And I? I go up, go down, up, down, up down, for who? Mem Mary, she suffer, Pushpa. Poor Mem is suffer here.'

His voice chimes a single note, flat, sucked free of passion. He lifts the pipe and with the other hand, gestures for her to come to him. She covers her head with her sari sash and holds parts of it over her mouth and nose. The flame of one candle has died, the other three quiver in small, orange leaf-like shapes. She takes languorous steps as she watches her feet in the dark. She squats over the lamp. The clutch that fastens the pipe-bowl to the lamp has come loose. She takes the tail end of the pipe and holds it over the lamp. The opium pill inside the pipe-bowl vaporizes. She watches Abu suck hard at the pipe and when he has taken a long drag, she grabs the hot pipe-bowl and scrapes the dross and ash with the scraper from the tray. She tips the bowl over into a small metal dish and gently knocks it against the dish until all the flecks have left the bowl.

'You cook more chandu for me, Pushpa?'

To the walls and air, she says, 'Maybe later.'

'You try with me, sister. Then never you will say "later". Opium always now. Now, now, now.'

A second candle burns out. She reaches for a candle beside a bottle of glistening oil opposite the tray.

'Sister, my blood singing. Now I go see Mem Mary and I tell her soft-soft, "Go back. Go back." Mem will happy in England. Tuan don't love her.' He turns his body and lays flat on his back. His eyes are suddenly alert, fixed on the darkness above.

'Abu, you only lit four short candles,' Pushpa says, 'next time, don't you think you should light more candles if you only have short ones? Or light one or two long candles with the short ones.' She strikes a match and lights the replacement candle. She lets the wax drip onto the floor, then sticks the candle in the liquid wax. The flame rises high, dips low, stabilizes in fresh bright yellow.

'I will tell him. Because, sister, time already come for we all. How long more I want to scrub his foot and cut his bread? You know what is freedom, sister?'

'My man, everywhere people think they're not free. Now is the time of the British. It won't last forever. Five more years and we'll already be in a brand new century. The twentieth century. Can you believe it?'

Abu remains stiff, like a cadaver on an operating table. 'You talking like Tuan also. Call me "my man". I nobody's man, you hear? My father fisherman. My mother cook rice for village—

'My dear, I am telling you, you are already free. You just have to realize it.'

'Then why I only seeing dark? My eyes open only, I seeing black. Black outside, black inside. Tuan, he live like God pluck him from heaven, put him here to eat all our chicken, all our fish, all our coconut, drink all our water, take, take, take. Everything also they take. His wife cry like waterfall in room upstairs; he cannot see?'

She suspends her hands over the fire and slowly brings them together, crosses her thumbs, fans her fingers out and flaps them. 'Like Tuan's butterfly,' she says, 'you become like Tuan's butterfly. See the shadow on the wall. The butterfly comes from a worm.'

Without looking at the result of her creative impulse, he says, 'Butterfly only live two week, sister.'

She stops flapping the shadow-wings. 'Why don't you just leave Charles and Mary? Go back to your village. If you cannot be free here, you can find something there.'

'White people everywhere, you don't see? Village or here, they poke their pink nose in toilet also. How come God give them all so much power? Take, take, take. They thinking their life more than mine.'

She drops her hands resignedly. The flame crackles and spits. 'Abu, something else is taking from you and it's not the British, it's not Tuan Charles or Mem Mary.'

'Take, take, take. And I left with nothing. My body inside black. This house black.'

She straightens her legs and gets up. 'Alright, Abu. It's getting late. I should get some sleep. Charles's guests will be arriving early tomorrow.'

'Everyday inside this den, my soul can scream and sleep.'

She stands over his reposing body. 'It's a bitter pill. The opium pill is bitter, Abu.'

'And suddenly, my blood singing. And suddenly, Abu know what to do.'

'From darkness comes darkness.'

'And Abu melting inside this den. No more Abu. Everything going like dirt in the drain.'

'For a while, for a while only. Remember the last time you didn't take opium? You were shaking and purging and wailing. You were mad like your Mem.'

'Then no Abu. No Abu. No Abu. Inside this den God bring his hand out and hold me like baby. Outside, God hold white man hand. Inside, Abu, Abu, Abu. No Abu. Abu. No Abu. Abu. No Abu.'

'My God, Abu! What a life you have chosen for yourself,' she says as she plods back to the entrance of the cellar.

*

'I think she woke up, I don't know.' Maxim sat on a chair facing the partially open front doors of the front hall. She folded her arms against her chest and looked out.

The viscous night seeped into the garden, licked its reds and greens and yellows with a long black tongue, but stopped at the edge of the veranda. A dimly lit light bulb threw a dull brownish orange light across the wooden planks.

Hadi stood inside the hall, leaning against one of the front doors. He casually pulled something out of his teeth and said, 'How can don't know?'

She crossed her legs, dusted the sarong, and with a chaste hand made sure most of it covered her legs and thighs. Over the sarong, the oversized T-shirt she'd worn when she first arrived at Yalpanam had acquired more tiny holes at the sleeves and collar. 'She said something, but her eyes were closed as if she was talking in her dream. Then she stopped and didn't speak again.'

He watched her face closely as though searching for a small object in a darkened room. 'Already three days like that. How can?'

A cricket shrieked from the veranda. Its long, vibrating screech filled the hall and dissipated.

'You think I know? I'm also confused. That's why I said to you—'

'Auntie already told me before you even came here. If she is sick, don't call a doctor.' He gripped his hair and pulled hard several times. The taut facial flesh stretched up and down, his face a mask woven from good leather or hide from a young animal.

'Then we just let her die?'

'Don't be so dramatic, lah. She's an old person. They take time to recover.'

'My father always said . . .'

Back against the door, he slowly slid towards the floor. He squatted, hung his arms over his knees. 'What did he say?'

She shook her head.

'Just say, lah.'

The cricket screeched again.

'Never mind,' he said, 'but for sure he knows a thing or two. Richest man on the island has to be clever.'

'Clever? How do you know?'

'It's not just luck that makes people rich. Got to be clever too.'

'And suddenly you know so much about my father?'

'I'm talking only. I don't know anything about your father. I only know the buildings he built. Twice I went to listen to him speak in the villages. That's all.'

She wiped her cheeks forcefully as though angry they were there. 'Even I never listened to his political speeches.'

'Don't worry, don't worry. There's still time'.

'Time?'

'Ya, ya. When you go back, you can hear him for the first time.'

She squirmed in her chair. 'I think I better go and see if Auntie is okay. Maybe she has woken up?'

'Wait!'

She shot him a sharp glance and lifted her eyebrows as if to ask, 'What?'

'I won't talk about your family anymore,' he said, drawing out his words, acquiring time, 'and I will help you, for Auntie's sake, and because . . .'

She rose from the chair and moved towards him. 'Because?'

'Never mind.'

'No, tell me, please.'

But he stared at the ceiling, his lips shut tight.

She went back to the chair, buried her face in her palms like someone who had lost all hope, and sulkily said, 'I'm not trying to play games here. It's been too long already. I can't go home now. You don't know my parents. You don't know my *mother*. Now she may be sad because deep inside, maybe she is thinking something happened to me, I'm dead.'

He lowered his gaze from the ceiling and transferred it to her.

'But if I go back now,' she continued, 'alive, maybe she will smile at first, but after that, it will be the end. Nothing I do is okay. She won't understand why I came to Yalpanam.'

'I understand—'

'No, you *don't* understand. I don't *want* to go back.'

She stood up. 'But,' she said, her voice breaking, 'thank you for buying food and helping to clean the house. I know I shouldn't be taking money from you. You are not . . .' She looked around the hall as if searching for the word she wanted. 'You are not, you know what I mean . . .'

'Not rich like your father?'

'Not like that. Only that you don't have much money.'

'Not everything in this world is about money.'

She nodded.

Silence flooded and cooled the hall. Even the crickets had stopped their passionate wails.

'OK,' he said, 'I have to go now. Late already. Tomorrow your phone charger will arrive. The order from KL took longer than expected. I'll bring it up after work.'

'Thank you.'

He lingered by the front doors for a moment, then slowly made his way out. She watched him until he disappeared into the black mouth of the night. The drone of a jerky motorbike engine rose and fell. When it faded entirely, she retreated to Pushpanayagi's room, lay down beside the old lady and closed her eyes.

As they slept, the shadows melted into the walls, the floor, the ceiling. They gazed at the two creatures from every direction in the room. They loved listening to the pumping of blood through Pushpanayagi's ancient veins, to her beating heart. They were soothed by the young girl's rhythmic breath. Only when the young girl joined Pushpanayagi in sleep did the shadows seep into the surfaces of the room. Otherwise, they simply went wherever the old lady went and trembled with every pinch, laughter, or tear she experienced. They roared with every pulse that, now and again, soared within her blood like a great bolt of lightning.

7

'The Monarch chrysalis hangs down, you see, Deborah. The swallowtails attach sideways.' Charles points at rows of little cocoons behind a glass cage on the floor. He leans forward, lowers his spectacles and inspects the pupa more thoroughly. Some cocoons dangle from the horizontal branches of a potted plant that sits like a miniature jungle in the middle of the cage. Others stick to twigs, leaves, vertical branches.

He clenches his lower back and rises, grunting. 'I dare say, my dear, I am far too young to be feeling far too old.' He straightens his back, pushes his chest out, forces his shoulders back. 'Stiff as a pole, my mother used to say. One must have one's back as stiff as a pole. Good posture is a reflection of good character. Wouldn't you say, Deborah?' He struts towards a large teak table in the centre of the room. Leafy plants cover the length of the table. He removes a stained handkerchief from his pocket and gathers with it little brown droppings scattered on the table's surface. He twists the tips of the handkerchief, makes a small bundle of his collection. Pushpanayagi eyes the potted plants lining the wall by the windows. There, the caterpillars are fat; they wriggle on leaves and shed bile-coloured liquid droppings.

'My little worms will soon be migrating to those plants by the window.' He flashes a paternal smile at the bundle. 'They really are clever little creatures. They know precisely when it's time for them to hide in their cocoons to gestate for the final production.' He chuckles to himself. 'My sweet little caterpillars. Look how much they eat. Hearty appetites! Look how fast they grow.'

Abruptly, his thin lips tighten and almost disappear into his mouth. He lowers the hand holding the bundle of droppings and adjusts his thick black-rimmed spectacles with the other. 'And I'll tell you one other very important detail, Deborah,' he says, suddenly serious, 'they take every care in the world to live for a mere few weeks. Except the Painted Lady of course. Oh, she! She is the queen incarnate. Why would she be called anything other than Vanessa Cardui? Elegant, august creature. No, she must live for twelve whole months to state her superiority. There is no other way for her.'

His attention is diverted to a wall where a black-green, spotted butterfly perches close to the ceiling. It flaps its wings and tucks them back in. 'Oh, Nymphalidae of Papilionoidea! How you live in exquisite ancestry. Your bloodline is strong and pure. If they could contemplate their condition, they would be filled with pride. Don't you think, Deborah?'

Pushpa nods enthusiastically. 'Yes, yes, Charles. There are clearly butterflies that are better made than other butterflies. And—'

'And the better butterflies should be treated accordingly.' He laughs joyously, the way people do when agreed with. 'You *do* listen to me pontificate, and ruminate, and gush about these winged creatures! I dare say, Deborah, only other lepidopterists listen with charmed ears the way you do.'

'My dear Charles.' She stands still, hands folded at her back and looks around the room as though also searching for newly emerged butterflies. 'I understand the importance of the work you and all these men are doing on the island. My eyes are always watching.'

'I do wish Abu felt the way you feel about my work. My deepest desire is that today the poor, foolish man will return with the *correct* eggs. Abu really does behave like a buffoon sometimes.

I suppose I have to expect this sort of thing from a boy raised in an illiterate village. But, really, Deborah . . .' He rips off his spectacles and presses them against his chest. 'Is it so hard to follow simple instructions? Perhaps he doesn't understand the gravity of the situation. How would he know just how important my discovery is going to be in the world of lepidopterists? A pure red butterfly, Deborah! The world has never seen it. I shall name it the Red Tanner. One has to keep the family name going.'

A shrill muffled scream enters the room. Charles swings his spectacles back over his eyes and hurries to the wastepaper basket in a discreet corner of the room. He empties the bundles and gazes into the bin as though he is not regarding the bin at all but contemplating an object in his head. Another scream, softer, turns into a barely audible sob.

Pushpanayagi's eyes dart from the caterpillars to Charles and back again.

'My dear Charles. You need not trouble yourself about Mary.' Her voice, soft, shaky, even nervous, is enough to call his attention.

He turns around, cheeks strangely bloated as though several tongues are pushing against the walls of his mouth. The blues of his eyes are firm, cold behind the thick lenses of his spectacles, watery glints flashing through the blue.

'Oh, I am always assured when you are around, Deborah.'

'Oh, I know. We both understand—'

'*We* most definitely do, despite—'

'The nonsense the island is saying—'

'Oh, they know *nothing*, my dear, absolutely nothing—'

'It's easy for people to spread lies about things—'

'They know nothing about. But we are wise—'

'Very wise. In this situation, we have no choice—'

'*But* to be wise. It's impossible to explain to people that Mary is only—'

'Listen to me, Charles. Mary is like a child, if you don't mind me saying—'

'Why would I mind when even you can see that the spirits have left her?'

'It's true, Charles. She is like a princess who cannot see the palace she is in.'

'What more could I want in this situation? You and Abu are doing a fine job—'

'Only one thing, Charles. Abu, he has got it in his head that somehow . . .'

'Mary is simply, what's the word you used the other day, Deborah?'

'Oh, Mary is a passionate—'

'That's the one. *Passionate*. Mary is a *passionate* woman who requires the company of herself and the creatures of her inventions—'

'Her imagination is big enough, so she'll never be lonely. What women like her . . . what people like her need is to be left alone. The best thing, Charles, is to not—'

'Encourage her. Yes, Deborah, I have been listening to your wisdom—'

'I have been going upstairs with Abu, and checking on her so you really need not trouble yourself.'

'That's a mark of your generosity of spirit,' he says, his words clipped, his voice flat. He glances over at the glass cage, his face immediately softening. 'Enough of that for now. Come, look at these beauties. The precision and order in the world of Lepidoptera have the capacity to break one's heart when one takes the time to ruminate over the matter.'

Pushpanayagi walks towards the glass cage and kneels before it. 'The cocoons look like the candlenuts people in the village used to use in Ceylon.' She taps on the glass with a finger. 'We . . . they put it in big pots of watery curry. That one pot could feed the whole village.'

Charles folds his arms over his chest and beams at her as though he has heard something spellbinding. 'Surely you were the aristocrat of your village.'

She beams back. 'Close enough,' she giggles, tapping the top of the cage. The chrysalises hang static from branches and twigs. 'Maybe you also are like these cocoons. When you first came to see me, you were so frightened.'

'Those were terrible days.' He closes his eyes and sighs. When he opens them again, the blues of his eyes are soft, dark. 'What luck Mary had. And, indeed, me too.'

She turns towards him and watches him carefully as though checking for signs of change. He stares at the ceiling, hands in the pockets of his beige trousers, his eyes blank, lost in the image of the ceiling. He looks as though he's sunk deep into a thought and the thought has birthed other thoughts, a whole generation.

Someone knocks lightly on the door, then knocks again, louder.

'Come in,' Pushpanayagi says.

Abu stumbles in holding a glass jar, his face shimmering with sweat. Bits of grass and weeds stick to his dark brown arms. A leaf the shape of a miniature boat sits on his head, close to the forehead, on the verge of falling. He shifts his head and the little leaf-boat floats downwards. 'Tuan, so much I collect already.' He points the jar in Charles's direction. Tiny terracotta-coloured eggs coat parts of the jar's interior. Charles rushes forward, takes the jar, removes his spectacles and squints. 'I suppose so. I suppose so,' he murmurs. He holds the jar so close his eyes begin to cross. 'Good, good,' Charles says, 'now you can prepare Mem's lunch. I've a lot of examining to do this afternoon.'

When Abu catches Pushpanayagi's eye, he glowers, raises his eyebrows, and flashes a look at Charles. Pushpanayagi shakes her head, puts her palm out as if to say, 'Wait', and promptly Abu clenches his fingers into fists.

'Well, what are you waiting for, my man? The fowl isn't going to roast itself,' Charles says to the jar of eggs.

'Yes, Tuan.' Abu turns around, ambles towards the entrance, and lingers by the door. 'Whiskey, Tuan?'

Charles looks up from the jar. He smiles and says, 'Your timing is always perfect, my man. The day has been far too long.'

*

A large cloud, pregnant with grey, sailed towards the sun. Other clouds, smaller, bruise-blue, glided, collided into one another, and waited. The large cloud pregnant with grey moved, faster now, propelled by the proximity of its beloved. It swallowed the sun in one, two, three gulps. The late morning light in Yalpanam's garden dimmed. As if encouraged by the devouring, more grey-blue clouds sprouted and merged and joined the first cloud that had eaten the sun. They flocked around the receding light like bees to flowers, lover to beloved. The island fell into shadow.

A flight of swallows sprinted across the darkening canvas—the moving picture changed again; now swallows, now two fat crows and a hawk, now a cloud split into two, four, uncountable parts. A wind deep in the gut of the island howled through foliage, river streams, wide open roads and open windows, fan blades and blades of grass; it screamed and screamed in high, metal-like tones through ten thousand ears that could not hear it. The islanders shut their windows, waved umbrellas, held newspapers over their heads, but they could not, would not hear the wild wail of the wind.

Off and on, the wail brushed against Maxim's eardrums and her ears twitched, but she continued to pat cabbages and blow little worms off the tomatoes. Her eyes darted up the veranda and back on the vegetables around her. She dusted soil off her hands and looked up at the sky. Speckles of lilac burgeoned amid bulging blues and greys. She looked back at the veranda where Hadi was crouched over, banging away at the wooden planks. She moved to the curling tomato plant and watched him lift a hammer and swing it down in one swift thud. The battering echoed through the garden and through the hearts of the sunbirds sleeping in the nest on the veranda. She scurried past rows of kailan and pak choy and went round to the back of the house.

Hadi threw the hammer on the floor and wiped his face with the sleeve of his T-shirt. Beams of sawn wood lay scattered, some tipped over, down the steps of the veranda. Mounds of sawdust gathered at the base of a woodblock where a rusted saw rested flat, its jagged teeth pointed towards the garden. He picked up the unused nails and dropped them into the pouch around his waist. He got up, turned around, and saw Maxim walking across the garden, on her way back to the veranda, her eyes on the glasses in her hands, filled to the brim with white, cloudy liquid. He zipped the pouch shut.

'Going to rain, lah,' he called out.

She minced towards the veranda, her eyes unwavering from the glasses tight in her grip. She took a cautious step up the veranda. Hadi watched, grimacing.

'What's all this?' He tugged a box of cigarettes out of his shorts pocket.

She placed a glass on the railing. He dashed forward, spontaneously, as though he had foreseen the act, and rescued it. 'No, no,' he said, 'it will fall.' He sniffed at the glass and settled it on the floor.

'I squeezed the limes I plucked yesterday. I put in the sugar you bought last week.'

He lit the cigarette and took a long puff.

'I thought you must be tired after all the work,' she said.

He sucked hard at the cigarette, winced and exhaled a stream of smoke into the air. 'The floor's all done. See the wood now?'

'It looks good. So many holes before.' She sipped from her glass and watched little ghostly smoke rings rise from his mouth, and disappear in the wind.

'Yesterday I used that thing you bought. The shiny one, you know? To scrub stains.' She angled her glass between two railing shafts. A gush of wind blew and the glass wobbled and nearly fell over.

'Better you hold the glass, Max.'

She grabbed the glass and set it on the floor next to his. 'You don't want to try the lime juice?' She studied the wall behind him and nervously pinched the folds of her sarong. The veranda was dark. The late morning sunlight had vanished. The wind deep in the gut of the island blew harder, stronger. It ruffled their hair, their clothes, and whirled through their ears, but they did not hear it.

He picked up the glass and drank.

'Tasty also,' he said, placing the glass back on the floor, 'Auntie's limes are just as good as the vegetables. Never tried her limes before.'

'You don't sell her limes?'

'Yes, I sell her limes. But I have never tasted them. Sometimes only I cook the pumpkin.' He leaned towards her and grinned. 'I don't like vegetables. Chicken is my favourite.'

'You cook yourself?'

A shadow flashed across Hadi's face. 'If I don't cook, who will cook?'

She smiled, disbelievingly. 'Your mother!'

He stumped the cigarette out with his foot. 'She cannot cook from the grave, can she?'

'I did not know. I'm sorry.'

He folded his arms and stepped back. 'My parents died a long time ago.'

Thunder clapped. The house shivered and rattled the glasses on the floor. 'Better we go inside,' he said. They looked into each other's eyes. She picked up the glasses and followed him into the hall.

Between the two wicker chairs, a box partially covered in an old sarong masqueraded as a table. A white phone charger, its wires in a neat reel, lay at the edge of the box. She placed the glasses down on the print of a large hibiscus in the middle of the sarong, snatched the charger and glanced at him guiltily.

'Sorry. I haven't used the charger.'

He ran his fingers through his hair, unconcerned.

She shrugged. 'I don't really need it.'

She dug the pointed tips of the adaptor into her palms. 'There's so much to do here. Never had the time to even *think* of looking at my phone. You know, the other day, it took me the whole evening to get the stains off the courtyard windows. And then, yesterday, I was weeding the *whole* morning. Then I had to prepare lunch and work on the kitchen walls. The black stuff there is *so* stubborn.'

He flicked his pouch up and down. The nails tinkled louder and louder as the flick grew into a shake and finally a rattle. Over the soft, strange music, he said, 'Don't worry about it.'

*

Pushpanayagi hesitates at the bottom of the spiral staircase, one foot on the first step, watching Abu trudging his way up, his back hunched. The crockery on the tray in his hands clatters. He pauses, grips the railing, attempts to stop the rattling by trying to remain still, but the cup and the saucer and the spoons tremble and he turns his head, beckons her. The light from the oil lamp in her hand is bright enough to illuminate his pained face. He pleads with his eyes. Come, come, they say, come quick. She follows the curves of the steps, spiralling, swirling, twirling, whirling upwards.

A meek voice from above calls out, 'Abu, sweet Abu?'

The tray in Abu's hands quivers so violently that he has to place it down on a step. He raises his arms and folds them against the back of his head as if to quell the tremor.

Pushpanayagi taps him on the back and he picks up the tray, and together, they tread lightly up the staircase.

'Charlie, my love, have you come?' The voice almost chirpy, like a bird about to burst into a song.

Abu nudges the half-open door with his foot. 'Sorry, Mem. Sorry.' He walks quickly to the four-poster bed and sets the tray on the table beside it. He slaps the edges of the mattress as if to dust it.

Mary raises a blanket over her chest. She tugs at it, pulls it close to her body. Locks of golden curls fall over her shoulders. She sits up, brings her knees close to her chest, and tightens her grasp of the blanket. At the foot of her bed, balls of crumpled paper lie strewn. 'I'm ever so pleased to see you,' she says. Her voice quavers, soft, polite.

Abu relights a candle fixed in a tall, finely embossed candlestick. The candle flame strong enough, he tips another candle over the flame, lighting it also. Pushpanayagi steps away from the door, one foot inside the room.

'Pushpa, my love, is that you?' Mary dips her head, attempting to catch a glimpse of Pushpanayagi's face.

Pushpanayagi abruptly raises the lamp to her face, bares her teeth in a grin, and just as abruptly lowers the lamp.

A dusky shadow falls over Mary's face. She gasps for air, clasps her neck. Abu extends a teacup over the bed, but as the gasping quickens, he hurriedly places the teacup back on the tray and fumbles in his shirt pocket.

Mary turns to face the heavy, dun-coloured curtains covering the windows. 'All day yesterday, when nobody came, she spoke to me.' She caresses her throat as if coaxing the words to the surface. Her eyes linger on the curtains that resemble swarthy ominous cloaks; then, with a slight shake of her head, she looks up at the stained glass window above the curtained windows. The Virgin Mary's face, cast in the shadows of the night, still bears the daytime gaze of sorrow.

'Pushpa,' Mary whispers. She fidgets with the blanket, snivels as she gazes at the stained glass window like a person bereft of hope. One fast tear falls down her cheek, a second one follows. She reaches for a handkerchief lying squashed beside her on the bed. 'Our Lady of Sorrows listened to me all day.' She dabs her nose with the handkerchief and wipes her eyes in deft, gentle strokes. 'When Abu only deposited the trays and both times said he was in a terrible hurry, I knew it was going to be one of those days. Abu, you mustn't think I am chiding you. Only, I get so frightfully lonely and frightened up here. The mouse . . .' She squeezes her eyes shut and shakes her head like a child rejecting instruction. 'The mouse,' she sobs, 'even the mouse has died and left me. He used to poke his sweet little twitching nose through the sheets and even permitted me to touch his darling head with a finger. What happened to him? I sense you want to ask, Pushpa, but you are far too dignified and respectful to do such a vulgar thing. But I will tell you. In the end, we are all compelled to confess, aren't we?' She half-heartedly flings the handkerchief beside her, makes the sign of the cross and looks at Pushpanayagi. 'Bless me, Sister, for I have sinned. It has been one quarter of an hour since my last confession. Yesterday, I committed a grave sin. In the morning, I heard the sad sound of crunching gravel. At first I thought it was Charlie going out, leaving me once again. Then I realized. Those were no ordinary horses. The Four Horsemen had come. I could smell it, Sister, my holy Sister. The pungent force of death. The dawning of the Apocalypse. I screamed and screamed, but no one came.'

'Not true, Mem,' Abu says, 'I come five time yesterday. All time Mem ring bell, Abu is coming.'

Silence ripples through the room.

Mary hugs her knees and rocks herself back and forth. 'And so,' she says, 'I knew the Devil had cursed us all. That we had faltered when we dirtied this land with blood that was not ours to spill. We denied God's grace when we murdered the elves and angels of the jungles. The Lord has abandoned our mission. The Lord has abandoned us!' She pulls the blanket over her head.

Abu leaps to her side, perches on the edge of the bed and gently removes the blanket from Mary's head.

'Mem is okay. Drink tea, Mem.'

'Oh, dear Abu!'

Pushpanayagi puts the lamp on the floor and heads for the tray of tea things. Abu watches her encouragingly, but she does not look at him, only forward, at the glinting floral teacup, at the little copper spoon, at the ball of opium the size of goat droppings. She spoons the pill into the teacup, stirs as soundlessly as she is able to, and holds the cup over the bed.

'Drink this, Mary.'

Mary, eyes fixed on the Virgin's face, absentmindedly picks up the handkerchief beside her on the bed, daintily dabs her nose with it and as though she has seen or heard something inaccessible to the other two in the room, she stops sobbing and starts to laugh. A noiseless laugh, accompanied by heaving shoulders, strains her face until the strain reaches an imperceptible limit and the laughter becomes a shriek, and the shriek gradually dies into a knowing smile. 'And so,' she says, 'to appease my Lord, I spoke to the Mother of His Son. Thus it was. Therefore, thereafter, it was so. And the Lord said it was so. I stabbed the mouse with my penknife and tossed him out the window. Then I wrote letters to Charlie.' She points a shivering finger at the balls of paper at the foot of the bed. 'Our Lady said to me, Blessed Child, if your husband is a true husband, he will not follow the Devil's plan. He will not murder butterflies so that they may be pressed into books, their ghosts trapped in the astral sphere with no salvation for their souls. He *denies* life. Most Blessed Child, if your husband is a true husband, he most certainly will not tear you away from your three daughters, their sweet young souls alone and frightened in England. If your husband is a true husband, he will at least . . .' She pauses and clutches at the neckline of her nightgown, her eyes glinting with tears. 'He will at least sit by your side and soothe you. And so it was. Therefore, thereafter. The Lord hath spoken through the Mother of His Son. When Charlie is asleep, one aims well with the penknife. It is the heart one must target after all is said and done. The heart is the seat of this life and the one after.'

Abu nods at Pushpa and swiftly, she makes her way around the bed and hands over the cup.

'Mem, you stop now. Drink tea.'

But Mary's attention is fixed on the sorrowful, compassionate face of the Virgin. She whispers, 'Batter my heart, three-personed God, for you as yet but knock, breathe, shine, and seek to mend; that I may rise and stand, o'erthrow me.'

Pushpa glares at the soft golden curls, at the sky blue eyes glittering with tears, at the small, perfectly aquiline, perfectly pink nose and, as though she cannot stand any longer to look at Mary's trembling, sniffling, whimpering form, blurts out, 'Stop feeling sorry for yourself, Mary, and drink the tea!'

But Mary, momentarily deaf or unaffected by outbursts as spiced with emotion as hers, blinks at the face of kindness on the window, at the face that knows exactly what is in her heart, and averts her gaze only when Abu tugs at the sheets, his habit of gaining her attention which she has early on learned to respond to.

Regaining her composure, Pushpanayagi says, 'It's best you drink the tea and rest, Mary. You shouldn't be talking too much.'

Abu taps on the mattress, another method he has invented to communicate with Mary, and slowly, she lowers her eyes; her mouth relaxes, and her breathing resumes its natural rhythm. She smiles, nods at the cup, and whispers to Abu, 'Yes, I think I shall have tea now, and then I shall sleep. I am ever so tired. Have you been this tired, Abu?'

He takes the cup from Pushpanayagi and holds it to Mary's lips. 'Mem, I know this kind of tire. Tire like never sleep for many, many year.'

'Yes, yes,' Mary murmurs sleepily, 'it does feel like that. It feels like my eyes have been open for centuries.'

'Like that, Mem.' He lifts the cup to her lips and she drinks thirstily.

'It's the fatigue,' she says, delicately licking tea off her lower lip, 'of coming this far and realising that something has been missing all this time, taken from you without your knowledge. Something that feels so far, far away and yet, without it, life is so devastatingly empty. What is one to do?'

*

Maxim squeezed through a gap in the wire fence close to the well and pushed out onto the grassy stretch opposite the mouth of the jungle. She stepped into a slushy pool of something. Mud, could even have been shit. She rubbed a foot against the grass, got some of the slime off, not nearly enough. What the heck. She squatted, stretched the sarong out over her knees, made a cosy tent of it. The cloth was too soft, scoured to death over so many years it was almost transparent.

Ooot. Ooot. Heee. Heee. A bird in the jungle called and called, straining its poor lungs. Perhaps it was a nice sound, maybe even beautiful. Sing again, sing, sing. But the bird was quiet. Sulking in a tree probably. Glum and morose. *Pull face for what? Who going to see you?*

Why must Auntie go into those epic sleeps? At least when she was awake, the ball of silence would come. Every time Auntie slept, stuff burst through Maxim's head like a frenzied volcano . . . but thank the vegetables, there was the weeding,the cobwebs to dust off from the ceiling, and there was the tray to prepare in case Auntie woke up. Then there was the Practice, talking to Tomatoes and Company. Are you ready to go down to the market? Did you enjoy last night's rain, Cucumber? How does the soil feel today, Cabbage? And when Hadi came, mucked about the house and stayed till dark, the crashing waves inside her head went down, cool and mute. Auntie said thoughts are nothing, as empty as air. Empty like time. Just ignore them. But sometimes they swirled like one of those twister tornados and who could ignore that?

She broke the squat and sat on the grass. She couldn't ask him for more. But if she just had two more T-shirts, another pair of shorts, and a pack of panties, she'd be fine. A bit of money to get some of the meals. Already, he'd bought cutlery, crockery, detergents, dinners. The dinners were cheap, from his favourite 'mamak' stall, but still. Ever since he realized she wasn't leaving Yalpanam, he always came with a packet of something. After Day Ten, she stopped counting. Time didn't seem to matter anymore. But *he* kept count. Yesterday was Day Twenty; today, Day Twenty-one.

We don't take charity from people, Daddy used to say when Auntie Bonnie wanted to buy a blow-up garden pool for the family or when one of his sub-contractors dropped a shiny TV at the front gate. *Self-sufficiency is the root of success. The moment you start depending on others, you're finished.* He'd never told her *directly*, but it was as if he meant for her to eavesdrop on his conversations with his workers, her mother, and his various assistants over the years.

And the charger. The stupid charger. Why had she asked Hadi for it? *Obviously,* his phone didn't use the same charger as hers. His was cheap, the kind Bangladeshi and Indonesian workers used. Made in China. Mother had bought hers, made sure it had all the latest functions. Of course, Hadi had to get the charger specially ordered. And now she couldn't even use the daft thing! Only later she'd realized it. When people went missing, they checked for pings. And if the police didn't, Mother would be sniffing on her own tracking device. Maybe, after three weeks, they would have stopped trying to find out the location of her phone, but it was too risky.

She picked at the grass, plucked a nice long stalk and stroked her chin with it. She peered into the blackish green jungle. So thickly foliaged, crammed with all kinds of creatures, crawling things. Daddy talked about leeches once. How when he was younger, he hiked through a jungle and his legs were covered in blood and leeches. That was before politics absorbed him, way before his business made him big.

A silver light flashed through the dark green leafage and disappeared. It was too faint. Could have been anything. Maybe even her eyes. It had to be her eyes. Lately, she'd been seeing things, stuff moving in her side-vision. Shadows, bits of light. The light flickered again. Or maybe it was something Auntie P was creating somehow, as she slept. The few times she woke up, the old lady looked like she'd been passing time with a ghost. But she never said which ghost or where they'd been meeting. She just looked wonderingly at the walls and smiled mysteriously as she ate, and often, she ended her meals with four, five sequential burps and, 'You're a good girl. Thank you, child.' That was enough. She let the old lady rest again. It didn't seem decent to probe about the letters in the box of things or about the locked room on the top floor. And Hadi apparently didn't know much at all about the house or about Auntie's past. Five years he'd been coming, and *nothing*. Didn't even know that there wasn't any detergent in the house.

But he was too good, too nice, so far. Visiting every day, bringing things, soaps, face creams, a tiny broken radio, as well as his big mouth. He always seemed a few words short of what he really wanted to say. *On the brink*, the edge of the cliff. Down below, words, stories, gossip, swimming in a pool of swampy gook. She didn't want the gook, didn't want his mouth, his knowledge. Something lived underneath his surface, very close to it, a force maybe, yes, a force with spumes that made her feel she was doing the wrong thing.

She leaned back and pressed her palms on the muddy ground. Something somersaulted in her belly, and stopped, and the old ball of silence slowly grew around her. The ball warmed her, as though she was soaking in a bath of treacle. It embraced her—Auntie must have woken up.

'There you are. Looking for you everywhere.'

Wet rubber slippers squeaked against crunching soil. It seemed like only hours ago when he said he'd be back tomorrow.

'Doing what here, Max?'

'Simply, lah. Wanted to see what's out here.'

She turned around. He stood behind the fence, still in Yalpanam's compound. 'Come back in,' he said.

She didn't feel like moving. The ball of silence hugged her, tighter, warmer.

'I have something for you,' he said.

She looked at his hands but they were empty. 'Not dinner?'

He pointed at the house. 'Dinner I left inside. This one,' he said and took a phone out of his pocket, 'I have an extra one. Since you're not using the charger, better you use this. Got data already.'

She stared at the phone, her heart pounding frantically. 'But I cannot take that from you.'

He pushed his hand through the fence. The phone glared back at her. 'I'm not using it. At least you can use it to play when you're bored.'

Somehow, she felt that he was lying, that he'd bought the phone. If he'd had it all this while, why did he wait *three weeks* to give it to her?

Her throat tightened. A cold tingle spread up her neck, her cheeks, and paused at her eyes. Tears fell. They fell so quickly she had no way of stopping them or wiping them off before he could see her crying.

'Come.' He gestured for her to take the phone. Very slowly, she touched it, but he nodded and she took the phone. 'Good,' he said. He kept his hand through the fence as though waiting for her to take it.

'Are you coming back?' he said.

Her voice had gone into the black space within. She nodded.

'Take my hand. I'll pull you up. If you're hungry, I bought roti canai.'

She grabbed his hand. In one swift motion, he pulled her up. She squeezed through the hole in the fence and went with him back into Yalpanam's compound.

*

The world of objects is here. There, a table lamp; here, a whistling kettle; there an embroidered cushion; here a slumbering cat. On and on, at every shift of the body, there is the eye that looks, the object looked upon, a boundary between here and there, this and that.

Newborn babies do not apprehend objects the way they will a year or two from their birth. The mother, the nurse, the overwhelmed father are not yet 'her' and 'him'; the mother shedding tears of joy-tinged fatigue is not 'mother', 'woman'—but what then? For we cannot ask *who* she is. The babe in her arms does not yet know of selves, of the who's who of its world. The mother is simply there, undifferentiated—ah ha—*undifferentiated* from it. She, it, the forceps used to grasp its soft bloodied head are all part of the same movement, the such-ness, the is-ness of the life it has found itself in. Twenty-two years later, the (hypothetical) baby, now a university student named Prajapati, lies on his dormitory bed, kept awake by lust and by what he believes is love, placing the object of his insomnia in a slew of mental pictures: she is bathing in a river; she is delicately walking down the steps of the campus hall in high-heeled shoes; she is nibbling on a samosa like a contented rabbit. Days and nights are passed in this way; she is there, oh so far away, and he, sadly, remains here; a year later, when he has forgotten her not because of anything as injurious as heartbreak but because of boredom, the images in his mind take on the shape of metallic-painted cars, elaborate scenes in which he is giving an inspired speech to a crowd of adoring citizens, fans, who will vote him in as the youngest MP in his constituency. Then, when he leaves his one-bedroom flat and steps out into the world beyond his imagination, he is confronted with object after object, 'all coming at me,' a voice in his head says, 'it is too much.' (Prajapati is a highly sensitive individual). Yet, only twenty-three years ago—half a speck in cosmic time—we who have known, knew it was otherwise: objects were not coming at him; there was no one to gurgle *at* (let alone give an inspired speech to); there was no loneliness, no desire because, well, 'me' and 'you' did not exist.

(And yet, ponder this: at what point does the object seen separate from sight? Do sounds appear apart from hearing? Where may the boundary between object and sight be? Or . . . in a whisper, may we say, 'The kettle I see is *here*, in my sight, my God, in *me*'?)

At age thirty-three, Prajapati says to himself, after reflecting upon his life which he has concluded is nothing more than a journey of confusion and sadness, a succession of failures: 'Wouldn't it be easier to have been born as two or three for company? Or perhaps it would have been lovelier if there were no edges between things? Or from time to time, I could enter the bodies of others and know what I have always longed to know? To actually breathe the breath of another, to sing with my lover's voice and feel the heavenly tremor vibrate through shared bones.'

But, perhaps, Prajapati wouldn't enjoy such a sacrifice—to give away what is his for the sake of union, no, disappearance. But, perhaps, it is not disappearance he yearns for, only a way out of loneliness, a means to feel friendly towards everything, to connect, to disengage, once and for all, with the ache of separation.

That may, in the end, be humanity's acknowledged or unacknowledged collective impetus, and therefore too, an impetus lodged deep in the old woman's heart, supine during the slow-winding years, years of misunderstanding the force and design of her own life.

Yawning, the old lady pushes through, pushes past, ordered, in some measure, by her rebelling heart, now, at last.

8

A long time ago, when the garden teemed with potted begonias and heliconias, morning glories peeked out in full violet blooms from hanging baskets, and daisies the colour of egg yolks littered the ground in ordered rows, visitors who came to Yalpanam gasped at the colours and shapes that fell upon their eyes. They paused and noticed the silken beauty of petals and stems—and time grew long. It deepened into a kaleidoscope of tender heartbeats and warm, soothed blood, jolts of sublime feeling and the thawing of thoughts about dinner, the latest play at the Coal Island Club, the rip in a skirt, the darkness prowling at the base of their souls. For those deep, long moments, the flowers filled the visitors' bodies with flamingo-pinks, rich magentas, and citrus yellows, with a naked spirit, free and unapologetic.

The spirit of the flowers followed the visitors as they cruised towards the veranda; it remained bubbling in their hearts as the women lifted the hems of their starched dresses and tripped up the steps to the veranda, the men beside or behind them, and when they turned around to cherish the view of the garden, the spirit welled through their blood and bones, and a quiet love for the world thrummed in their hearts like the gentle song of the river not far from Yalpanam. The men and the women looked at one another with clear, resplendent eyes, their hearts firm and drenched in love's subtle tune.

Up they went, past the dark wooden doors and into the front room, their veins burring with loaned nectar from the garden, their souls alive with silence. They marvelled at the paintings of English seascapes and meadows on the walls, at the tall gold-gilded vases that sat next to thickly upholstered armchairs and sofas, and at the miniature porcelain dolls behind a locked glass cabinet; and they exclaimed to their host about the beauty of the house, about its glorious charm that had conquered their hearts. As they sat down and ate little sponge cakes, they forgot about the flowers and the spirit that had once, not very long ago, cleansed their hearts and blended into their own spirits. Soon, they forgot everything about the garden and they talked about the latest play at the Coal Island Club, about newly arrived British Officials, about the terrible hygiene of native cooks, and eventually, about the poor ailing wife of their host. The women blew their noses into starched handkerchiefs, lowered their eyes and said, 'Poor darling Charles. Poor darling Mary. You must let us see her when she's feeling better.' Soon, their own minds were filled with memories of lovers lost or dead, of inheritances snatched by surreptitious relatives, of the flirtations of spouses with local islanders. They ate more cakes, laughed as much as they permitted themselves to, and when an appropriate amount of time had passed, they left in their carriages, too preoccupied to shift their eyes once more upon the garden that had fostered light and colours in their bodies.

Decades passed and the garden wore many different masks and when, eventually, in the mid-twentieth century, most of the flowers had gone, the spirit of the flowers settled in a corner where a small row of roses bloomed. It slipped into the soil, burrowed deeper into the earth and reposed in a long serpentine coil. When it rained or when Pushpanayagi watered the roses, a thin swirl rose from the coil and returned to the stems and petals but within hours, it slithered back to the coil and the spirit slept in a bed of perfume and humid air. Occasionally a silver current sparked through it and a very quiet, almost unheard clashing of cymbals reverberated in the soil and for a moment, the spirit nearly uncoiled itself, thinking the time had come for it to return to the garden. But it soon resumed its slumber until the next shock of current stirred it awake again.

As the young girl sat by the roses and gazed dreamily at the grass, the silver current flickered through the coiled spirit and specks of light flashed in the soil beneath the roots of the roses. She lowered her head and sniffed at the flowers. The dots of light twinkled, expanded. She twirled a finger around the rims of the petals, stroked the sides of the petals and dug two fingers into the soil. She pulled the fingers out and smelled them and the spirit yawned. She stretched her arms up and stared out at the garden; her eyes blank, tired. She yawned. And yawned again. Across the dirt path, Pushpanayagi sat on an old towel by the vegetables, a rag on her head to shield her eyes from the potent light of the afternoon sun. She hoisted the cloth, looked at the girl at the other end of the garden and waved.

'How are you, Auntie?' the girl yelled.

Pushpanayagi tipped her body over to one side and tried rising. She groaned, pressed her palms on the ground and pushed her lower back up. The girl dusted her hands, got up, and jogged towards Pushpanayagi. The thick tuberous head of the spirit darted through the soil, slipped out onto the land above and simmered on the hot pebbles on the grass. The rest of its self slowly followed.

The girl took Pushpanayagi's arm and the old woman grabbed the girl's arm and through a cacophony of moans and whimpers, Pushpanayagi rose and finally stood up. She nodded at the girl and the girl snatched the old towel and a small rattan basket filled with tomatoes, stalks of mustard greens, and baby cucumbers.

'Bathe the tomatoes and the dark leaves properly, okay, child? Do that one first. They are for the market. Keep a few for us. After that, you can bathe the rest.'

The girl smiled and interlocked her arm with the old woman's. They meandered back towards the house and stopped at the veranda. Pushpanayagi placed a hand on her chest and breathed loudly.

'You don't have to come out, Auntie. I know what to do.'

The old woman shook her head. 'Ever since I woke up, I feel I must come out into the garden. My body is still a bit weak, but I am not dead.'

'I've never seen someone sleep for so long.'

Pushpanayagi massaged her chest with a whole palm. The palm went round in clockwise circles, then up and down. A loud burp escaped her mouth. It went on and on. When it stopped, she said, 'Let's go in, child. I want to work in the courtyard.'

The spirit slinked through the grass. It twisted upwards and swelled out over the garden, then cascaded down and spilled between sheaves of grass and fallen leaves, in the nooks between pebbles and grit, and through the small beating heart of every plant.

*

'Of course, on Touching Bones, if you don't want to say anything, you don't have to say.' Maxim sat on a chair beside Pushpanayagi, the machine in the girl's hands casting a ghostly blue light on her face. Almost possessed, the girl looked at the thing in front of her eyes, her eyes never moving from the screen. The thing looked like a black version of the ice-cream wafer sandwiches the man with the box and the bell used to sell a long time ago. Ting, ting, ting, the bell went from down the slope and many minutes later, the poor man would be huffing and puffing on his bicycle outside the gate, screaming at the top of his voice, 'Wanilla vafer, wanilla vafer, wanilla vaferrrrrrr!'

'You see or not, Auntie?'

Pushpanayagi tried looking at the thing the girl loved so much, but its light produced a nauseating metallic flavour on her tongue. As though she had eaten a steel bowl. She couldn't explain it. 'What all more?' She raised her eyebrows at the thing.

'You wanted to know what I always do on the phone, right?' The girl looked almost irritated as she tore her eyes away from the thing and quickly glanced at Pushpanayagi, as if to confirm that she was still a part of the conversation.

Pushpanayagi shifted her bottom, too long in the wicker chair. Something in her lower back cracked. A cold wave shot through her spine and twitched at her neck. A dark flash sprinted past the front doors. She closed her eyes and listened to her breath. As we come, we also go. Ever since she woke up, it felt like a stone was sitting in her stomach. A stone that moved from time to time. When she became the stone, the tears straightaway collected in her eyes. And all the images would come, thousands of pictures of feet, leaves, elephant trunks, motor cars, lips, flowers never before seen on this earth, spinning pools of wind. As though her mind had come loose and was going wild, storming out every single item it had collected. She opened her eyes. The girl's finger moved up and down the screen, so quick like a knitting needle.

'Nothing, really,' Pushpanayagi said, 'I only wanted to see what you all like to do. What all these new things are.' The dark flash darted up towards the ceiling. Her heart fluttered. Once in a while, a fish leapt in her chest. Hare Rama, the world is lifting its curtain. She stretched her head but it was no use. She couldn't reach the girl all the way in the chair beside her. Her body was too stiff to move.

'We call it the Internet, Auntie.' The girl finally looked away from the machine. Her eyes darkened, her eyebrows close to touching, she seemed troubled all of a sudden. 'It's a place,' the girl continued, staring at nothing before her, 'I guess it's a place where people go to find stuff out? And also, talk to each other.'

Pushpanayagi chuckled. 'Why go to a machine to talk?'

The girl shook her head. Strands of hair stuck to her cheeks and lips. She blew them away violently. 'It's not just about that, Auntie. You can talk to anyone, anywhere in the world.' Her eyes brightened. A pleasant smile grew like the first bloom of a rose bush. 'I write letters to someone in America and we talk about everything under the sun. He likes to write about things like planets and stars, the universe, stuff like that. Ever since, ever since . . .' She bit her lip and quickly moved a finger on the screen. The finger seemed angry, eager to travel up and down the machine as fast as it could go.

'Very nice. I see. People on the island can go to places they would never be able to go to otherwise. They can talk to people they would never be able to talk to.'

The finger stopped moving. The girl looked up. Her face glowed as though the eerie light from the machine had transformed into the warm embrace of the sun. 'Exactly, Auntie. You get to know more about people. What they do. What they think.'

Pushpanayagi smiled. 'You show me first, child, then I will tell you. But I feel a person is more than what they do and think.'

The girl looked at some invisible spot in the air. She hemmed and hawed and finally said, 'As in . . . a person is more than what they do and think because they have *feelings*?'

'Something like that, but also not like that.'

The girl threw a puzzled look at Pushpanayagi. Her face collapsed into a frown. Slowly, the frown smoothed out and the light around the girl shone again. 'It would be nice to talk like you.'

The girl obviously enjoyed the newness of their language—the fresh, exciting fact that having spent days in the same house, the girl could say certain things with ease because now she had the right.

'Talk like yourself. Don't let other people's shadow get mixed up with you.'

'How would I know if the shadows are already mixed?'

'You will do things a certain way if the shadows are stuck to you.'

'What way?'

'I don't know. You have to find out.'

'But there are so many people, and so many shadows.'

'That's the problem.'

The finger dipped down onto the machine again. It silently tapped on the screen. Once again, the blue light ate the girl up, took her away from the hall. Where did the light transport this mouse that didn't know it was a tiger? The girl felt so far away. In an instant, the blue light swallowed her whole like the python that gobbled up the poor rubber tapper on the plantation, decades and decades ago.

'Yalpanam,' the girl said. At last, she looked up from the machine, eyes close together, mouth shrunk back to its original shape, serious, as though at any moment now, she would be talking about world affairs or about the level of pollution on the island. Pushpanayagi leaned forward and waited.

The girl cleared her throat and read from the machine. 'The Yal is a lute. In ancient times, a blind Panan lute player visited a king in Ceylon. The king was so captivated by the Yal player's music that he gifted the blind Panan musician with land on his island. Soon, the lute player filled this new land with people from his homeland in India. This new settlement was called Yalpanam, land of the blind minstrel. 'Jaffna' is a corruption of the Tamil word 'Yalpanam'.'

Pushpanayagi stared at the little machine trembling in the girl's hands. The stone in her belly shifted, moved up and settled in her throat. She pressed her hands against her chest, her heart beating loudly. Hare Rama, it was still regular like the metronome that used to sit on the piano in the hall. 'So many years have passed, I've forgotten this story,' she said, 'I suppose you can say the Yal player's music is in my blood.'

The girl shot a sharp look at Pushpanayagi. 'You came from this place? Jaffna in Sri Lanka, formerly known as Ceylon?'

'Yalpanam, yes. Those days, long, long ago, the year I was born, the British had already been there for almost twenty years. All the names they changed. How many times they said Yalpanam, Yalpanam, Yalpanam. Always they twist the words. They don't know how to say it properly. Maybe they don't want to. Yalpanam, Yalpanam, suddenly they were calling it Jaffna.' Pushpanayagi stroked her chest. With no warning, the words had come like bullets flying through the air. But they were enough to take the girl away from the machine, to get the glow around her strong again.

'You mean, all those years ago, you were there?' The girl looked at Pushpanayagi with eyes that seemed to long for something more. Deep in the darkness of the worlds she had travelled through when she'd been asleep, Pushpanayagi had seen those very same eyes, lit by the sparkling flames of candles, wet from the tears of bondage. Pining eyes. Something about the glaze that covered the pupils made the eyes porous. Anything could enter them. Aching eyes. Blue eyes ached, brown eyes ached, down in the darkness of those worlds.

'Auntie?'

'How come the machine knows so much?' Pushpanayagi studied the thinness of the object in the girl's hands. Earlier, the girl had tried to explain the magical appearance and disappearance of words and pictures. But the girl was too comfortable with this new magic, she didn't even know it was magic.

'It's full of information, Auntie. People from all around the world load stuff up. You can try with anything. Think of something you want to know more about and I'll find it for you.'

'Wood apples'.

The girl's face creased into a frown. 'Really?'

'Charles Tanner.'

The girl's eyes grew into two big dark discs. The finger began its sprint on the screen even as the girl continued to look away from it. It was hard to tell exactly where the girl was looking. The eyes hardly blinked like she was in some kind of trance. Slowly, her mouth opened. The finger hovered over the screen. 'Is he someone famous?'

But the words had sneaked out of Pushpanayagi's mouth. Somehow, her will and her actions missed each other, fell away before they could join up. Better if she didn't speak at all. But a hollow sphere inside her—maybe it was even the stone in her belly—wanted to push up for air and it wanted her to stay and to use words. It was as if there were two selves within. One chose the peace that passes all understanding. The other wanted to enter the monsoon.

'Famous? I don't know. That's why I am asking you to check.'

The girl's eyes settled on the machine. 'Tanner, Charles. Born 1853. Died Unknown. Minor British Lepidopterist. Published several papers on tropical butterflies and moths. Worked mainly on Coal Island in present day Malaysia.'

The girl's face paled. The big dark discs that had pined for something more widened into even bigger discs. 'You knew him, didn't you, Auntie?'

Pushpanayagi's head moved up and down.

'The man in the letters?'

Pushpanayagi's head moved again.

'The man who had the crazy wife? The one who wrote that she was slipping or wilting or something like that? Something about her delicate spirit, I can't remember exactly.' Red blossomed on the girl's cheeks as though the tomatoes from the garden had lent their colour. Perhaps the girl had spoken too soon, too much, and now she was frightened.

'Sorry,' the girl said to the floor, 'I read the letters in the box in that room. I know I shouldn't have, but I thought . . .' She picked at the sarong she was wearing. 'I thought, since the letters were not written to you, it was okay. But I *know* that's wrong.'

'That's dust from a long time ago.'

'They are yours?'

'They are in this house, yes. They were written to me, yes. But I don't know if I can say they are mine.'

'Deborah, Penelope? These are you?'

'As I said, child. That's what the British used to do. They created new names for everything.'

Pushpanayagi closed her eyes and felt the stone in her belly. It lay very still, its presence heavy. Her skin became cold.

'And . . . Savitri . . . the one who wrote that letter to you . . . begging you . . . did all Indians speak and write like English people in those days?'

'She was . . . Savitri was different. Brought up by Irish nuns in a convent on the mainland. Nobody knows why she came to Coal Island.'

'You didn't *ask* her? She said you were like a sister—'

'What's past is past, child. No need to ask questions that can't be answered.'

Silence grew around them. Pushpanayagi gripped the armrests of her chair and sighed.

The girl looked at her thoughtfully and said, 'Maybe it would be interesting if you brought Deborah or Penelope back to life. Not *literally*. Just on Touching Bones.'

The stone thumped against her belly, waiting to explode. 'Who knows what happens to our old selves, whether we can ever bring them back to life. I suppose—

'Not a big deal, Auntie. You can do anything you like. Make Deborah into whatever you want.'

Pushpanayagi caressed her stomach. She poked the thick flesh, hoping somehow to reach inside and haul it out, or at least quicken its eruption. 'Who knows what is being planned for us. All I know now is that I'm very hungry. You carry on. I'm going to chop some vegetables.'

*

Mingled with the roots of the mango tree in the garden are bones, mostly animal, some human; ancient, laid in the ground centuries before the old woman was even born. There are bones beneath the tomatoes, cabbages, and insect-chewed leafy vegetables too, but they are more scattered and live deeper in the soil. When worms and other subterranean creatures crawl over the bones, something in the bones sighs, shivers with a mild flickering of life. This is the normal way of bones. They feed the earth in their dark beds of cold, pungent soil and welcome the worms with the soul of a lover. For a long, long time, well before the house was built, the bones nourished the earth, claimed it as their home, an inheritance from life departed. When the land was touched again, probed and poked by men with intention, ambition, the bones lay very still and the worms wriggled away, closer to the earth beneath the jungle. As the first bricks were laid, the bones jounced and shuffled and as the feet of the living stomped on the ground, they migrated, with the help of underground spirits, deeper into the soil. As the years passed, and as men, women and animals associated with the house died, and new bones entered the earth, some of the old bones rose closer to the surface of the earth, touched new seeds and roots, and were transported back down into the soil by the underground spirits. But, somehow—whether because the spirits had forgotten or because it was simply fate—the thick, hard roots of the mango tree reached down towards the bones and the bones inched upwards, and with each monsoon season, the bones and the roots grew closer and closer together.

After the Japanese left the island, and the house witnessed four deaths of its own, more flesh entered the earth and more bones emerged to remain years after the bodies had festered and disintegrated. The first burial of the twentieth century opened up the land wide for there were two deaths the earth had to nurse. The rain had come down hard that day and the soil was saturated, pliable to the shovels the four men used to dig the earth behind the house, close to the jungle. Savitri wailed and wept as the ground slowly opened up for her husband and his servant. Days later, two of the four men returned and cleaved the earth open again, a few feet away from the previous grave, and Savitri herself was lowered into the ground, her flesh and bones now a part of the land. Drowned in the sea, accidentally or purposefully—Pushpanayagi was too frightened to find out—but she did know that Savitri wanted to be buried next to the husband she had spent most of her time trying to understand, so that she could continue her endeavours in death.

But who remembers these bones? They are nothing special, it seems. They cannot be seen with fleshly eyes. They belong to bodies long dead, to temperaments, personalities, souls, whose words, expressions, mannerisms have evaporated into the winds. When those who can remember forget or die, the ways of the dead evanesce into nothing. Who is left to gaze at the image of a dead wife's giggle turning into a gentle hiccup? Or at the fastidious hands of a loved one dusting pillows before sleep? The way a father combs his hair back until there is not a single stray strand. The lilt in the speech of a friend inspired by the full yellow moon hanging low on a midnight picnic in the garden. These fade. As time turns its wheel and darkness inches closer, these remembrances slink away from the light and disappear completely.

But something joins the earth. The embraces and sighs, tears and rage from four hundred years ago join the earth. The warm, panicked breath of a woman as she admonished her child three hundred years ago joins the earth. When two Portuguese merchants stopped by the land six hundred years ago and ate rose apples as they lay on their backs and gazed at the dawn sky, their terrible longing for home joins the earth. Absorbed into bones. Absorbed into the body of the land. In the trunks of trees is the memory of the first plant.

*

Silvery clouds flocked around the crescent moon. Soon, more clouds gathered and the moon disappeared. Maxim turned around and glanced at Pushpanayagi and Hadi in the front hall. 'Don't think it's going to rain,' she shouted. Their eyes fixed on the phone in Hadi's hand, they laughed, talked, the old lady pointing at the object like a child with a novel toy. They hadn't heard her. From deep within the foliage of the mango tree, an owl hooted, and as if that was her cue, Maxim shuffled back into the house.

'Finished already, Auntie?' She sat by the old lady's feet.

'Acha, acha. What a thing this thing is.' The old woman laughed and the laughter grew into a cough, and the cough turned into a fit of coughs. Hadi patted her on the back and slowly, the coughs died down until the only sound the old lady emitted was an erratic sniffing. Maxim reached for the Huntley & Palmer's biscuit tin she'd kept underneath one of the wicker chairs.

'Take care, Auntie,' Hadi said. He tapped Pushpanayagi's back lightly and the old lady let out a long, slow burp.

Maxim removed a crumpled handkerchief from the tin and held it in her hands, her eyes fixed on the old lady's face as though to make sure she didn't cough again.

'Sometimes, when I get too excited, the coughing comes,' the old lady said as if in response to the girl's stare.

Hadi shook his head, chuckling. 'Auntie was showing me the page you made for her on Touching Bones—

'I cannot imagine this, child. Not in one thousand years would I have thought this kind of thing was possible.' Pushpanayagi smiled. 'Let me tell you . . . all these *people* on my page.'

Maxim loosened her grip of the handkerchief and dabbed her neck with it. She examined the cream-colored cloth that used to be starch white a long time ago. Embroidered at the bottom right corner of the handkerchief were the initials M.T.

'The grandchildren and the great-grandchildren of pork sellers, tailors, shopkeepers, tin miners, doctors, fishmongers, rubber tappers. In the flesh, I talked with their ancestors and I bought things from them. And now, what is happening?' Pushpanayagi took the phone from Hadi's hands and flashed it at the young girl. Maxim squinted, trying to read the words on the screen.

'Chi, chi, chi. Come here, child.'

Maxim got up and peered over at the phone, but Pushpanayagi gestured for her to come closer and the girl went to stand behind the old woman. Hadi crept towards Maxim and together the three of them stared at the screen.

'Inside one face, you can see a whole line of people.' Pushpanayagi pointed at a photograph of a middle-aged woman with lightly permed hair and burgundy lipstick. 'Her eyes I know so well. Do you believe I've never met this woman? But suddenly, I look at her, and a feeling is coming. Deep in her face is a man who sold shoes. I cannot tell you when, but I bought something from him. Maybe it was sandals.'

Pushpanayagi touched the screen and another photograph emerged. Under the picture of a sneering, curly-haired man was the name George Chelliah. 'When I look into this man's eyes, I see nothing. No other men or women inside him. But see what he is saying about himself. Owner of Family Business. Chelliah Chimes Clockmakers. Attends the Coal Island Lutheran Church. His ancestors lived in a big house near the sea. Cannot remember the big man's name. Maybe it was Paul.'

The old lady clicked on the photograph of a plump floral-shirted man with very dark sunglasses. 'You see that smile? A bit crooked, crooked. I have seen it years ago. But I cannot tell you where I saw it or on whom. Maybe if this man took off his black glasses, I can say something more.' Pushpanayagi tapped on another face. 'Ah, this one I don't know, but maybe the next one we will—

'You never told me also . . .' Hadi gazed at the front doors, his eyes distant as though he'd seen something long forgotten.

Pushpanayagi paused a finger over the screen. 'Told you what?'

His eyes remained on the front doors.

'I also didn't know who this George Chelliah was or that Teng woman—

'Not that, Auntie.' Hadi's eyelids wavered. He ran his fingers through his hair and cleared his throat. 'About my parents. That's all.' He folded his arms and pushed his chest out slightly. 'You didn't see them inside my face?' He dropped his hands and picked at the straying fibres from the chair, his eyes fastened on the back of Pushpanayagi's head.

The old lady closed her eyes for a moment and opened them again. 'By that time,' she said, her voice trembling, 'I stopped going down the hill.'

A thick surge of silence swept through the hall. It washed over the three people and tore their eyes away from one another.

Hadi snapped his fingers. 'I better go then'. He hurried towards the front doors and without looking back, ran through the veranda and down the steps into the garden.

Maxim sat on the chair next to the old woman and together, they watched Hadi scurry towards the front gate. Trails of the earlier silence danced between them but a deeper, more viscous force shot through the remnants and the girl said, 'People are still adding you to their pages, even though there's no photo of Deborah Siva?'

The old lady yawned. 'Maybe it's the same light that has always gone through the island from those, those days. If you're on the island, the people here don't care what you have or don't have. They want to know you anyway.'

A smirk appeared on the girl's face. 'You mean they want gossip.'

'Maybe. But also, if any speck of you has fallen on this island, somehow people know and something clicks together.'

'So, what about your neighbours? They *never* come up here.'

Pushpanayagi sighed. 'What is there to talk about with them? So much time has passed.' She closed her eyes. 'Nobody should be living this long,' she whispered, opening her eyes.

'Maybe you're like a tortoise. They can live for over two hundred years.'

'Maybe. Maybe that's my secret.'

The girl twisted in her seat. 'Do you know my father is also on Touching Bones?'

Pushpanayagi held the phone out to Maxim.

'No, no,' the girl said, 'that's not what I meant. *I* don't want to look at his page.' She took the phone and nestled it in the handkerchief. 'Not at all. It's not for *me*. I was only thinking, as a *joke*, Deborah could ask Cheah Lee Kong to be friends. As a *joke*. Who knows, when you see his picture, you might suddenly see me inside his face.' She forced a laugh and tapped on the phone's screen. 'Just as a *joke*.'

Hadi's motorcycle engine groaned and shot staccato thuds through the air. It hummed more smoothly and soon faded into silence.

'Then you must do that. If that is what you want to do, do it.' Pushpanayagi closed her eyes and a small, peaceful smile illuminated her face.

*

It is a small world. How often this adage is heard and people find themselves agreeing! When, in fact, as Charles would say, the planet, relative to our existence, is large in diameter—over twelve thousand kilometres, Mars, a mere six-seven thousand; the moon even less at under four thousand—and in the twenty-first century, with the population reaching the highest in the history of the human race, the still-repeated maxim—'the world is so small'; 'what a small world it is!', whatever the variation—is swallowed as easily and as spontaneously as water, as though people have forgotten that there will always be more people they do not know than those they do. How else could they explain the fact that most days, and for some people it is every day, without fail, for the past twenty, thirty or forty years, their eyes fall upon, whether they realize it or not, brand new faces. On a trip to the sundry shop, for instance, how many fresh, one-of-a-kind eyes and noses and lips are seen? Most likely never to be seen again, most certainly never to be seen again fifty, sixty, seventy years in the future.

But, countering this, a more inclusive temperament would say that interconnections are abundant, too prevalent to be ignored, ignored only by those who are determined to gaze elsewhere, at a clear sky, for example, where everything looks clean.

'Isn't the world small, darling?' Mary had asked her distracted husband, not long after they disembarked the SS Indian Ocean and stood on the Coal Island pier, waiting for the arrival of Charles' cousin, Richard Miller. Metres away, a bulbous-eyed, overly tanned woman of Mary's height and age, fanned herself beneath a coconut tree and upon catching sight of the newly arrived couple—Mary in cream and pink stripes, smiling through joy-induced hiccups; Charles in a grey linen suit, flustered, cursing at midges flying in circles around his head—the bulbous-eyed woman dropped her fan, strode towards Mary, caught her by the arm and exclaimed, 'Mary Charlotte Tanner, as I live and breathe!' The woman had taken knitting classes with Mary in London and, while they had not continued their friendship, they had, on several occasions shared intimate secrets over tea, as Mary would later tell Charles, much later when they had moved into Yalpanam and Mary's primary agenda was to unload every memory, every dream, every hope, every single facet of herself onto a progressively uncomfortable Charles. 'Do you remember that sweet woman, Charlie?' she said, her eyes pining for his attention, 'the one we met when we first arrived on the island? Georgina Fawkes? Oh, Charlie! When I saw her, I knew it was a sign from above. No matter where we go in this life, rest assured that the Lord will grant us a few kindly souls for comfort. It is His way of revealing His love. What a shame sweet Georgina left days after our arrival! We would have been the *best* of friends had she stayed! Here we are, on a dream island, miles and miles away from home, and who do we see but Georgina Fawkes? Isn't the world small, darling?'

To avoid multiplications of what Charles termed his wife's 'emotional waste', he agreed with her and excused himself, but when a lepidopterist friend—a brief, short-term friend as all of

Charles' friends were—dropped by for whiskey on the veranda that evening, he said, with long-awaited relief, and to his glass, for on some level he knew his friend had very early on learned to deafen himself when Charles spoke about his wife, 'women are terrible, terrible believers of anything and everything. The world is *not* small. It is, in fact, very, very large and we are but half-drops in the ocean. The human population counts for a fraction of the stars in the galaxy.' Sipping his whiskey, his face took on a pained, pensive look, and unable to bear the silence manufactured by his friend's avoidance of the topic, continued, 'One of these days, I must examine Mary's lexicon; for there is no other way but to use her language to get her to see that the world is not what she thinks it is. It most definitely is not a triumph of the heavens. The love she speaks of is pure fabrication, an invention of her own desperation—

And here, his friend, perhaps as a token of his parting—for this was to be his final visit to the house, out of choice, not fate—or perhaps because something had rudely unblocked his ears, or perhaps because he decided to tap into that bounteous resource of bravery specially gifted to the inebriated, opened his deceptively small mouth and said, 'What in the world is wrong with you, Charles? If she troubles you so, why don't you simply send her back home? At least, she will be surrounded by what she knows and may, in the end, be happy.'

Unaccustomed to such directness (the arrow landing shockingly in the centre of the dot), Charles fell into the heart of the kind of moment he had always treated from the peripheries: chaotic, unknown, suffused with 'emotional waste'. The next morning, as he brushed his strawberry-blonde hair, every strand tucked into a flat pomaded bed, he regretted his words in such a deep and mournful way that the words trailed behind him like menacing shadows for the rest of the day, and when Pushpanayagi, his trusted Deborah, asked him at dinner if he would like another bowl of mulligatawny soup, his non-response and distant gaze were enough for her to brush Abu away with an impatient hand and urge Charles to consume another glass of wine in order to lift his spirits, which he willingly did. At last, after a whole carafe had been consumed, Pushpanayagi watching with maternal eyes, he indulged in a brand of 'emotional waste' he later considered not dissimilar to his wife's.

'In a moment of haste,' he told Pushpanayagi—Abu clandestinely listening from the corridor—'I allowed myself to reveal too much. The audacity of that man! Do any of these people *know* what it is like to feel such helplessness? Nay, it is more than that, much more than that. It is the terror of utmost loneliness. Why would it happen *here?* Now? Mother's words play over in my head, again and again, taunting me. My dear Charles, she had told me uncountable times, do not do to Mary what your father did to me. My father, that lowly, despicable man, lover of the bottle and of women, vile philandering drunk! I would *never* be like him. Whatever the situation, however difficult it may be, Mother said, do not abandon her. I, abandon her? Never! I only wish her insanity would lift. It is so frightening. She *frightens* me. Her joy is *large*, her melancholy *larger*. How do I fathom such things? I knew something had to be done. Something, anything, had to be done—but what? I prayed to a God I fashioned for this unholy predicament, a God not Christian, not heathen, but a God of mud and rot. Days later, on that dark morning, thunder rumbling—do you remember, Deborah?—I walked up the hill and there you were, beneath the Banyan tree, ready, as if you knew, as if the God I created had spoken to you. Oh, they may speak, all those imbeciles who know *nothing*. Would they sit with a woman whose eyes, one moment, are permeated with horror, and naive excitement, the next? A woman who converses with flowers and birds, who claims to be communing with angels in the grass? I *dare* them to! Perhaps my single concession to Mary's strange mind is her insistence that, darling Richard, as she so often calls him, has brought us to this house from the dead.'

Upon listening to his outpouring of 'emotional waste', Pushpanayagi, who had thus far assumed that Mary was a spoilt Colonial wife who had the luxury of accessing insanity, converted that assumption into fact. If Charles had forgotten to muse on the small world his wife had talked about, maintaining throughout his life that the world had more space than intimacy, Pushpanayagi did, after Charles' sole display of emotional extravagance, think aloud in her room that the world was indeed quite small. Of all the people who could have moved into her home, the one chosen by this small world was the first cousin of her ex-lover. Small, cosy, yes, the world was small, especially when it (by 'it' she did not mean God of the World, but more an assumed collective intelligence) ordered the right people to fall into a situation at the right place at the right time, so that they may astound themselves by their proximity to one another: this so-and-so's cousin once served with that so-and-so's father in the Boer War and now, both so-and-so's are prominent shareholders of a thriving tea company in London. Links, logic-defying connections, harlequin strings pulling the right people into the right time and place, pulling, another version may go, the wrong people into the wrong time and place. Right or wrong, Pushpa did muse on the smallness of the world, but only briefly and superficially. She did not get as far as the magnanimous reasoning that serendipity, coincidence, and mysterious connections were part of a grand design—in one is a need fulfilled by another whose own need is met in the need fulfilled. A need, liked or loathed, a need, nevertheless.

But Pushpa, not sensing this need, chose to pity Charles, in silence, for she knew that once the alcoholic haze had lifted, he would be abiding by the implied rule in the house that, during the sobriety of daytime, work came first, and personal affairs were to be held in abeyance. The subject of Charles' outburst was never mentioned again, and after some time, it was as if it had never happened at all.

9

Of all the people, she'd listened to Mother. Worst of all, she'd *remembered* the story about Mother and Auntie Mei-Mei sneaking off into the jungle when they were children, picking and eating 'jungle berries'—whatever those were—and having diarrhea all night long. One of the few stories from those bedroom-moments when Mother's extra eyelashes came off and she blinked at the mirror like a lonely movie star. She just happened to be standing outside The Parents' bedroom past her bedtime and got invited in. Something in Mother went wobbly past midnight. Mostly, she gave a roundup of the evening's outing. Once in a while, an actual story got told that suddenly made Mother seem real, like she wasn't always a well-dressed woman with precise ideas about porcelain vases and butter dishes imported from France.

But she'd never really kept those stories in her memory, or at least that's what she thought; because now, all of a sudden, she'd remembered the story and opened her big mouth and told Hadi. She stood inches away behind him, watching him hunch slightly on the patch of land behind Yalpanam, the grass here wilder, rougher. He leaned forward, not looking for 'jungle berries', no, he *knew* there was no such thing, but for edible mushrooms. She couldn't even find a Malay translation of 'berries' for him. She'd only said fruit, jungle fruit. Of course, he couldn't take her seriously.

'Come lah, Max. Help me look.' He straightened up and turned around. His back was so long, his head so much closer to the trees than hers. He smiled proudly. By now the cigarettes should have yellowed his teeth, but they were as white as the teeth on the toothpaste box he bought for the house yesterday. He shook a plastic bag at her, telling her to come take a look. She dragged her feet towards him and peeked into the bag.

'So few? I thought you would have collected at least a hundred by now.'

'Always talking big,' he laughed and twirled the bag as though he was going to fling it away.

She caught the bag and ran, his hurried footsteps behind her. 'Oi, oi,' he shouted. He clenched part of her T-shirt and she laughed and laughed and screamed and he tugged harder. She threw the bag to the ground, tripped over one of her slippers. He stood above her, laughing. 'That's what happens to thieves,' he said. He extended his hand towards her. 'Don't want,' she said, 'you come and sit down. Your shorts are too clean.'

He sat on the ground and crossed his legs. 'Haaaaiiiihhh,' he fake sighed. Traces of the laugh lingered on his lips. When he smiled or laughed, the terrible seriousness that sometimes fell over his face like a mountain broke apart in an instant. The dimples shattered the darkness like clumps of sugar dissolving in lime juice. Then he'd remember something or she'd say something, and the mountain grew back again so fast it was almost as if it never went away.

He lay down and rested his hands on his stomach. He stared at the overcast sky. 'You need anything?' he murmured. The way his voice suddenly went raspy, he might as well have been talking poetry to the clouds.

'Only mushrooms. That's all I need.' She giggled.

'Max . . .'

Lately, this new voice popped up from time to time, always when it was just the two of them, after the chores had been done and Auntie was resting. Like when they sat in the courtyard eating lychees he brought back from the market, or when he came down the ladder she was holding after he'd fixed the light bulb and he'd accidentally looked too deeply into her eyes, and now, the voice was back, a little huskier.

'You talk like this with your customers also?' she laughed.

The mountain slowly crawled back into his eyes. 'Enough lah, Max. Enough.' His voice was softer, deeper than usual. Sometimes, Daddy spoke like that on the phone when the lights were off and he thought the whole house was asleep.

'What? I didn't say anything.'

'You don't care about the future, is it?'

'Future? What you talking about?'

He closed his eyes. His face hardened as though it had taken on the qualities of brick. He opened his eyes, turned to his side, and faced her. One hand supported his head, the other pinched the grass. 'I'm not your brother. I'm not your boyfriend. I'm no one from your family.' He plucked a fistful of grass and chucked it back on the ground. The hand began playing with the grass again. 'But I see myself as your friend. So, I must ask you. How much longer can you stay here?'

Her heart pounded and the old dryness took over her mouth. The full mountain had come back. She glanced at the jungle. It looked portentous, thick with all kinds of alien life. 'I don't know,' she said.

The entire mountain sat on his face. He looked so old, so much older than when he picked a worm from the ground and shoved it in her face, or when he told her that his lime juice needed some salt. 'Yesterday, Mrs. Fatima told me your mother, Mrs. Cheah, is talking about what kind of funeral they can have for you. Your mother is saying that if you've been missing for one month already, how can you still be alive? The police also have stopped looking as much. No clues, no signs, no one saw you leave or be taken—'

'So? You want me to suddenly ring my mother's bell? Then everyone will be happy.'

He grunted as though she'd said something stupid.

'Is that what you want, Hadi? I must go to them and live in my house like a normal person?'

'No, I am only saying that—'

'That, what?'

'It's no longer only about you, Maxim Cheah!'

He sat up. His face softened. 'I'm sorry. I didn't mean to shout'. The mountain floated away, but within seconds, it came back. 'It's just that . . .' He ran his fingers through his hair, the boy-band bangs falling perfectly in place above his forehead. 'Just that . . . you have a family, a mother, a father, but you act . . .'

She bit her lip and swallowed hard. 'If you had bothered to ask me, I would have told you that I'm planning to call my father. But you seem to think I'm stupid. I can't live here forever. I *know* that.'

'What are you waiting for?'

'You want me gone so you can get Auntie and Yalpanam all to yourself. That's why you are forcing me to go back, aren't you?'

He shot up. He shook his head as though she'd said the most poisonous thing. 'I can't talk to you like this.' He looked at her, then at the plastic bag on the ground. 'Make sure you cook the mushrooms properly,' he said and stomped towards the gap in the fence.

'You don't understand,' she shouted, but he did not turn back.

He pushed apart the fence where the gap was, fitted through it, and marched ahead, down the grassy slope that led to the front of the house, not looking back once; not even once to show that he knew he'd crossed a line he had nothing to do with.

Who was he to prance around, telling her what she should or should not do? *Just a friend.* Someone who was just a friend didn't have the luxury of barging into her life and pointing a finger at her, saying she was wrong. Just friends picked jungle mushrooms, shared stories, ate exotic fruits together, and eventually said goodbye. *That was it.*

She yanked the phone out from her shorts pocket and took a deep breath. The soil smelt strong, like a blend of metal, wood, and the musky oil Mother rubbed on her temples on hot afternoons. The sunbird songs travelled all the way from the veranda. It mixed with the shrill call of the mynah birds and the screech of another bird. One day, soon, the bird would screech again and Auntie would be there to tell her its name. It seemed to work out that way for some reason. She'd have a thought and then hours later, or maybe the next day, Auntie would talk about that very thought even though she hadn't said a single thing about it. Maybe Auntie would also explain why Hadi was behaving like a dumb fool.

A tiny green light blinked on the top right corner of the phone. She clicked on Deborah Siva's page and scrolled through it. She tapped on 'Cheah Lee Kong'. For two days, each time she touched his name, she clicked out, went to Google, and ended up finding out about skin cancer symptoms, celebrities who did Botox, Jupiter and its moons, how to make earrings. Sometimes it was Footsy's blog, but he was getting quiet these days. Whatever it was, she kept clicking on things, on and on until her eyes smarted, or Auntie called her to brush the moss off the bench in the courtyard, or Hadi's motorbike putted outside the gate. But she had to see, at some point, she had to see what was happening down the hill, *if* anything was happening at all. If Hadi was right, she'd see a whole storm. At least now, once she saw, she'd have something to throw at him. She could tell him the storm was not on the island, it was in a stupid little *teacup*.

She clicked on the pictures folder. She'd seen most of them before when Daddy used to leave his laptop on the kitchen table. Photograph after photograph of political party gatherings. All the people wearing green, blue and white shirts with the party logo of one dark brown hand and one light brown hand, interlocked, stuck on the breast pocket. Behind podiums, holding microphones, one arm in the air, hand in a fist, then standing at buffet lines, or smiling in a crowd of orphans, schoolchildren, it didn't matter as long as there were children to make them all look good. She scrolled further down, back to the really old photographs, before he ran for MP, when he put up pictures of his buildings. The clock tower in town, the fire station, Sea Front Square. The last building-related picture was of the huge signboard for D'Place Mall before the building was even constructed. She clicked on 'Posts' and scrolled down.

Something rustled behind her. If Hadi thought she'd forgive him so quickly, he was stupider than he looked. Did he think she was as blind as the bats that flew over the garden at night? Probably decided to come back to tell her the people in town were saying she'd finally escaped the Cheah House or that Daddy was using her disappearance to win votes. She turned around. An empty plastic bag lay between the fence and the ground where she sat. A light breeze blew and the bag swished.

She scrolled down Cheah Lee Kong's posts, her heart suddenly flip-flopping as though she was sitting for an exam.

Cheah Lee Kong wrote on 24 March, 11.39 p.m.: Puff, Puff, where are you, Puff?

Cheah Lee Long wrote on 25 March, 5.46 a.m.: Puff is magical, but where has he put his magic? Inside a shoe, or up on a tree? Could he be swimming in the river with the crocodiles? No one knows. Only Puff can bring his magic back into the world.

Cheah Lee Kong wrote on 25 March, 7.24 a.m.: Puff can fly, but he doesn't know he can fly. Fly, Puff, fly! Fly home where you belong.

Her hands began to tremble. The cold feeling in her throat stormed up her face. Tears came fast. They gushed down her cheeks. She threw the phone on the ground and sobbed into her T-shirt. Her belly felt so dark and empty, her chest tight, as though someone was pulling a rough string around it. The pain in her chest grew sharper and sharper. More tears fell. It was as if the island's sea was inside her body and it had to flow back out onto land. She wiped her eyes with her hands and stared at the jungle. Somehow, she knew the darkness between the leaves and the trees, how the vines twisted around the tree trunks. She knew it. Somehow, the darkness and the twisted vines were what her body felt like. It was as if she was looking directly at herself. And from somewhere in the darkness of the jungle, Puff's purple snout released a cloud of purple smoke.

*

The shadows skulked outside Pushpanayagi's bedroom, waiting for the speckles of light flickering through the windows to stop, but the lights kept sparking and soon, a warm inky emptiness filled the room, and the terrazzo tiles gently heated up, and through two long cracks in the wall facing the old lady's mat, a sapphire current coursed up and down, sending warm incandescent rays through the bricks. Space-time curved around Pushpanayagi, cradled her like an egg and its embryo. As she leaned against a pile of sarongs, neatly folded by the girl earlier in the day, and as she yawned and adjusted her snag-tooth that had been slowly loosening over the days, the larger shadow crept into the room, despite the scintilla of light and sapphire current, and hovered close to the old lady. Its lunar-silver glow was murky that evening. Indigo light drizzled from the ceiling. The shadow shrivelled, then melted onto the floor, formed a black rivulet, glided slowly, unwavering from its passage, towards the other shadow by the door, and wrapped itself around the silver nimbus of the shadow. One shadow, swarthy, immense, it slithered into the room.

The rain of light fell harder. Flecks of indigo light pelted down on the shadow, seeped into the floor, and the shadow, shrinking from the light, spread farther, closer to the old lady, past the windows, into the garden, into the crevices of curling cabbage leaves, past the dirt path, into the trembling roses. It paused at the edge of the fence. The roots of the mango tree stirred, and the bones that had mixed in with the roots shifted, and these bones spilled an odour of sour musk through the soil that reached the other bones by the jungle and those bones rattled in their cold, wet beds.

The land quaked, sending the underground spirits to the surface of the soil. They waited for the spirit of the flowers to ascend, to consume the shadow, but the spirit slackened beneath the earth, and the shadow, blacker now, stronger, crept back past the garden, slithered through the windows and, the rain of indigo light over, it slipped quietly into the old lady's body.

Pushpanayagi coughed, patted her chest and called for the girl, but the girl was far away on the stone bench in the courtyard, studying the stars that were springing and twisting for her. The old lady closed her eyes, but sleep did not come. A dark fog bellied out within her. She turned to her side and the snag-tooth that had been threatening to drop fell onto the mat like the little ivory ball that had fallen from the eye of the stone tiger on the pillar by the front gate one day, all by itself.

*

All the windows are open, even the four, square windows beneath the stained glass window in the topmost room of the house. The air is so still, not even the tips of leaves flutter, not the grass recently sheared by Abu as he sang morose dirges about his days in the village, not the paper lanterns shaped like fish and stars and flowers festooning the veranda, not the flames of candles inside the lanterns; nothing has the will, a reason or the heart to move. Not even the swallows that love to dive low in the garden and swoop in rapid circles over the daisies and tiger-lilies. The bees have not come to suck at the milkweeds. Inside Charles's butterfly room, the butterflies do not spread their wings or flit, as they often do, from wall to wall and above the glass cage where the cocoons hang in rows like cocoa fruit. The indoor lizards hide behind cupboards and chests of drawers, their tails unmoving, their eyes closed even as a lost fly spirals up in the air, pauses, and falls dead on the floor of the master bedroom.

This stillness does not enter the hearts of those who shuffle about inside the house. Bowties are tied with stiff, adroit fingers, sashes wrapped around dresses in mesmerising strokes of the hand, and in the hot, sunless kitchen, pots and pans clash in minor-key rhythms, unlike the gentle, wistful melody that wafts through the front hall from the piano that has been rolled closer to the centre of the space for all to see—for all to see Pushpanayagi's fingers that gracefully lift this way and that on the ivory keys, and her celestial smile in union with eyes half-open in joy, and the slow swaying of her body as the music rises and falls. Notes are struck and the walls loosen. The little people in the paintings on the walls sigh and begin to whistle to one another over cadmium-blue ocean waves, or stacks of hay. Their souls in paint heave quietly in their worlds and awaken through pigment. The song is finished. Pushpanayagi lowers her hands, presses them against her chest as though she herself had been moved by her playing. The guests have not arrived.

She has worn the single festive sari she had packed in an old leather bag the night before her journey through the Indian Ocean. Its silver flowers twinkle against coral red fabric. She rises, smooths the pleats that have deviated from their neat rows, and saunters towards the table, laid out with a large sylvan-themed punch bowl and delicate crystal cups, by the courtyard windows.

'Well, well. If it isn't the guest of honour doing her rounds! Does she approve? Ha! Ha!' Charles hurries from the entrance of the corridor into the hall. He fits his hands into his trouser pockets and scans the room.

'Everything is looking splendid, Charles. And all these honourable people coming—'

'For *you*. They are coming here for *you*. And, rightly so, I may add.'

Suddenly shy, Pushpanayagi lowers her head and gazes into the deep red liquid in the punch bowl. Slices of oranges and cubes of pineapple float on its surface like little objects lost at sea.

'The heat is abominable!' Kitty Miller dusts the skirt of her silken gown. She pauses midway through the corridor, spins around and says to her husband, 'If you come any closer, you'll be welded to my dress!' She sashays down the corridor, then skips when she enters the hall, as though taking pains to avoid the floor. She glares at Charles. 'If a tiny breeze doesn't blow in the next few minutes, I'll scream into my glass of punch.' She darts an accusatory look at him. 'Well, dear cousin, you dragged us out here into the pit of hell, don't you think you should at the very least hydrate us?'

Pushpanayagi pours a ladleful of punch into two cups and hands one over to Kitty, who takes the cup grudgingly. She flashes a quick smile at Pushpanayagi. 'Why, thank you.' Kitty twirls around. Her eyes land on her husband who is standing by the piano, fidgeting with his bowtie. 'Percy, please! If it bothers you that much, you might as well take it off and run wild with the natives.' She turns to Charles. 'Singapore is nothing like this, you know,' she whispers loudly.

'Come now, Kitty. Our guests will be arriving at any moment now. In fact . . . that's the first carriage approaching.' He adjusts his bowtie and runs the palm of his hand down his shirt. He watches as the boy—specially hired for the evening—holds a hand out in greeting, while a foot shod in sparkling blue appears on the carriage step.

'I still fail to fathom the point of this whole circus,' Kitty mutters. She sips from her cup and waves at her husband to join her. 'Honestly, Charles. This punch is diabolical. I can taste the cheap moonshine on my tongue and it is *far* from pleasant.'

Pushpanayagi hoists parts of her sari to drape over her head but, changing her mind, quickly lets it fall and strides away from the punch table, heading for the front entrance, and changing her mind again, takes a detour to Charles's favourite armchair, moved for the evening to a corner by the front windows. She strokes the voluminous tassel that hangs off the top edge of the chair and stares out into the garden.

'We absolutely adore those exotic little lanterns hanging from the beams!'

'Victoria, Johnny, please, please, come in. Indeed, Victoria, you'll be surprised what wonders occur when you tell the houseboy to scout for decent decorations. One enters a whole new world of aesthetics!' Charles's laugh is loose, guttural.

'We were saying, weren't we, darling, that the lanterns were so quaint? We thought so immediately. What sweet, quaint lanterns, we said.'

Pushpanayagi releases the tassel and inches closer to the windows. She grips a windowpane and pokes her head out. The close, sultry air hangs like a heavy stone. Across from the house, the jungle-covered slope of the neighbouring hill slowly swallows the sun; the last refulgent pinks and purples in the sky dwindle away and leave a wash of dark ultramarine cloud. The hooves of horses crunch gravel on the path leading to the house. Another carriage has arrived. Pushpanayagi darts away from the window, levels the fabric of her sari, pats the bun on her head, and struts out from behind the chair, chest out.

Charles is by the door, smiling, shaking hands, a debonair host. 'Do come in, George, Anna, Philip, Clara. It is terribly hot, is it not?'

'Charles, you must tell me your secret. How does one create paradise on this island? Your garden takes one's breath away!'

'It's simple, dear Anna. One hires the best of the natives.' Laughter trickles into the hall. 'My man Abu is a Jack of all trades. In another life, he would be a star at Eton.'

Pushpanayagi steps forward and extends her hand. 'Welcome, welcome,' she says, nodding enthusiastically, 'I hope you've had a good carriage ride?'

The women smile weakly. 'Yes, thank you,' one says, 'but the heat—'

'Oh, enough about the heat!' the other says, 'We must talk about Charles' stupendous garden! Is your man Abu responsible for the glorious begonias?'

'Yes, yes,' Charles says, 'he is such a queer fellow. The garden is very much his preoccupation. He tells me it gives him great joy—

'Imagine that!'

They guffaw, and Pushpanayagi, watching their faces like an eagle about to descend on its prey, guffaws along.

'Marvellous, Charlie. I must say you are doing rather splendidly for yourself.'

Charles ushers the guests into the hall, Pushpanayagi trailing behind.

'Kitty!'

'Clara!'

Kitty and Clara, reunited, take their excitement to the veranda, away from the rising din in the hall, clinking glasses, tinny laughter, a cacophony of jovial voices.

'Oh, but we must say happy birthday to Deborah!'

'Oh yes, we are here after all for a birthday!'

'A birthday is always a grand excuse for having as much wine as one likes!'

'Birthdays are excellent creations!'

'Thank you, all. Thank you for coming—'

But quickly, the conversation switches again and Pushpanayagi slowly worms her way out of the circle.

'Is our old girl feeling up to joining us this evening?'

'Mary is too fatigued to grace us with her presence this evening. It's the weather, really, dear George. Her constitution is too delicate to handle such crude temperatures.'

Pushpanayagi drifts towards the front windows, to her previous niche by the armchair, close enough to the veranda for Kitty's voice, spiked with passion, to ring clear.

'Honestly, Clara. I simply do not understand *how* you do it! The world is so heartbreakingly small here. Do you mean to say you *never* tire of this primitive little island?'

'Oh, at least we have the club. I do manage to meet almost everyone there. I know all the ladies here . . . all except, well, Charles' wife.'

'Got the morbs, that Charlie's wife . . . oh, dear Clara, I *do* need a break from all that island talk. Mad as hops, if you ask me in all honesty. *Why* does he keep her here? I've been telling Percy, he's got to tell his cousin to send his wife *back*. Their poor daughters in England! My heart absolutely breaks—

'Oh, but they can't ship the girls all the way over here, now, can they?'

'Of course not! Charlie should at the very least send Mary *back* to Surrey. The poor woman has been *infected* by this godforsaken island. Do you know what he did when he realized he had absolutely *no* power over her?'

'Do tell, Kitty.'

'Shouldn't you know by now? Tsk, tsk, Clara. Oh, but I suppose you and Philip have only just arrived in this festering place. He went where all our men—I should say where all *your* men went. There's nothing of this sort in Singapore—to that quack of a woman, Deborah. When I remember, I thank the stars Percy's brother Richard got away from that witch as soon as he realized—'

'Richard Miller? Of the Miller & Johnson plantation?'

'The very same one. Do you know he *built* this house?'

'Oh, I never!'

'Precisely, Clara. This was *his* house. When he died at sea, God bless his soul, Percy was ready to transport us all here. *Percy* was going to take over the plantation and move us into this very house—'

'My word, Kitty.'

'Precisely, Clara. Or at the very least, *Charles,* who was already on the island, but even in death, poor Richard was still being twirled around a little brown finger. He willed the house to *her*—'

'Deborah?'

'What humiliation, Clara! What vermin does Charles take himself to be? *Living* in a house that rightfully belongs to the Miller family, now owned by a woman who probably makes frequent pacts with Lucifer.'

'Is she that dangerous?'

'Some sort of oriental mystic, they say. I am sure you're acquainted with the sort. Contemplate it, Clara. How else do you think she keeps this family here? I hear Charles pays her a small fee every month as rent. What in the world is Charlie running away from?'

Pushpanayagi retreats from the armchair. She fiddles with her hair bun, tugs the sleeves of her sari blouse, and looks at the floor in a daze. Her hand rests quietly on her chest as she slowly, shakily, raises her head. Her eyes are sombre, distant; the rest of her face taut. Charles and the guests are deep in merriment by the punch table, oblivious to her place by the windows. Perhaps it is the curtains that create an illusory veil over her, but as she trudges closer towards the centre of the hall, the veil lifts and Kitty, who has now relocated to the entrance, screeches, 'There you are!' and the cup in Kitty's hand plunges to the floor, shattering into a glittering web of glass.

The guests turn their heads in Kitty's direction. Hastily, some of the eyes revert to Pushpanayagi standing by herself at the centre of the hall.

'Abu! I say, Abu! Careful, Kitty. Not to worry. Abu will clean this mess up immediately.' Charles fumbles through his pockets for his handkerchief and wipes his forehead.

'Happy birthday, Deborah!' Anna says and the other guests promptly mimic in amplified tones, 'Happy birthday, happy birthday!'

Pushpanayagi walks towards the piano, traces a finger along the ivory keys, and strikes the lowest one. A deep funereal note echoes through the hall.

'What a super idea! We do need music to brighten up this party, don't we?' George whisks his wife over to the piano.

'Charming, yes. Come over to the piano, Kitty, Clara. You mustn't worry about the broken glass. Charlie's man will take care of it.' Anna smiles in Pushpanayagi's direction. 'What a delightful costume you have on, my dear. Perfectly appropriate for one's birthday.'

'Quite fitting,' Kitty chimes in, 'Quite, quite fitting, Deborah.'

'My name is Pushpanayagi. Goddess of Flowers,' says Pushpanayagi, quietly.

The hall falls silent.

Pushpanayagi clears her throat. 'But I do not mind. English names are . . .'

'What the devil has possessed you, Abu?' Charles' voice cuts in as Abu dashes into the hall, panting, dripping with sweat.

'Tiger, Tuan!'

'What tiger?'

'Eat lady!'

'What lady?'

'Mem lady.'

'Mem? Mem who?'

'Don't know name, Tuan.'

10

I am sorry, Max. Your mother's sadness entered my own self. How can you do that? You have no—*I was holding one of Auntie's pumpkins. The clouds were grey. I could already feel one or two drops of rain. I saw your mother walking through Market Square. Suddenly*—Suddenly, what?—*She looked up and from the sweetcorn stall, she stared straight into my eyes. I dropped the pumpkin on my foot.* And then? *And then my foot started to burn and . . .* And? *I realized something. Maybe it was the pain in my foot. Maybe it was the rain. But I felt something in her heart. I saw it in her eyes.* I think you saw another woman. My mother is not like that. She's strong. *Then I took a pen and wrote in the receipt book. I wrote a note to your mother. I told her to forgive you. I told her where you are*—You *gave* this note to my mother? *I put it in an envelope and dropped it in your letterbox.* Now what will I do? Where will I go? *Everything will be fine. Allah is kind. Your mother will love you till the day she dies.* No, she won't. You don't know her. You think all mothers are the same. It's not true. *You cannot see the love. You're blind. Blind.* Blind? If there is so much love, then why has even my father stopped writing posts about me? Seven days he's not written a single thing about Puff. *Puff?* It's nothing. Nothing matters. Puff is stupid. All of this is so stupid!

Maxim ran towards the front door and as she ran, the floor creaked and as it creaked, a vibrating blue light coursed up from the floor and seeped into the hearts of Pushpanayagi and Hadi, and before Maxim could step out of the hall, the blue light seeped into her heart too, and she stopped.

The blue light glowed bright through them all. It was a simple blue light, the kind that pours into a person when they look deeply into the eyes of someone else. Your mother's mud-brown eyes, for instance, in your sphere of sight, different, apart, out there, yet eyes also, like yours, happening, existing in your vision, yours. Or the hand of your friend? Touching yours, a long-fingered hand, fingernails chewed down to the quick, warm against yours—apart, no matter how close or warm or pulsating, another pulse, another system of veins, blood, tissue. Your lover, for instance, running towards you, one body approaching another body, meeting, fusing warmth, lip upon lip, and suddenly, tragically, one day, you ask on a gloomy, mauve-clouded night: what lies inside my lover? When will I know? When will I ever know?

The loneliness of every object.

The loneliness of birth and of death.

The loneliness of not knowing.

The loneliness of being oneself.

The deeper loneliness of not being oneself.

*

The warm, black thing was coming again. Always—now she could feel it so clearly minutes before it spread everywhere—it nibbled at the bones. Always, a nice, small biting of the bones, and then the little lights started flashing and then, and then. Hare Rama, if this is you, Rama, coming on the chariot after exile, please come closer and quickly. The belly-stone hopped once, twice—she closed her eyes and placed her hands over her navel; the stone was asking her to speak. Something moved through her legs and shook the stone. Rama, the body has not been talked to since those days. 'What do you want, stone?' The stone settled back in its place.

Lights shot through the warm, black nothingness. She sank, deeper and deeper, into eddying darkness. Her head spun, her heart leapt. A shower of golden-orange light fell upon her, upon every spot of nothingness. She opened her mouth, drank in the light and sank deeper and deeper out of the light, into capering darkness.

The jungle is cool, dark, noisy with insects hiding in leaves and branches, inside cracks in the soil from which plants sprout, tall, short, wide, decaying, ferns, spikes, thorns, spores, vines, twisting, erect, curling, so close they kiss, so close the taller plants provide shelter for the shorter ones.

'Tuan.'

'Sssshhhh!'

Abu lowers the rifle in his hands, shakes his head at the dimly lit lamp at his feet and taps the armrest of the chair. Pushpanayagi watches him from the corner of her eye, then turns towards him and lifts her eyebrows. He shakes his head again, rolls his eyes, and points at Charles in the chair.

'Tuan'.

Charles jerks back and sighs. 'What the devil do you want?'

Abu rushes forward, parks himself by the edge of the chair. He hugs the rifle to his chest. 'Tiger not come, Tuan. Now much dark, Tuan. Mem need for food.'

Charles glares at the rifle in Abu's arms. His gaze slowly travels up to his servant's neck, chin, nose, finally the eyes. 'We're doing this for *her*, can't you see?' He rests his own rifle on the armrests of his chair; it lies over his lap like a bar keeping him in his seat. 'Kitty is perfectly capable of babysitting for one measly evening. I would think so! For God's sakes, man, we're saving the bloody island!'

Abu hangs his head and steps back. 'Yes, Tuan.'

Charles lifts the rifle and points ahead. 'When the beast comes, we simply aim and shoot. Now, please be quiet. To conquer the beast, one has to trick the beast. It mustn't know we're here.'

Pushpanayagi tiptoes to the chair next to Charles and sits down. It squeaks. She clenches its armrests and whispers, 'Sorry, sorry.'

'Not to worry, Deborah. Somehow I don't think the tiger would mind you. In fact . . . if you could do whatever it was you did when that blasted baboon stole mangoes from the tree, that would be splendid.' He lowers the rifle. 'What did you do, exactly?'

Pushpa flips her single plait over her shoulders and looks to the ground. The earth is damp, littered with leaves and pebbles, twigs, a few crawling insects. She breathes in deeply. The air is stagnant, filled with the smells of soil and wet bark; woody, a little blood-like. 'I told it to go. That's all.'

'Just like that. Well, do ask the tiger to come. We can't have it killing all our women. What a beast! To know exactly what it wants. Quite a will.' He raises the rifle and aims at the darkness.

'You don't have to kill, Charles. If it's eating people, it's already old—'

'Nonsense! What sort of a human being allows a beast to take what isn't its right to take? And with no fight? Never will I live such a life! It is the life of a worm.'

Abu taps the armrest of Charles's chair. 'Tuan, Tuan,' he whispers, 'tiger come.' Abu directs their gaze with his rifle. A slow squelching of leaves blends in with the insects' song. Down below, the frayed tip of a tail flashes behind a Meranti tree and disappears. Charles angles his rifle at the space between the Meranti tree and a slender palm. The animal darts out from behind the tree. Charles fires his weapon. He reloads and fires again. The tiger staggers drunkenly and drops to the ground. He reloads and fires, again, and again, five, six, seven, eight shots. He charges up from his seat and bolts down the slope towards the beast. Abu trails close behind, rifle tightly clutched in one hand, lamp in the other. Pushpanayagi watches them, hand over mouth, and scrambles after them.

Charles looms over the dead animal, Pushpanayagi inching closer. A single, long fang peeks out of the animal's slightly parted mouth, its eyes frozen in death. Blood blooms from a wound on its chest. Charles reloads the rifle, aims at the tiger's neck and shoots. The shot echoes thunderously through the jungle. He reloads again, points the weapon at the animal's stomach, and fires again. Abu chucks his rifle on the ground and creeps in the direction of the tiger. Charles lifts the rifle high and in one quick sweep, swings the weapon down, and thrusts it into the tiger's chest. He pierces the animal's flesh with the stock of the rifle, pounds and hammers and pulps the beast over and over and over again.

'Stop, Tuan! Stop! Tiger die already.'

Charles stabs the tiger's head, stabs it so hard that its skull cracks. He releases the rifle and falls to his knees. Abu scurries forward. 'Tuan. Tuan. What happen, Tuan?' Charles buries his face in his palms.

Clumps of flesh litter the ground. Streaks of muscle and tissue lie between and over bones. Only the paws and the tail remain whole. Pushpanayagi turns away from the carcass, from Charles and Abu. She covers her mouth with her hands and begins to convulse. She leans against the closest tree, vomits, and massages her belly, and vomits again.

The insects stop singing. A grave quiet fills the jungle.

Charles rises, his face catatonic, frozen like the eyes of the tiger he has just killed. 'Well, I . . .' he mutters. He glances at Abu, then at Pushpanayagi. A look of horror falls over his face. It slowly turns into a vacant glare, then the hollowness departs and gradually, something soft infuses his eyes, cheeks, lips. Pushpanayagi recognises the softness. She has seen it many times on many faces, and on her own, when in rare moments, she looks into a mirror and sees the fear bubble beneath a sheen of shame.

*

It had rained all night and all morning. Pools of water formed glistening patches in the garden. The wind peeled clouds away from the sun and birds returned to their favourite spots in the garden. Four mynah birds stood around a pool by the pumpkin patch and gawked, squawked at the water. One hopped in and plunged its head into the water; it rose for air, shook its head in a shiver. The other birds watched the spectacle in silence. The bathed bird waddled out of the pool and a second one entered. Like that, they took turns until each bird was fully wet and the feathers on their heads spiked from the dipping and the shaking, their abandonment to the little pool that was slowly evaporating in the lightly glowing sun. They toddled away from the pool and began hopping towards the cabbages. They squawked from the depths of their lungs. They cawed and yelped and Pushpanayagi poked Maxim's shoulder. The girl held the old woman's arm and led her down the veranda steps. The warmth of the sun tore away more cloud and the sunrays poured in through the pumpkin patch.

'Come, child. What is happening with the mynahs?'

'Careful of the water, Auntie. So much already collected in the garden. What kind of rain is this?'

Pushpanayagi clicked her tongue and tugged at the girl's arm. The ground was still wet and soft. They strolled towards the vegetable patch, their slippers noisy in the clayey soil, but the earth held their feet.

'One hundred years ago—something like that—it rained nonstop for one week. The garden was flooded and you know what happened?'

They stopped by the tomato plant and the girl leaned over to see what the birds had congregated around. The squawking stopped.

'The water came up so high, frogs started swimming like fish. Then my . . .' The old lady sighed and jabbed her tongue through the little gap left by her departed snag tooth. 'Savitri, you know, Charles's other wife, she was new to the house when it happened. She put flowers on the water and with God knows what paper, some kind of hard paper, she made boats and put the frogs in the boats. For one whole day, we watched frogs in paper boats going round and round the flowers.'

The girl laughed prodigiously. Each time the laughing threatened to fade, it miraculously rose, until Pushpanayagi tapped the girl's back and the laughing stopped for good.

'Suddenly, I am remembering the sound of the water as the boats went up and down. Swasshh, swassh, susshhh, sussshhh. Charles also liked it. Savitri did things like that sometimes and Charles would smile.'

'Grumpy puss Charles.'

The old lady's face tightened. 'He had something heavy inside. Like a dark, very old rock. Too hard to move. But I think, in the end—'

'What happened in the end?'

Pushpanayagi stared at the fence beyond the vegetable patch. A darkish gleam grew over her eyes. 'He died the normal way. One afternoon, he went to sleep and kept on sleeping.'

The old lady kept her eyes on the fence and stroked a tomato, bright red and plump. The other hand rested on her chest. Maxim looked at the fence to see what the old lady was seeing, but there was nothing there.

'Do you think he thought about his first wife before he died?'

Pushpanayagi shook her head as though the question hadn't crossed her mind. 'I can never know that. She had been gone for so long. Who knows what people keep deep inside their souls. No one really knows actually. No one really knows another person.' She gripped the tomato and kept her eyes fixed on the fence. Maxim watched her face closely and said, 'Is that why you keep the room at the top locked?'

Pushpanayagi's fingers tightened around the tomato in her hand until some of its juice seeped out. She glanced at her hand and quickly pulled it away. 'That key was lost years and years ago. I don't need to go there, so I never tried to open it.'

Pretending not to have seen what happened, Maxim stepped towards the congregation of birds. 'I think it's a dead bird or something,' she said. 'They're standing around . . .' she continued. Pushpanayagi rubbed the hand on her sarong. 'Acha, ok. We don't need to disturb them, then. They also just want to quietly say goodbye.'

The girl edged closer to the birds and the birds began to shriek and flap their wings. A few hopped back from the object of their fascination to reveal a dead bird, lying toy-like and drenched, its black feathers shimmering. She squealed and looked away.

'They know what to do. You don't have to worry. Like we have funerals, so are the birds grieving.'

'That's what they're screaming about? Like the women who wail at Indian funerals?'

'Something like that. Now, we say a prayer for the bird'. Pushpanayagi brought her palms together in prayer and closed her eyes. The girl followed suit.

'Just whisper after me, in your heart. Dear Lord, bless this baby of yours who has died on our land. Take him away from this earth with the respect he deserves, dear Lord. Feed him with your honey as his soul flies to the astral worlds. Do not keep the pain in his heart going and also take away the pain in the hearts of those who are still living. Dear Lord, we are saying this prayer—.'

A hollow clanging stabbed the air. Maxim and Pushpanayagi turned their heads. A short, plump woman in jogging pants and an oversized T-shirt stood at the gate, a pink unopened umbrella in her hand. She gaped through the bars of the gate. Her eyes found the young girl and the old woman. For a long moment, the eyes stayed on the two people in the garden. Then the woman began banging on the gate with the umbrella, lips pursed tight, eyes tapering as they took in more of the young girl and the old woman.

Maxim, rooted, petrified, hands hung in the air in its stance of prayer, watched the woman at the gate like a person witnessing a tragedy unravel before their eyes and, slowly, her hands came tremblingly down, and she rasped, 'Mummy'.

Pushpanayagi stared at the visitor as though a strange, new life had emerged from the earth. She wiped her hands on her sarong and ran her tongue over her teeth. The tongue lingered over the new gap in the centre of the upper row of teeth and quickly retreated into its cave. 'It's your mother?'

The woman struck the gate, again and again, but nobody moved. Then she slid the umbrella through the space between two bars of the gate, as if, denied entry, she had to somehow stake a claim on the garden, and all she had for a weapon was the umbrella. Pushpanayagi grabbed the girl's hand and pulled her towards the dirt path that led to the entrance of the compound. They stopped midway through the path. The old woman said, 'Go and open the gate for your mother.'

The woman gripped the bars of the gate, the umbrella squeezed into her grip, a sad smile on her face, watched her daughter take slow, hesitant steps towards the gate. She nodded approvingly as though the girl was a toddler learning to walk, the woman's smile progressing as the walk progressed with more skill, and her daughter came nearer to the gate, but the sadness lining every contour of her faintly wrinkled face remained. 'Maxim, ah,' the woman said softly. A bird flew out of the mouth of the stone tiger on the pillar beside the gate. It flitted above the visitor and flew back into the tiger's mouth.

'Mummy, ah.' Maxim gently pushed the gate open.

The woman dropped the umbrella, pulled her daughter into her clasp, oblivious to or uncaring of the girl's resistance, and planted her face in the girl's unwelcoming chest. The more the girl tried to jerk back, the tighter the woman gripped, and soon the tightness wore down the daughter's aversion, until, at last, the woman looked up into her daughter's eyes, and the girl allowed her mother to fondle her cheeks, and brush a finger in wonderment on her lips. 'Why you go so long?' the woman whispered.

Finally, the maternal grip loosened and Maxim stepped back. 'Better take your umbrella, Mummy. Today is very muddy.' She took another step back and furtively dabbed a cheek as though attempting the futile task of erasing her mother's fingerprints.

'Hailah, hailah. Mummy take later.' She glanced at her daughter, then at Pushpanayagi, who was still standing in the middle of the dirt path. The soft sadness promptly vacated the woman's face. She pushed past her daughter and stomped towards the old woman. 'Looking-looking for what, ah?' she said. She clenched her fists and stood, feet slightly apart, inches away from Pushpanayagi, far enough only to narrowly escape the smell of each other's breath.

Pushpanayagi stared vacuously at the woman.

'You is it?' the woman bellowed.

Pushpanayagi held her hand out but the woman did not seem to notice it. 'Please . . . forgive . . . me,' the old woman stammered.

Eyebrows knitted, a scowl on her face, cheeks brighter than the tomatoes in the garden, the woman grunted and peered into Pushpanayagi's eyes as though the answers to her problems lay there. 'You don't try fool me! Understand or not?' The woman made to spit on the ground, then quickly looked back into the old woman's eyes, her dark glare confronting. 'You think what? Kidnap my girl, then I do what? Hug-kiss you, is it?'

'She didn't *kidnap* me.' Maxim hastened towards the two women.

'I calling police after this. What kind of game you playing?'

Maxim landed a jittering hand on her mother's shoulder. The woman turned towards her daughter, her eyes suddenly yielding. 'Auntie didn't do anything, Mummy,' Maxim said quietly. She withdrew her hand from her mother's shoulder. 'No, Mummy. Auntie didn't *keep* me here.'

The woman's face dropped. 'You say what? How long already Mummy wait and wait like fool. Everyday cry, everyday cry, until my eye also burn, burn like got fire inside'. The woman looked at

Pushpanayagi with eyes like two dark stones. 'Girl ah, you don't know. This witch *tell* you nothing happen. She *play* your head. You don't be fool, girl.'

'Please forgive me . . .' Pushpanayagi murmured.

'You think what? Say sorry then all people happy, ah?' She waved a hand in dismissal. 'You no think other people, ah? You no think I crying in my house, ah? You think my husband no feel sad, ah?'

'My words may not mean anything to you, but your daughter has been happy here. You can see for yourself.'

The woman turned towards her daughter. 'We go now,' she said.

Maxim inched back from her mother. 'I can't go now. Auntie and I are praying for a dead bird.'

The woman's cheeks coloured a shade brighter than her umbrella. She held her hand out to her daughter. 'Come, better go now.'

'I'm not going *anywhere.*' Maxim turned towards the old woman, her eyes begging for collusion, for agreement, for aid, but the old woman was staring at the ground, at the pebbles, at the ants, at the weeds, her ears suddenly deaf, her presence suddenly gone.

The woman teetered forward. 'Girl have to come *back.*'

'No, I *don't.*'

The woman's eyes darkened with tears. A few fell rapidly, then more tears gushed down. Maxim lurched towards her mother. She suspended a hand over her mother's arm and pulled it away quickly. 'Mummy, ah,' she muttered. Her mother wiped the tears with her fingers as though making room for the fresh tears that were falling fast. 'Girl don't understand,' she said, her voice trembling, 'Girl have to come back. Mummy cannot. Mummy cannot already. Daddy also go away. Mummy don't know where he go. Mummy alone now.'

*

The shadows whizzed around the old lady, teased her eyes open, and gently lapped back into her chest. She sat up, pressed her hands against her breasts as though touched by sentiment, and rose. She swayed towards the door of her bedroom and, guided by the shadows within, walked like a somnambulist to the foot of the spiral staircase.

For many years, the shadows roosted on the walls. They dirtied the ceiling with their black ether. They tightened the tiles, brick, wood, made the indoor air small as though the house was a cave visited by nomads, the interior climate now too cool, now too tepid for comfort, but at least it was shelter. Indeed, the old woman spent her days and nights sheltered, alive, in the shadow of the shadows. Would she have looked up once, her eyes immersed in the boon of extra vision, and seen them flashing across the courtyard, through the kitchen, into the cellar? Or floating like feathers up to the topmost room? Would she have looked and seen? Maybe. But such is the quality that endures in the cells, generation after generation—the quality anchored in the blood since men began to fashion tools out of bones, wood, iron. Men and women chanted incantations into fire and looked at the stars and computed; they studied the elements and pried into the earth and they built, invented, constructed, erected, added details, components, features to their lives, and soon, time was filled to the brim with objects, wishes, ambitions, desires, worries, grief, solitude, lack. So it was. So it is. The old lady ignored the shadows, neglected their movements, and fell into a passage of time moulded by her own hands.

It is also true that the vegetables spoke to her and that—in the nights before the shadows grew bold—the beetles and the frogs, forgetting their diurnal dynamic, lay by her bedroom windowsill and fell in love with her breathing, and the love soaked into her breath, and the breathing slowed down, went quiet, until there was almost nothing. Then the walls began to fracture and the air expanded, and the shadows contracted. Nobody—if there was anyone to see—could have denied the beauty of the dome of golden light that arched over the old lady's head as she slept. It was similar to the soothing glow of the morning sun an hour after dawn. For a moment, when a person pauses for no reason at the gate of their home, and something tells them to look, not directly at the sun, but at a single blade of grass absorbedly still, flooded in the morning light, they sense into something so tender, so deeply alive, it fills their bones with forgetfulness—they don't know who they are anymore, or about anything else in this world; only the blade of grass soaked in the soft golden light is real. Perhaps it is too soon to utter, perhaps such things should not be said at all, but the life bursting through the blade of grass, through the golden dome over the old lady's head, pushes apology out of the way, thrusts timidity into its hole, rams doubt headlong into its metal wall, and, from the belly of the earth, the words lift, 'Love. Love. What else could there have been, all this while, all that while, what other thing could we have wanted?'

The shadows leapt and twisted inside Pushpanayagi's chest. They moved her feet up the spiral staircase. They took care that her steps were small and slow. They placed her hand on the railing and gently, gently, assisted her up the stairs.

*

Mary sits in bed, knees to her chest, arms around her knees, wiping her tears with the handkerchief Abu has brought in—washed, starched and folded—with the tea tray. He slouches a few feet away from her, by the edge of the bed, close to one of the posts of the four-poster bed. 'Drink tea, Mem,' he says, but he does not move to reach for the cup on the tray at the foot of the bed. She clutches the handkerchief and rocks her body back and forth. 'If he had come but once to simply glance at me, I might've been happy,' she says, glaring at the flame of the oil lamp in Abu's hand, as though her words originated from its orange glow, 'but I know, I must understand his predicament.'

Pushpanayagi stands by the door, in her nightgown, watching. She cups the doorknob as if she is about to fling the door open but she keeps standing, very still, like a woman in a painting.

'I used to be downstairs,' Mary says, lovingly caressing her cheek with the handkerchief, 'oh, in the old house, of course. Not here, never here. In this house . . .' She focuses her wilting eyes on Pushpanayagi. 'May the grace of the good Lord be with you, my sweet Pushpanayagi. But in this house, my heart was caged. Like the birds they hang in painted cages in the market.' Her eyes widen as if she has uttered something abominable. 'Would you believe, in those days, the earliest days on the island, I was allowed to roam the streets? When Charles was busy on the plantation, Abu—dear, sweet Abu—would accompany me in the carriage and we would embark on adventures—oh, a myriad of adventures! We had a marvellous time, did we not, Abu?' She swings her head back in Abu's direction. Her eyes beseech him for something it seems only he can know. He smiles and raises the lamp as if to shed light on her memory.

'We picked shells by the sea, ate custard apples from his grandmother's tree, talked to the Malay women in villages, all sorts of adventures.' She leans back against two large, plumped up pillows, then turns to face the stained glass window. 'One night—I remember the night so vividly—Our Lady of Sorrows appeared before me in the old house. I was sitting on the swing in the garden, smelling the perfume from the jasmine plant dancing in the warm air. The moon was as round as a pregnant belly, as yellow as the eyes of wolves. Then Our Sweet Mother walked out from behind a bush, sat next to me and said—'

The doorknob creaks. Pushpanayagi pulls her hand away from it and quickly says, 'I'm sorry, Mary. Slip of the hand.'

Mary smiles sadly, as though she has learned a difficult truth. 'You are right, Pushpanayagi. What use is it talking about a past that no longer matters? Even if Our Lady had told me that night that in one year my life would shatter for I was too prone to smelling violence and my heart would cower at the sight of falsity, that I would be relegated to a room where I would have her gaze constantly upon me—even if she had spoken to me thus, what is the use of it?' She looks intently at Pushpanayagi, the deep blues of her eyes brown in the dimly lit room.

Pushpanayagi shifts her eyes to the floor, then gradually raises them in Abu's direction, but his gaze is fixed on Mary as though his whole being has been pulled into her gravitational centre, as though his whole being has found a place to rest.

'It's late, Mary. Perhaps you should try to get some sleep.'

'I've woken all of you up, haven't I?' Mary's voice quivers, suddenly riddled with doubt. 'It's useless. I cannot live like this any longer. Would Charles want to see me? I know he doesn't want to even glance at me. Look at what I've become. Nothing but a pox on his life, on this land. That's why he moved us all to this house.' Tears glide down her face. 'He moved us here so he wouldn't have to feel his burden. Is that not so, Pushpa?'

Pushpanayagi squints as though the room is too bright for her eyes.

'I really do not mind, my darling. You needn't feel afraid or wrack your heart with guilt. I know Charles thinks I'm incapable of anything, but my eyes still see and, more than anything else, my heart still feels.'

Abu tilts the lamp. Light falls on the tray arranged with a teapot, a tea cup, and a small copper spoon set on a wooden slat across the edge of the mattress where Mary's feet would have been. 'Drink tea, Mem?' he asks, but Mary does not show signs of having heard him.

'It isn't romance. No, I know it isn't that. Something else, is it not, Pushpa? Something deeper than romance.' Mary pulls the blanket closer to her chest. The objects on the tray clatter. Abu darts forward and soothes the din with a steady hand. 'Perhaps the teacup knows. Perhaps the walls know. Perhaps the floors know. Perhaps the courtyard knows. Perhaps the kitchen knows. Perhaps the cellar knows. What secret do you keep together, Pushpa?' Mary's eyes glimmer as though, suddenly, she has found words not from the flame of a lamp, but from a hidden cavern in her heart. 'What creates your friendship, Pushpa? It was as if, one day, I went mad. And Charlie came home with the news that we would go to a place where my worries would cease. Were you supposed to have cured me or him?'

Pushpa ambles towards the bed, sits on the end opposite Mary and smooths the creases on the sheets with one palm. To the sheets, she says, 'I gave him my ear.'

'Is that the secret? Is that the secret of everything?'

Pushpa's ears twitch, her hands motionless on the sheets.

'I have heard the crows croak. I have heard the coal miners cough. I have heard overseers call men at the coffee plantations pigs, idiots, fools. I have heard Charles call the natives imbeciles who need to learn the ways of sophistication. I have heard frogs shrieking in the mouths of snakes. I have heard Abu crying softly behind curtains. Do I not have ears too?'

Pushpanayagi crosses her hands on her lap.

'I have failed, Pushpa. My life has been a mistake. But all is well, all is well. Abu is a good man. He knows what I speak of. I receive his gift with the gratitude of a saint. With this tea, peace shall finally come, and peace shall finally come unto you all, and, at last, into this house.' She nods at Abu and he nods back. He takes the teacup to the table beside Mary's bed. He removes a tiny ball from the breast pocket of his shirt, drops it into the cup, then fishes out two more from the pocket and drops them in too. He hurries back to the foot of the bed, grabs the copper spoon, returns to the cup and begins to stir the tea.

Mary sits up. She makes the sign of the cross and says, 'Bless me, Father, for I am about to sin.'

Abu hands her the cup. A pitying sadness fills his eyes. 'Drink tea, Mem.'

Pushpa watches as Mary blinks tenderly at Abu; she watches as Abu's hand falls on Mary's and tightens around her wrist; she watches as Mary's hand slowly breaks free and her fingers lift to intertwine with Abu's; she watches as Mary finally raises the cup to her lips and drinks.

She watches for a long time, even after Abu has left, and Mary's eyes have finally stopped moving, her arms rigid, her face taut in death. She stays on the edge of the bed, glancing at Mary, then at the curtains, then at Our Lady of Sorrows, then at Mary. For a long time, she stays and watches the waxen body, the skin like polished marble, the hair like rings of gold, so shimmering that they appear divorced from death, still alive and impossibly belonging to the same body that houses the two blue stones that were once eyes, and even when Abu returns the next day, she refuses to go down the spiral staircase with him. She sits for hours after he leaves, and at last, when she knows it is time for her to go, she covers the body with the blanket, making sure every corner of the beautiful cadaverous face and every golden lock is no longer visible, and when she is satisfied that the lifeless body has been secured in its shroud of Indian cotton, she shuts the door behind her.

11

Day three and the bread was back. Did they forget that she'd said *umpteenth* times over the years that she'd grown bored of Chinese coffee shop bread? Sure, there were other things on the breakfast table and she didn't need to eat the damn bread, but why bother putting the bread out when she'd said *very clearly* that she would never touch the stuff? Maxim jabbed a finger into a spot of water on the plastic sheet over the mango-print tablecloth. The cloth was new, so was the sheet. Maybe when she was six or seven, she'd loved the bread, dipped chunks of it into one of those Pyrex bowls of Kak Isma's homemade kaya. Then, later, when the bread appeared at every breakfast table, she ate cornflakes, noodles, whatever else was on the table. Obviously they didn't get it, couldn't see she'd moved on to other things.

Mother sat across the table, on the edge of her seat, hands palm-down on the table, watching like a stressed-out hawk. Each time Maxim looked up from her bowl of porridge, Mother tilted her head as if she wanted a report on it. Didn't make the porridge, but acted like she'd grown the rice herself.

'Drink Milo, girl. Mummy see you don't drink much.' Mother leaned over her own empty plate, eyes as big as fifty-cent coins, a strange eager smile on her strange unpainted face.

Maxim nodded, glanced at the sweating carton of orange juice, at the plates of Malay cakes and chee cheong fun, at the little triangular packets of nasi lemak arranged at the centre of the table. Yesterday, there'd been roti canai instead of chee cheong fun, and the day before a giant steaming bowl of oily noodles. All Mother's philosophies on green foods, super foods, clean foods, were far, far away, buried with the tubes of lipstick and pots of concealer.

She ate another spoonful of porridge and wiped her lips with the napkin Mother had insisted she lay on her lap, as though they were at a restaurant. Mother's eyes moved over the breakfast things. A weird new look flashed across her face, like she was gulping down the food with her eyes and growing more and more satisfied. Mother had never, in all the eighteen years Maxim had been alive, sat at the dining table with *anyone*. She ate solo in the guest dining room, or in front of whatever Chinese soap opera she was obsessing over at the time.

'Eat some more lah, girl. So thin already.'

She sipped the mug of Milo Mother had made Kak Isma prepare despite her saying no a thousand times. Minerals and Vitamin B, Mother said, all of a sudden, after giving long speeches for years about how the sugar in drinks like Milo and Horlicks was evil. Poison to the system. Maybe Mother was finally going mad. Nobody could live like that for too long without something finally snapping. Screws loose. Fallen off the wagon of life.

'Thank you, Mummy. Full already.' She sat back in her chair. In her side vision, Kak Isma scurried here and there, polishing, preparing, probably already starting on lunch.

'Girl ah. After eat, you want help Mummy upstair?' Mother smiled. For a moment, the dark rings under her eyes lightened and her pale, puffy cheeks looked firm, a little pink. The question felt genuine as though there was something terribly exciting to be done, now that the house was quiet, now that only Maxim, Mother and Kak Isma remained. In the three days since she'd been back, there were no guests, no Lunching Ladies, no gardeners, no gossipers, nothing, only Mother's words and the silence between the words.

'I might do some reading.' Maxim zig-zagged a finger across the tiny spots of water on the plastic cover. She lifted the finger and examined the glistening pink flesh.

'Mummy going clean all the room. Gwailo call spring clean. Ha! Ha! Ha! Fun also, girl. We can put song on radio. Got music only nice, lor.' Mother's smile faded. A wave of something dark, something sad fell over her face. It looked a bit like Hadi's mountain. Suddenly, Mother seemed small, as though she wasn't really the hawk, but a mouse the hawk was eyeing.

'Ok. Maybe I will join you for a while.'

Mother shot up, dusted her hands and screamed, 'Isma, Isma.'

'Don't bother Kak Isma, Mummy. She doesn't have to come upstairs.'

Kak Isma rushed into the dining room, hands drenched in soapy foam, hair all over the place, looking like someone had lifted her out of a warm, sleepy bath, forced her to go somewhere she wasn't ready to go. She glanced at Maxim, smiled and winked, but turned away too quickly before Maxim could respond.

'Clean up the table, Isma. Maxim and I going to clean Kong's study.' Mother smiled. She purred, her sudden baffling transformation into something as soft and as excitable as a blind kitten. 'Maxim agree she come spring clean. She going to take Kong's study.'

Maxim's face grew hot. Her heart fluttered. She pinched the plastic sheet that covered the table. Something in her wanted to rip the sheet apart, fling every single pot and plate of food onto the floor. What the hell was Mother thinking bringing vulgar amounts of food into the house? Who the hell was she trying to feed?

'Ah, come, come, girl. We go upstair now. Actually, better you take Daddy's study. Then girl can read all your book there. Nice ah, girl?'

Mother waved a hurried hand at Kak Isma, then shuffled around the table and touched Maxim's arm. Maxim pulled away, sprang up from the chair and glared at the little glimmering square cakes on the table, at the packets of nasi lemak tightly wrapped in old newspaper, at the stack of plates and bowls, at the tray of gold-plated forks and spoons, at the untouched loaf of Chinese coffee shop bread. She kicked the foot of the table, but nothing moved. Her toes throbbed. The table, *solid*. As solid as Mother's out-of-the-blue niceness, as solid as Mother's out-of-the-blue *mock* niceness. Murderers acted like this, exterminating the object of their hatred, pretending to be overflowing with sadness, but the sadness is filled with holes and cracks. Between the gaps, they make their mistakes: cash in the insurance cheque too soon; use their victim's ATM card; give away their victim's possessions like a lottery-winner with a pathological people-pleasing problem. A husband's shirts, a wife's jewellery collection, a father's study.

'What happen, girl? What problem you got?' Mother attempted to touch her arm again. She stepped back and peered into Mother's eyes. Dark, empty, glossed over with mock worry.

'Where's *Daddy*?'

Mother's eyes deepened into its dark emptiness. Her lips parted and tightened. 'How Mummy know? Daddy think he got no family. Man is like that. They do what they want. They no *think* of other people. That why better woman support woman.'

'What is that supposed to mean?'

The scowl loosened into a look of mild irritation. 'You better don't worry about Daddy.'

'What are the police saying? Aren't you checking with them?'

Mother gently pushed the chair Maxim had been sitting on towards the table. She gestured at Kak Isma to start the clearing of the table, then tottered away from the breakfast madness of her own making. She paused at the foot of the staircase and turned around. 'Girl ah,' she said, her voice suddenly composed again, 'you too young go worry about police and all that big-time problem. Don't worry, girl, every day Mummy praying to Lord Jesus Christ. Now better we go upstair and clean Daddy's study.'

*

Pushpanayagi sat up on her sleeping mat in her bedroom, popped another chunk of pineapple into her mouth and chewed, carefully avoiding the gap left by her fallen snag tooth. The girl had been so good at chopping and shaping fruit, cubes, slim slices, so neat and nice. And cleaning, yes, the girl cleaned with magic hands. Every spot, every corner, free from dust and the build-up of years, as though the girl was born to purify. Purify, purify, yes, the girl knew somehow. Pushpanayagi felt for another chunk of pineapple from the bowl on the floor but there was nothing left. The bowl was not as wet as when the girl was still in the house. She always washed; every bowl and plate that came to the bedroom was scrubbed, still shining with water when the girl walked into the room like a graceful angel and said, 'Come, Auntie.' Then, she would sit cross-legged on the floor and watch Pushpanayagi eat whatever had been prepared. Sometimes a hand held up the girl's chin as though Pushpanayagi's midday meal or dinner snack was a play the girl had paid a lot of money to watch. If the food had not been finished, the girl blinked her eyes so fast, puckered her face, and asked if something was wrong, but before Pushpanayagi could say anything, the girl would be behind her, gently caressing her back, pressing the shoulders, making sure the blood flowed properly. No one had told the girl to do these things. No one had given her a lesson on how to tenderly pinch and knead the aching spots on an old lady's back, or how to make circular movements on the head to keep the skull and the brain happy. But somehow, the girl did these things as though she'd been trained since she was a baby. The mother would be taking care of her now. Was the girl all right? That was their family, their responsibility. She had no right anyway, couldn't interfere. The girl would be fine, is fine.

She lowered herself, very slowly on the mat. Tonight there was no pillow, no girl to prepare the pillow. The pile of sarongs had collapsed at some point after the girl's mother had appeared and taken her away. Hadi still came to deliver things like the big pineapple from the market, but he couldn't do what the girl did, didn't know how, what. It wasn't his fault. The boy had other things on his mind, old things, future things. And she could not re-fold the sarongs, one by one, so carefully, so lovingly, the way the girl had done. How Maxim would stand by the bedroom windows, flung open 'for air, Auntie. Always must have new air coming into the house. Why do you want to breathe the same air you've already breathed?' and she would hold each sarong up in the sunlight, and shake the dust off over and over again before she began to fold. Pushpanayagi stroked her chest gently. The girl is fine. The mother came to the house. Nothing could have been done. She had to go.

Sleep would not come nicely tonight. The way her mind was feeling, it wasn't going to listen to her body. But something was working inside her blood. These days, she felt it, something—Rama, what is the thing inside the blood? A thin crack in the ceiling looked like it had spread well beyond her eye-range. Another crack, and another, so many cracks in the ceiling never seen before. If the girl was here and wanted to know about the thing inside the blood, what could she tell her? It was like something pushing through the blood, something—no it wasn't pushing, it was like something had mixed with the blood, a new force with its own tingling and vibrating sensations, a bit cold like seawater at dawn. Those days, in the old days, dipping feet into the sea down the road, before there was even a road for the horses to trot their sweet feet on.

She sighed. The past is an illusion, they said. Swami B, Swami T, and Swami D, spinning somewhere in the old land, so many decades already dead. Then the trees spoke on this island and said, 'You were born to open yourself to others.' She had. She had! She gripped a sarong from the collapsed pillow-pile. She squashed it tight in a fist. Something flew across the ceiling. A flicker, a shadow, something. Probably an illusion, *the* illusion. She'd given, they'd taken. They spoke and spoke and spoke: the illusion of their suffering. How was she to tell them that the Buddha was wrong? Life is not suffering. They suffer life. In God's world, which is also this world, there is no suffering. Yet, they spoke. They only had to close their eyes and move into the peace that was already there. But, so what? They are long dead, even their bones have putrefied. The past is an illusion and she had helped in the past—it was over.

The thing flashed across the ceiling, disappeared, and reappeared in the corner of the ceiling. The shadow drifted above her and expanded slightly. Her blood grew warm. The shadow stayed like that for a few moments, then floated down and wavered over her chest. Her heart thumped. She closed her eyes. 'Go away. My house doesn't welcome black magic,' she whispered. She opened her eyes. The shadow still hung above her like a raincloud. 'Gently go back to your source,' she said, louder this time. But the shadow did not move. She closed her eyes. If this is my death, Rama, so be it.

*

'No! Stay *away*.' Maxim spun around and leaned against the door of the study. Her palms were wet with sweat, soaked right through her flesh it seemed. She slid into a squat. Thank the stars Mother had stopped banging on the door, so rough, so *vulgar*. Auntie would never act this way. She could *feel* Mother—the bulldozer, that's exactly what she was—on the other side of the door. No breathing, no huffing and puffing, nothing of that kind, but there was *something*, a heavy nothingness, that pricked every part of her body and told her, 'Mummy is here.' If she said anything about 'heavy nothingness', Mother would tell her to stop reading books that filled her head with 'stupid thing'. Auntie would know. She lived with talking vegetables, in a house that . . . in a house that was something unfathomable. In the house, even Hadi could do things. Talk big, talk like he knew stuff just like a wise, old man, but he was foolish, really, as foolish as Mother. Opened his big, fat mouth and all the flies went to his putrid tongue.

She pressed her ear against the door and closed her eyes. *Everything that really matters is behind the eyes.* The heavy nothingness trembled like bolts of slow-moving electricity. It smelled of something. Beyond the smell of bottled perfume (a pungent, heavy-sharp, artificial smell), another smell lingered. A bit like festering flowers. Something cold pulsated through her chest. Her head felt so heavy as though fists were punching her skull. How *dare* Mother strut around the house as if Daddy had never even lived here?

'You clean by yourself, ah girl?'

Maxim opened her eyes and struck the door once. 'It's time you shut up!'

Heat seethed through every cell in her body, seethed strong in her face. Her legs weakened, floundered in the squat, felt like they were disappearing. She sat down.

On the other side of the door, the silence sizzled and spat. A silence full of noise. There was no ball of silence here, that excellent ball that sometimes just grew around her for no reason and kept her in a happy, homely cocoon. It sprouted like something from Alice's Wonderland on that first walk up the hill, came now and again when she was doing things around Yalpanam. A stinging, inky feeling filled her throat. She held her head up, waited for the tears to flow back into her eyes, slowly got up and walked towards Daddy's desk, still strewn with papers and files, little gift boxes, a few half-drunk bottles of mineral water, an industrial-sized hole-puncher. She ran a finger along the edges of the table. She hardly came into this room. Nobody had said she couldn't, but somehow, somewhere, someone had written a rule with an invisible pen that only Daddy and his men could come in here. But a few times, one or two years ago, when Mother was out and Daddy was at a construction site, she opened the door and sat on the squeaky leather sofa in the corner of the room, buried her face in a groove between the back of the sofa and its hand-rest, and breathed in the smell of stale whiskey and peanut halves that had fallen into the cracks.

She faced the olive green sofa next to the bookshelf, still only half-filled with books. Shapeless patches shone here and there on the sofa as though someone had smeared oily hands on the leather. Her breath quickened. She hurried towards the sofa and collapsed into it, the old squeak louder than she remembered. The leather was cool against her thighs and arms. She sat very still. Slowly, the coolness turned into the squishy warmth she'd loved when, before, feeling she could forget embarrassment because nobody was looking, she closed her eyes and pretended she was sitting on Puff's giant stomach. But it was different now. She couldn't feel Puff anywhere. She leaned forward and sniffed along the grooves of the sofa. Eyes closed. Black, warm, whiskey, peanuts. Daddy. She felt faint, cold inside, the tips of her toes like ice, as though she was in a huge, empty hole, air everywhere, ghostly sounds like the voices in dreams floating through, and she was alone, unable to get out. Trapped in a world of echoes. She got up quickly. Her heart pounded as though there was a threat in the room. Nothing, nothing. No one here, nothing to see.

She hastened back to the desk. Nothing, nothing. No one here, nothing. She scanned the surface for the jar of blackcurrant sweets he always kept full, the thick oval sweets so bright and purple twinkling in the sunlight that flooded in through the large, wall-length windows. Then, Daddy played the song on the gramophone by his desk and the sweets looked even shinier, like they belonged in a fairy tale. But there weren't any jars on the desk, only a mess of papers, notebooks, and tiny boxes. When was it that he'd chased her around the room, laughing his head off, calling her Puff, the Magic Dragon? Ages ago, before the leather sofa perhaps. Years later, after Daddy's lips had already twisted into the scowl he borrowed from his wife, the sweets raged hot plum-purple in the sunlight, the song in the background, in her head. Always only in her head.

She sat in his swivel chair and looked into one of the gift boxes. A single sweet lay in a heap of translucent wrappers. The other boxes were filled with packs of staples, small mounds of paperclips, pins, caps of pens. Not burnished cufflinks, old foreign coins, news clippings folded into precise squares like before. She'd pick a coin, hold it up in the air and stare at the strange words and pictures, then Daddy would tell her about the countries of the world. Now they were gone, transported to the bedroom where the Bulldozer could manage them.

She reached for the last sweet, unwrapped it, popped it into her mouth and opened the top drawer of the desk. The sweet tasted more pungent than she'd remembered, almost like perfume. She rested it on her tongue like an object she was keeping for later. The top drawer was jammed tight with papers. She shut it and opened the second drawer. An empty pen holder stood next to a stack of accounts books, the one on top torn at the front and faded. She bent down and took a deep breath. The drawer smelt of him. That smell. That smell she knew him to be. Like wood that had been kept in the dark for a long time. Sweet, musty wood. Her heart felt so weak as though it was going to drop into the huge, empty hole and vanish forever. She slammed the drawer shut. She watched her fingers tremble, suspended in the air, slowly move down, as though her hands were made of tissue, or leaves, down, down to the last drawer. She watched her fingers pull the drawer open. A black hardcover book, glossy, with the word "Journal" embossed in gold, lay alone in the pale brown interior of the drawer, so obviously there as though it wanted to be seen. Her fingers reached the book; they grasped it, brought it to her nose as though they wanted her to feel its reality, Daddy's reality, full of sweet woody musk. The hand slowly lowered the book. The fingers moved, opened it, flipped the first few empty pages, stopped when a page appeared with handwriting, unusually neat, in thick, black ballpoint ink. *Ballpoint pens are for teachers and shopkeepers. Fountain pens are for businessmen and politicians like myself who take their roles seriously, with dignity.* Maybe the journal was old, the words written before he acquired dignity. The fingers flicked. They flicked and flicked through the pages. 6.9.2017. 4.5.2017. 8.8.2016, the most recent entry only a month ago. No 'Dear Diary'. The words looked heavy, smothered with stuff. 'Cannot do this.' 'Maxim is too young to know.' 'The heat builds inside my body like a—'

She shut the book, pressed it close to her chest, and waited.

*

They call out to the winds, to the stars, to the moon, like wolves they call, and howl. As the branches of trees wave in the sweltering island air and as the gummy black night, spilling over with stars, listens to the hissing of the monsoon winds blowing over oceans from the East, their voices emerge from the seed within, merges with the winds, the stars, the moon, the dark gelatinous night. What are they looking for? Is the call a plea for everything to be lifted? Or a cry for lives to be mended? Between the cracks and tears, in the crevices of their desperation, a little weed—a few inches tall, upright—weaves its body, defiant of stone and concrete, insistent on its right to live. The old woman would not pluck it; the numerous and various people before her would not pluck the weed that had been here before this weed was able to be. Some may gaze upon the weed that has thrust its way through what little space it has been given. Others may look beyond it, at the roses shimmering with dew for example, or at the mangoes hanging low from thickly foliaged branches. A few, like the old woman, have eyes that cannot waver from the tiny, clover-shaped leaves of this plant that would not be. Through a gap in the veranda steps, the weed pushes forth, mad for air, touched by moonlight.

It had happened before. In the old days, when the house was still fresh, and Charles Tanner cringed at the sight of monitor lizards that sometimes promenaded at the back of the house, close to the mouth of the jungle, in those older days, small, tender plants grew through unseen fissures in wooden planks from time to time, as though they knew when to begin living, despite their fate. Who would see them? There were plantations to oversee, land to be dug, trees to transplant, tea-parties to be had, wildlife to capture, offices to run, coal to be shipped. But amidst all this, after she had been under the banyan tree that had once stood like a courtly umbrella opposite the house, Pushpanayagi returned to the garden, her heart heavy with stories told by the island's men, the roots of their fears and loneliness curling, pullulating through her belly, and she sat in the quietest corner of the compound, near the well, where only the frogs dared to croak and the birds dared to warble. There, where the back of the house faced the jungle, where the beams of wood were rarely noticed, a single weed, sometimes an inkling of a plant, germinated through one of those apertures famous for welcoming neglected things.

It may have been because the frogs and the visiting birds cried out to the most malleable corner of Pushpanayagi's heart, or because she was born with eyes destined to look at small objects—a lens for specks and flecks and grit—but she gazed at whatever tiny life was growing out of the house with a look very close to grief. Perhaps it was what the men had said—confessions heard by her, by the pores of the island, by the universe—that made her look the way she did. Or maybe it was the mystery of why only men sought her ears. But the indisputable truth, acknowledged or unacknowledged by her, was that the weed that she watched also watched back. A faint line of light stretched between her eyes and the weed, and as she fell deeper into its form, its little tip bowed and a smile appeared on her face, a smile not small, not wide, a smile that marked comfort. Then the frogs and the birds would grow still and silent, and she spoke. She told them what she had never told anyone and would, over the years, stop telling any sentient thing, even herself. But on those days, when a weed or hint of a plant chose to emerge through a dark cleft, she spoke of the hatred that burned in the hearts of certain local islanders towards the British, of the fear that coursed through the blood of British officers that brought darkness into their faces, of the worthlessness that had leaked into bones and made them cold, of the loneliness that moored at the base of every man like a disease. She spoke of what she was doing on the island, so far away from her original island on the Indian Ocean, of her suspicions that she had come all this way for nothing but to ingest every microscopic element the island brought to her, of her fears that one day she would go deaf. It has to be said that the weed or potential of a plant—both essentially weeds since they are unwanted, unseen—whichever it was at the time of her declarations—listened, but gave no advice. It is not in the life-stream of weeds, particularly weeds that choose to live through cracks, to goad and soothe and whisper decisions or plans of action to whoever is spending time with them. No, these weeds only welcome the time given to them and the gazes bestowed upon them. They offer their whole being with every wilt and every flutter, whether reciprocated or not.

Tonight, after a long, long time, a weed has sprouted from the veranda steps. The air is so warm, so prosperous with the anthems of soil and dust, with the smell of iron-rich mud, so loud in its announcement that soon, any minute now, the monsoon will be here. What more is left to do? Lift! Lift! Howl like everything is finally in love with the river of madness that courses like new blood through veins! The weed is not frightened. The spirits circumnavigating it know it is a night for howls, for any voice that wants to fling itself out of bodies. The old woman sits alone in the garden, beside the steps leading up to the veranda. Every star that can be out is out, blinking so fiercely, so benevolently, for any eye that wishes to see. She strokes the weed, knows it is there, with or without her eyes. The moon, too, is out. Full, flame-yellow, as big as a plate, ready. The old lady is ready too. She turns towards the weed, gets up, then kneels on the veranda step, and bows her head. But when she raises her head, nothing escapes her lips, not a murmur, not a groan, not even a whimper.

*

Maxim's palms perspired on the diary cover; her fingers warm, the space between her hand and the cover like a lava pit—or at least that's what a lava pit would be in miniature form, in a 3D, virtual reality popup book. Mad, she was going mad like Mother. Half an hour and still she couldn't open the journal again or move. She rested the journal on her lap. Weirdly, Mother didn't come back to bang on the door and spout poison from her own lava pit of abuse. Something was different.

She rested her hands on the handles of Daddy's swivel chair and pushed herself back until she felt the support of the chair on her shoulders. Through the open window behind her, Muthu and Mother were chatting away in the compound below. How fast she got over her banishment from her husband's study. How fast she was to—all of a sudden, out of the blue, using every cliché possible—make mealtimes an occasion for her maternal madness. Not only mealtimes, but everything. Everything. Acting like the mother in mourning now rejoicing, making *sacrifices*. No makeup, no jewellery, no Jimmy Choos, no friends.

'That bunga kertas, you throw ah, Muthu. I want plant sunflower that side. Girl come back must have happy flower, hah, okay, Muthu?'

'OK, OK, good ah, Muthu. You sure ah got good seed? Last time your seed no good.'

If there ever was an emergency in this house, everyone would be saved because Mother's voice would carry even up to Uncle

Colonel's house, even up to Yalpanam—but the whole time Maxim lived there, not a sound from down the hill reached the gate. Auntie's voice was mellow, buttery, fluid: it was like listening to the sea at low tide when the waves gurgled against the shore with ease.

She flung the journal cover open and closed her eyes. She turned the pages quickly. Wherever she stopped, that would be the page. Auntie said we always *think* there's order in this world, but in truth, everything is random. Auntie's heart was all the oceans combined, maybe it was even the sky that let the birds be, like the ocean let the fish and the octopuses and the whales and the prawns all just be. Her fingers stopped. She opened her eyes. A little past the midpoint of the journal, the page glaring back at her was crowded with small writing, the words crammed next to one another as though there wasn't enough paper. She read the page, then read it again and again. *M is the product of lovelessness.* Heat singed her ears; the left lobe twitched. Something lead-like clung around her neck, sapped the air out of her mouth. *M is the product of lovelessness.* She couldn't breathe. She couldn't *breathe!* She hurled the book on the desk. She made a fist and slammed it on the journal.

It was stupid, so utterly *stupid*. Why the hell was she here, locked in his study, reading his hateful words, when she should have been out, like a normal person, watching a movie, hanging out with friends she could have made if they had *let* her? Shouldn't she be packing up, going somewhere, to fill her head with knowledge like a normal person? How did it happen? This body burning; heart pumping like a broken machine; alone in this room; filled with ick; everything going white, perishing; gone, gone; who are these *people*?

She jerked the phone out from her shorts pocket. Fire flared through her body. How dare he, how *dare* he! Her hands shook, terribly, uncontrollably. She punched fingers on the keypad, dialled his number. Her heart beat as though it would burst out of her chest.

'Max!'

The phone trembled in her hand. 'Don't say my name.' She gritted her teeth. Her jaw tensed up so hard it hurt.

Cars zipped past in the background; deeper in, voices murmured, rose and fell.

'That's right,' she said, loosening her clenched jaw, 'you don't have a right to say anything.'

A woman shouted, 'Two kilo chicken.' Voices clustered, clotted into a loud, muddled noise.

'Go to a quieter place, Hadi! Can't you hear me trying to say something here?' She swivelled the chair away from the desk and faced the windows.

The voices gradually thinned out until there was a hollow quiet as though he'd entered a room.

'I called to tell you that, that . . .' Her hand shivered. She firmed her grip on the phone.

'I am telling you that—are you listening, Hadi?'

His breath quickened. A blowing sound cut through the breathing.

'Speak,' he said, his voice choked with smoke.

'Your mouth is so big. You should keep it just for smoking. Hear that? You keep your mouth to yourself.'

The breathing became more rapid, louder, as though he was exercising.

'Die from smoking. I don't care! But don't try to kill other people. Second-hand smoking is worse!'

A clinking sound broke the hollow quiet.

'Oh, so that's how, is it? So, now you've got all the keys to Auntie P's house, is it?' She turned the swivel chair around and faced the desk. The smudges on the journal gave off a dull shine. She looked away from it.

'You've no *right* to do what I never asked you to do!'

'Max, I need to go back to the stall.'

'I never *asked* you to tell my mother where I was.'

'Come to the market. We can talk face to face.'

'You think people want you to speak for them? *Nobody* wants to be treated like they're stupid! Like they don't know what they're doing!'

Heat filled her face. Tears formed fast and fell in warm rivers down her burning cheeks. She felt him over the phone, distant like the echoes in the pit she was disappearing into. She clicked out of the call and threw the phone on the floor, the phone he'd supposedly given her for comfort, filthy, clogged to its edges with the things people do not say. Stuffed with the dark, dirty gaps between people's words, the gaps that stink of stale eggs. She grabbed the journal and hurried to the door of the study, her heart-machine thumping like one of Daddy's pile drivers, but her own machine, slowly breaking down, un-oiled, exhausted.

12

Over the years, the land across from Yalpanam, separated from the house by a mud track in the early days, by a shimmering tarred road towards the end of the twentieth century, has witnessed a carnival of feeding insects and mating birds, wild pigs, pythons and cobras, spiders the size of an average human fist, sometimes even birthing cats, and twice in the span of three hundred years, the murders of first a woman, then a man. Lovers occasionally cavorted around the flame tree in the corner of the land, or, devoid of imagination, carved their initials on the trunk of the jacaranda tree. The land is not quite a jungle, unlike the space behind the house, but neither is it an easy space to clear for the construction of buildings or for the creation of a field. Half and half, as the British and later, the top men in the local council would say: the land has trees; the land has wildlife, but the land is neither completely tame, nor completely wild. Therefore, it is useless. The land is unremarkable to most eyes until a person slows down and sees that, really, this land is a wild garden. And if anyone had bothered to ask—which Pushpanayagi did when she first came up the hill in a horse-drawn carriage over one hundred years ago, but no one had answers and they mainly suspected her of eccentricity—whether human hands had any part to play in the strange arboreal arrangement, they would have learned that the trees grew through natural pollination. But, truly, the wasps have to be thanked. When they spread the seeds of the banyan tree on its host tree, they buzzed for days, and the wind brought along more seeds and other insects and soon, the air was full of the promise of new life.

Thus, there is the flame tree with its bright, vermillion-orange flowers, and the Jacaranda tree blooming with the pride of a thousand purple flowers. There is also the laburnum tree in between these two trees, filled with golden-yellow flowers that emit the crisp sweet smell only flowers have. Wild bushes and spindly plants, their stalks sometimes nearly half as tall as the trees they grow around. Next to the laburnum, is the star and curse of the wild garden: the banyan that, before it was chopped down, used to stand like an inside-out cave, its thick long branches like stalactites reaching to the earth. It was not terrible the way a monster is terrible in a child's mind; it lived more in the realm of the awe-inspiring, the way certain monsters can be to children—colossal, strange, other-worldly. In fact, the aborigines who lived in a small village close to the land, in the days before the British took over the island, knew that the banyan was indwelled by spirits and ghosts. In the twilight hours, amidst the hooting of the owls that lived in the tree, the spirits and the ghosts of those who had wandered there by chance or misfortune and died, reached for a way back to what they had lost. For although they were no longer flesh, they were still bound to the earth.

By the time Pushpanayagi arrived on the land and before she walked across the mud track to the house she'd been invited to visit by her prospective lover Richard Miller, she stopped by the wild garden, arrested by the roaring colours of the flowers, but more than the carnival of colours, she was struck by the banyan tree which by that point was already one hundred and fifty years old and housing angels instead of unsettled ghosts. It could have been the warm glow that emanated from the tree like a cupola of honey-yellow light, or the force of peace that pulled anyone who looked at the banyan with eyes yearning for rest, or the sheer magnitude of its presence—whichever it was, indeed, it was probably all those factors—but the simplest fact was that Pushpanayagi, then still supple-looking and some may even say beautiful, gravitated towards the tree, sat beneath it, and not long after her back rested against its branches, a look of completion filled her face.

What is a look of completion? Well, it is similar to when a person has eaten just the right amount of food to satisfy their mind and body—but more profound. Similar to the moment a person marries their beloved and looks into their eyes and sees their unfulfilled wishes vanish—but longer. It is a bit like a person doing the thing they love most in the world and time turns into a dream, a myth. But all these things do not last. They cannot last. Such is the law of the universe. Two days later, the belly bloats from the extra bowl of rice wolfed down because its whitish gleam caused spontaneous salivation. The beloved, it turns out, is a bed-wetter and despises animals. And, suddenly, horribly, the thing a person loves to do most in the world isn't enough because, because—there is no reason; it is the descent of the dark irrational cloud. Dissatisfaction. Boredom. Irritation. Nothing is ever truly enough.

So, when Pushpanayagi sat under the banyan tree and its entire being encased her like a nourishing womb holds a foetus, she felt complete in a way, she would later tell the tree itself, she did not think was possible for a human being to feel. Certainly not with the kind of depth that felt permanent and more real than even the love of a mother for her child. Could it be that the tree felt so touched by her adoration of it, by her devotion to its power that it graced her with its magic? For she returned to it, day after day, sometimes at night, and allowed it to sing through her until, finally, on an ordinary morning with ordinary birdsong wafting from the other trees in the wild garden, a man angered by his employer wandered up the hill, stopped right in front of the tree and, upon seeing Pushpanayagi, was drawn to sit with her. Thus, it began. Each day, under the banyan tree, men appeared, told their stories, paid her a few shillings, and left. Some began to call her the Banyan Woman, and others, Sibyl. And it is true that she looked placid and kind and strong beneath the tree. But when she walked away and crossed the mud track, something else conquered her face, unseen by others, unfelt by herself. Slowly, the look of completion that naturally appeared on her face when she sat beneath the tree competed with another look, a murky look as though the mud from the track had somehow coloured her cheeks and more pronouncedly, her eyes.

*

7

If Amah had known, all this wouldn't have happened. Only child getting too old. Fear. Couldn't she have seen? They lied so well. Brought all those oranges. Then the siew yoke. Gifts. So many gifts. Amah couldn't see.

35 years. Never thought I'd live this long with her. Thought she would have done something by now. Who knows what. Why couldn't T's family just have been honest?? That Ah Hock so clever, could smell Amah's desperation. Filthy man. Dared to tell Amah T was the perfect wife? My blood boils, even now. More now. Looking at M, how not to be angry? But T is M's mother.

This week I thought I saw the signs again. T went so quiet, didn't want to eat, didn't sleep. But only for two days. If M was never born, I wouldn't be here. Left long, long time ago. People do it all the time. Put up, tolerate, make the best of things. I don't hate T. But no love. How to love?? Tried so many times. Too many times. It's not just the thing, it's everything. The way she nags M, forces her to go for tuition, forces her to eat whatever the ladies at the club say is good for the brain. I give up. M is turning out to be a misfit.

Maxim shut the journal. *Misfit.* She crept to the top of the staircase and paused. *Misfit.* She took a step down. And he did nothing. As the Misfit formed, developed arms and legs, a heart, couldn't he have stopped it from growing bigger? She took another step down. Busy. Too many things to do, so cannot stop the Misfit from growing. Oh, well. Her body trembled. Her legs felt like they would melt into the nicely shellacked steps, but she went anyway, down to where Mother was instructing Kak Isma about the latest thing that needed to be done in the house. *Loveless misfit.* But able to walk, at least. She stopped at the second last step and held on to the railing. Coward. Mother sat, arrogantly upright, in the second living room opposite the dining area, Kak Isma, saintly servant, nodding in front of her.

'After that, wash the pipe. Got lot of dirt there.'

She took the last step down the staircase and tiptoed towards the second living room.

'Must scrub properly. We don't see pipe, so don't see dirt.'

'Mummy. Kak Isma.'

They both turned to look at her. Mother's face was pale, paler than it had been at the breakfast table. She raised her eyebrows and smiled, her lips hardly pink, more a sick yellow.

'Girl ah, Mummy already tell Kak Isma, we want take down the painting, go put what you want. Girl pick lah, Mummy buy. Then later, for dinner ah—'

'No!' Maxim hugged the journal tightly against her chest. A thousand strings strummed through her insides, her body shaking as though it would fall apart at any moment.

Kak Isma glanced at her, smiled sadly as though she knew what was coming, and scurried off towards the kitchen.

'I'm not doing anything anymore. I'm not going to *pretend*.' She heard herself, the words fully formed, fully felt, as though something other than her was speaking. She strode into the second living room and faced Mother.

'*Stop* telling lies! I'm not a child anymore, do you hear? Not a child!'

Mother's mouth opened and closed. The dark browns of her eyes softened. She touched her hair, the permed curls so fixed in place they barely moved.

'I'm telling you *now*. I am *done* with the bullshit. I want you to be straight with me. What's going on between you and Daddy?'

Mother leaned back in her seat, decidedly, as though she'd been struck by inspiration and could now be confident. Her small feet, the paint on her toenails chipped, pitiful, dangled from the chair specially ordered from Bali, crafted by a white man in the East, as Daddy had said. Mother's face hardened. 'Daddy, Daddy, Daddy! Always think Daddy! I not here, ah? I am Devil in this house—'

'That's *not* what I'm saying. I just want to know the truth!'

'True? You want to know true? True is this.' Mother leaned forward, her face twisted in a horrendous scowl as though, yes, she was the damn Devil. 'True is your Daddy care only himself. He make money, but what money, you know?' Mother mock-spit on the floor. 'Tui! Mummy know you love Daddy. You think Daddy God. Of course lah! He buy you thing. Anything you want, Daddy buy for you. But is dirty money, girl. He cheating people. You never ask your Daddy God? When he come back, you better ask.'

Maxim thrust the journal in her mother's face. 'I know more than you think! I read Daddy's diary. What are you hiding? What did your family hide from Daddy and Popo?'

Mother glared at the book as though she'd been shown a dead rat, and in an instant, slapped it out of her hand. It landed on the carpet without a sound. 'Your Daddy always talking nonsense. Why you believe him?'

'You know where he is, don't you?'

Mother shook her head as though Maxim had said the most shocking thing. She began to mock-laugh. 'Girl, the way you act, Mummy can see you still young—'

'Tell me where he is!'

'Go lah, go lah! Go after Daddy. You love him more than Mummy. Go! Go! He sitting like fool in hutan—'

'The jungle? *The* jungle?'

Mother fell silent.

She waited for Mother to divulge more information, but she had already purposefully angled her body towards the sliding door and it was clear, all of a sudden, that Mother did not treat her own familial revelations with the same urgency as the stories she collected from the rest of the island.

*

Abu kneels beside Charles. His elbow relaxes on the wheel of Charles's wheelchair; his mouth moves sluggishly as he chews on a betel nut. He stares out into the garden through the open front doors, a look of ease on his face as though he is half-dreaming, half-listening to Charles's sporadic grunts, guttural, more for effect than a real expression of pain or discomfort. A metallic spittoon, peppered with scratches and haphazard marks, balances on Abu's lap. Every other minute, he spits blood-red liquid into it, without thought, as though his mouth has memorised the act. Charles's hands are folded across his chest, his shoulders slumped, his ice-blue eyes, glassy with age, glaring at the same garden. From time to time, he slaps his knee in an attempt to shoo away a phantom insect and grunts, sometimes mutters a profanity that Abu does not seem to hear or is purposefully ignoring.

'Blasted bastards!'

Pushpanayagi flinches in her seat across from them. She opens her mouth as if wanting to say something but she clutches the handles of her chair and purses her lips. Her eyes travel from Charles to the floor, from the floor to Abu, from Abu to the empty wall across from her.

The muffled sound of a bomb interrupts the silence. Charles stamps his feet, but there is little to cause either Abu or Pushpanayagi alarm. His feet are feeble, too old to produce effect. 'We *never* behaved like this when we first came to the island,' Charles says loudly, almost as if he is making sure his audience is listening. He gapes at Abu's balding head, the ice-blue of his eyes quickly turning darker, deeper. Abu smiles. His whole mouth is red; even his two remaining teeth look like they have been dipped in red ink or blood. 'The audacity!' Charles threatens to spit at Abu's face, then adjusts his head, aiming for the spittoon, but soon turns away and resumes his cantankerous mood. 'Don't worry, Tuan,' Abu says, his voice soft, paternal, 'this all happening for reason. Pushpanayagi talk karma. This Hindu people believe we pay for everything we do. Good means we get good thing. Bad means . . . hah, like now, Tuan, everything got a price.'

Charles snatches the cane resting against his wheelchair and strikes the floor with it, then waves it at Pushpanayagi, but she is looking intently at the empty wall, lost in its pale purple paint. 'Do you hear this fool, Deborah? Would you really use such a pitiful excuse as karma to justify this catastrophe? Japanese butchery. Are you going to sit there and allow Abu to misuse . . .' He hurls the cane to the floor. It lands with a thud. A look of panic engulfs Pushpanayagi's face. She rushes over to Charles, and stands in front of him, unsure of what to do next.

'You'd better calm down, Charles. The doctor has said that at your age—'

'My age! Do you want to know a secret, Deborah?'

Abu stops chewing. Suddenly, the hall is quiet, the air infused with expectation. 'The secret is this: I am at my sharpest. You think—and here I refer primarily to Abu, partly to Savitri—that I am incapable of listening and seeing. My God, stop walking on glass around me!' He laughs a joyless, almost sinister laugh. 'Abu, you aren't exactly young either. Look at your skin. As wrinkled as elephant hide. And yet . . .' He sighs. A sudden sadness muddies his eyes. 'Why do you insist on beating my back with looks and pats as though you foresee the shape of my tombstone? Oh, but you won't understand! None of you do.'

Abu spits into the spittoon, gets up and, laughingly, buoyantly, takes the handles of the wheelchair and gently pushes it back and forth like a baby's pram. In a low, tuneless voice, he sings, 'Rasa sayang, eh, rasa sayang, sayang eh. Rasa sayang, eh, rasa sayang, sayang eh,' over and over again until a faint smile emerges on Charles's face.

'The Japanese are lucky,' Charles says, 'If I were forty, even thirty years younger, I would have stood for none of their nonsense. If they can slash heads, so can I, and more.'

'Charles, I must advise you to rest now. It's no use trying to imagine what can't happen. You'll only make yourself tired and—'

'Do you see them with your third eye, Deborah? Do you foresee as Abu foresees my tombstone? Different, of course. Abu's is malicious, laced with human desire.'

Pushpanayagi watches the wheelchair go forth and back, and Charles's head lolling, lifting, lolling again and lifting as though it is doing a slow waltz. She looks around as if for something specific and not finding it, takes the untied part of her sari draped over her shoulder, brings it over her arm, crumples a fistful of the fabric and clutches it preciously to her chest.

'Pushpa, she not see anything,' Abu sniggers. He stops the wheelchair by her. 'Tuan, all this years, you are thinking Pushpa is magic woman? She just like us, Tuan. She don't got special power.'

Pushpanayagi brings the fistful of fabric to her neck, then, as though suddenly conscious of herself, releases it and quickly casts the cloth back over her shoulder.

'Utter rot, Abu! Look at her, my man. How long have we known her? Nearly fifty years! Now, look at yourself. You don't need to look at me again. We are all aware of your poisonous mutterings about my liver spots.' Charles points at Pushpanayagi.

'Are you looking?' Charles asks, 'Are you *looking*?'

Abu taps a fingernail on the handle of the wheelchair.

'Good! Now, what do you see, Abu?'

Abu stares at Pushpanayagi as though he is looking at an exotic statue. She is frozen in a pose so mundane, so ordinary, that it would have been easy to look away, except for her eyes that are suddenly resplendent—as if a new life has entered them and other eyes are naturally drawn to look at their own potential.

'Is Indian woman, Tuan. That all.'

Charles hits a wheel of the chair with his palm and Abu swings the wheelchair around to face Pushpanayagi.

'You are a complete fool, Abu.' Charles stamps his feet but the effect, like before, is weak. 'She hasn't *aged*,' he shouts.

Abu shrugs and looks around on the floor for his spittoon but it is inches away, too far from his reach. He swallows the excess liquid in his mouth and says, 'Good family, Tuan. Maybe you see mother, father, brother, sister, you will see also young like Pushpa.'

Charles smirks. 'And I am supposed to be the rational British gentleman! Anyone with intelligent, non-delusional eyes can see, nay, may even *profess* that the woman standing before us is unusual. Special, different, a mystic.'

Abu chuckles. 'Pushpa nice woman, Tuan, but not mystic, not like you say.'

'Well, Deborah, what do you have to say?'

Pushpanayagi scrutinizes the top end of the wall as though she is deep in thought, as though her thoughts will remain within, an enigma to everyone else. She interlocks her fingers behind her back, adding to her look of mystery, of being given a puzzle only she can solve. A serene smile appears on her face. 'There has to be some truth in what Charles says. We have, after all, known each other for a long time. In those days, even before I met Charles, people came to me. They saw what Charles saw. Abu, maybe you cannot see because the opium has blackened your blood too much. It's been a long time since you left the pipe, but I think the opium still talks through you. Some of us are made to shine as brightly as the afternoon sun. There will always be people envious of a strong sun. But of course, the sun doesn't care. It's the *sun.* It will always be here. It's one of those everlasting things, Abu. A divine thing. Maybe you'll understand in your next life. This life, it seems, you were made to be a shadow. Now, I better go and help Savitri. She can't handle the poor Communist all by herself.'

*

Maxim stumbled out the front gate and stopped to catch her breath by the culvert attached to the gate's pillar. She held the journal up in the air, as far away from her face as possible, her hands shaking, her heart flipping about as though it was going to jump out of her chest and fall into the drain beside the culvert. If it did, it would somehow seem right. Not only did her heart belong in the drain, her entire body too, everything of herself. Her legs wobbled dangerously as though they also wanted to disappear. She moved the book a little to the left, a little more to the left, until the whole object covered the sun. For a moment, it was as if nothing had happened, was happening. Footsy might have liked a short piece on optical perspective, the illusion of sight. How is it that a thing that can fit in a hand is able to block out the entire sun? But it didn't matter. She'd never read Footsy's blog again. The sky isn't *actually* blue. Neither is the sea. All lies. The stars are dead. Even Footsy is dead. The real Footsy from before; not the Footsy revealed last week, a *girl,* not blonde, not pretty, a Goth with black lipstick, a *girl.* All lies. All bloody lies. Every single thing in the whole world is a bluff. She threw the book on the ground. It landed close enough to the drain. Rightly so. Dirty pages, dirty words, dirty dreams. Who was *he* to say anything? Where was he *now*? *Loveless misfit.*

She stamped on the book, twisted her heel to make sure enough dust and dirt from her slippers came off on the front cover, and stamped on it again. She folded her arms, fought back the tears that were rising fast. The gate gently whirred open. She flinched but did not turn around. She could feel Mother's heavy nothingness approaching, bringing with it its stink of maternal madness.

Her back facing the gate, facing Mother, she said, 'Don't you *dare* come any closer. Go back into the house and don't come looking for me.'

Shuffling of feet, mumbling. She could *feel* the scowl filling out on Mother's face, could almost see the green tattooed eyebrows rising and falling. Pause. Waiting. Waiting for *her* to turn around as always, as always apologizing, trying to find words that will sound right and make everyone happy. The fire roared in her belly, sent its flames everywhere, up her arms, to her face, even to the back of her ears. Over the roar, she heard feet shuffling away as if Mother too could feel the heat of her fire. She picked up the journal, dusted it, and marched towards Yalpanam. So what if Mrs Teng was poking her head through her gate. So what if Uncle Colonel was lurking behind his fence. She turned the corner and went up the road.

From her trouser pocket, she pulled out the phone Hadi had given her. The palm that held it burned so hot as if the heat could've singed the phone, singed even the damn fool who'd given her the thing in the first place. Her throat ached with fire. *He* brought her back in touch with the world she had left. Insisted she go back into it when she was already getting used to Auntie, to Yalpanam. It wasn't just that he'd gone and opened his big mouth and ratted on her, it was bringing the phone to her *at all.* She squeezed the phone in her damp palm. Her arm felt electric. She stopped outside Yalpanam. The air was big, as wide as a whole galaxy. Birds twittered in the old silence. The ball of silence swelled around her, kept her in its pool of treacle, warm, ambrosial, quelling the fire in her body. She let the ball take her, move her feet to the huge tree stump across from Yalpanam. She sat on it and took a deep breath. Inside the ball of silence, everything went away. She glanced at Yalpanam's front gate, at the pillars, at the little dirt path that divided the two bright green parts of the garden. Suddenly, the fire blazed again in her belly, shot up her chest. She stood up. The stone tiger perched like a demon on top of the pillar. How Mother had banged on that stupid gate, forced herself in, taken her away, and Auntie had looked. She *looked.* Allowed the thing to happen. Didn't care. If she cared, she would have proposed something, an arrangement. Said nothing that would mean anything when she *knew*—but so what? Everyone does what works for them. Nobody actually cares about anyone else. People lie, yes, they keep secrets, but isn't this whole world a lie?

She stabbed a finger on the phone. He *owed* her. He created the whole mess. They *all* created the whole mess. Everyone, everyone, liars! She punched buttons, clicked on his name. One ring and he picked up.

'Listen to me. I don't want to hear you speak. All I am asking you is to meet me outside Yalpanam. Now. I have to go into the jungle and you will take me. My father is in there and I need to see him, I need to ask him why, why . . .' But her voice was too rich with heat, too hot for words.

'Ok, Max. Please take care of yourself. You don't need—'

She disconnected the call and sat back on the stump. She placed the book on her lap, opened it, and flicked through the pages until she found the entry with the stones. He'd *been* up this area, had *seen* the four stones outside Auntie's compound, yet he never said, pretended with everyone else on the island that he'd never touch Yalpanam or anything near it with a ten-foot pole. She didn't know him at all. He lived one life for her, kept his real life for himself.

June 1st, 2017.

I don't know why it suddenly turns into something and then I start obsessing again. See him everywhere, dreaming about him etc. Haunting me. Wants me to know something. I don't know what. Sometimes I feel I won't know. Every time this happens, I feel this is the place, but I never find anything. Shouldn't have come here. Last time I walked around the four strange stones near the old lady's house. Graves, obviously, but I won't go near that entrance again. Too risky. The old lady doesn't seem like she'd be friendly.

T is upset. Said I am getting carried away with Papa. Died before I was born, what you want to find, she said. But I can't keep trying to do what she wants. She doesn't listen. Has never listened. Doesn't see what she's doing to M but I still see it (the fear/care) in her eyes, at least that's (somewhat) good, even if it's fear, but it's only fear that she'll lose the child she waited and waited for. So many doctors. Too many weeping sessions, praying, throwing plates. Why didn't I leave then?? Before the child came. I think it was pity. Pity for T. What else could it have been? Then M was born. And T began to wrap herself around M, suffocated her, made M build a shell to live in, the poor child.

I can't explain to T what this feeling is. Even I don't know. Urgent. Emergency. Don't know what I'm supposed to do here. Waiting for something. Waiting for Papa to talk. My God! If people could see me. They won't look at me the same. My name spoilt. No one needs to know. Feeling like a child again. Why does anyone need to know? Even Amah didn't know I was playing the game every day, for who knows how many years. Do Not Disturb, I think I called it. Papa always hiding, Communist in hiding. Close eyes. One, two, three . . . nine, ten, open. Papa in the sand, the trees, the sea. In the hibiscus bush reading his Communist principles. Why did all those people have to keep saying it? Your Papa, they said over and over again, your Papa the brave Communist. Cheah Soon Bee, hero of Malaya, hero who died fighting for a cause (not like the son). Fire in his blood, Amah said, selfless, always thinking about the community, society, always outside himself, always thinking about other people (not like the son). Amah sad all the time. Useless son dreaming, chasing girls, smoking cigarettes, drinking beer, rowdy. Not like the father, they said and Amah also said. Poor woman was frustrated. No point saying sorry now. What she really wanted was a son like her husband. Too average. Too ready to follow people. Not a leader. No cause. No principles. What to fight for? Money is nothing much, she said. Never came for any of the dinners, too old, she said, but we all know she thought I was missing the point. No need to flash money around. But what was I supposed to do?? That's what I became. Rich. Important. Not enough, Amah? Maybe it wasn't enough. Because all this feeling is . . . it's black in colour, it is the one taking me here to this jungle. Failure.

Feels like I'm losing the game. I see it in M's eyes. She used to adore me. Everything I did was special. Even drinking tea. Driving the car. Playing music. Whatever it was, I'd feel like I was the only person in the world. She made me feel like that, and then suddenly, it stopped. She looked at me differently. Like she was far away. Somewhere else.

*

Pushpanayagi opened her eyes and gasped for air. She clutched the collar of her blouse, caressed her throat and tried calling for the girl, but her voice was gone. The air was hot, humid, salty, as though the gentle fan-breeze had come from the sea. She felt around her throat for the lump that seemed to stop the air from going in. It was like a ball of mucus strangling her; she could feel it expand at the bottom of her throat, trying to kill her. In an instant, she tore her hands away from her throat and the strangling feeling went away. She sat up, reached for the small pot of Tiger Balm on the floor beside her, unscrewed the lid and dug out a slab of balm, nearly half the pot, with her index finger. She slathered it on her neck, and threw the pot on the floor. It rotated on the edges of its base. The lizard in a corner of the room chit-chitted. The pot continued to spin like a top. 'Please forgive me,' she said, softly, then more loudly, 'please forgive me.' The pot stopped moving.

'Maxim! Maxim!'

But the house was quiet. Not even the crickets chirped. No frogs croaked. The owl wasn't hooting tonight. Windless night, so heavy and dark through the windows. A feeling of being trapped in a vast hole fell over her like a blanket that didn't soothe, but stuck to the skin, gluey and smelling of the mint oil they used to preserve bodies. She got up, hobbled over to the windows and swung one open as the girl would have done. She poked her head out, felt the air on her face, less hot than in the room, perfumed with jasmine. She breathed it in, felt the fragrance fill her body, even though she knew it wasn't real. How could it be? Charles had ripped the jasmine plant out of the garden days after Mary died. The smell was coming from somewhere else. So much sadness in the smell, on its own, even before Mary had talked about it as her favourite flower. Soft, beautiful smell, but filled with tears, with the loneliness in everyone's heart whether they wanted to admit it or not. Had she, in another lifetime, woven strings of jasmine into her hair? On this land or on the other, older land? Why should it matter? Something awful was happening. The world that had never had the chance to turn against her was turning against her now.

God? She had waited, dragged her feet, eaten food, toiled the earth, crossed an ocean, listened to human suffering, toiled the earth, waited, waited, waited. God! She breathed in the perfume of the ghost flower. The dead! The dead! What? Coming back now? Coming for what? Sinking their rotten teeth into my ears, telling me things buried long ago with the bones, opening unnatural eyes, coming to life. Go! Go! Of course, yes, they are pounding at the door. What Mary wants? She got it how she dreamed it. Nobody told her to curse at God. These people, forever taking and grumbling, everything is too hard, too dark. Order! Order! Go and find your order at the bottom of your empty heart. I am afraid of my wife, Sibyl, I am sad all the time, Sibyl, I can't look people in the eye, I am frightened of holes in the ground, I killed a cat, Sibyl, what shall I do? I was. I *was*! I didn't need to do anything. There is no doer, they said. No, I do not *do*. God *does*. Universe *does*. Not my fault if God made me better, not because I had something to give to God. Listen to me for once. I did good things before I was born. You know how blessed is this island that God put me on the boat and the boat went nicely on the sea all the way down to Malaya? Richard, you want to use your small British thinking on me? Look at Charles for one moment. Everyone thinks he is too stiff, too narrow, too fixed, too everything. Saw how he could *see* I had something extra? No, I never lied. I can see through your skin.

Pushpanayagi flung another window open. It banged against the window next to it. No, she had been good, had done what was right. She'd even given people a home, her home, and stood back, allowed them to be what they needed to be as God allows his children to be what they need to be. And they had all come to her, the sun that illuminates, gives life back to life, a sun so enchanting it burned and blinded those who could not see what she had been born to do. But the tight, heavy feeling, the stone in her stomach, kept pushing, moving, vibrating, saying no, no, no. No, you have not actually been.

13

The stairway leading down to the second door of the cellar is pitch black. Pushpanayagi stands by the first door, hands behind her back, without a lamp. She turns around, catches a glimpse of the last light of dusk in the courtyard, and mesmerized by the display of dark golden light, by the melancholy of departure the light inspires, she stares in a daze at the place that, before the war, before the new century, had once been as pruned and groomed as the garden at the front of the house. Now the garden alone boasts of well-watered, well-clipped plants. But there is little time for trivialities like flowers, seeds and gardens: on poles and fences all over town are Chinese heads death-staring at passersby on their way to the market. But Pushpanayagi has not seen them. Yalpanam remains safe on its hill, away from the muddle of war, but close enough for those in the house to feel something in their chests as bombs go off, close enough to feel gloom upon hearing stories of bodies bursting open from Japanese 'water torture', of decapitations in broad daylight and girls raped in front of their families—a gloom like a monsoon rain-cloud that arrives in the sky, briefly unloads, and leaves a trail of grey on the moments that follow. It is the grey that sneaks into houses and brings shades and shadows to the walls, infuses the steam from kettles and boiling pots with memories of water, tears. Time stretches in grief. A scream reverberates through the stairwell.

Clenching the frame of the door, she turns back towards the stairway and pauses. She jerks forward when she senses a hand on her shoulder.

'Only me.'

Abu holds out a brightly-lit kerosene lamp.

'Don't scare me, Abu.'

'I see just now you didn't take lamp. Sorry.' He extends the lamp and smiles through his betel-chewing as if to reassure her, and she gingerly receives his offering.

'Now go back to Charles. I'll help Savitri.'

'You become better, yes?'

'Better? Better at what?'

'Make sure Communist don't die.' A sly look comes over his face. 'You help this man?' he says and stops chewing, anticipating her reply.

'Don't you think you should be with Charles?'

'You so hurry for me to leave, Pushpa? Why you don't go down yet?'

'I'm going.' Then, as if she hasn't said enough, she whispers, 'I don't care about Communists the way you do. I've nothing against them.'

He saunters to the courtyard windows and gestures for her to join him. She hesitates for a moment, but makes her way towards him, and sets the lamp on the floor.

'Last night I dream of my father-mother. You believe, Pushpa? I am eighty-years old man dreaming of father-mother.' He forces a laugh and spits out of the window.

'Why shouldn't you dream of them? It's normal to dream of the dead.'

He nods spiritedly as though she has said a truth he had been thinking. 'Now so old, must dream about dead people.' A pensive look on his face, he smiles knowingly. 'Tuan sleeping. Sometime when Savitri too happy, too sad, he get very tired.'

He lowers his body and props his arms on the window pane. 'Now the time when British not here. I think so Tuan feel . . .' He brings a hand towards his chest and, grandiosely, taps it with all his fingers. 'In here, he feel like nothing there. Abu know. I know what he feeling.' The pensive tide returning to his face, he rests his arms again on the window sill. 'Tuan don't know what we like about Japanese. Japanese people . . . they like we.' He turns to face the dusty glass of the open window beside him, Pushpanayagi slightly apart from the windows, out of his eye-range, and, not finding her face, her eyes, he turns back towards the courtyard. 'Asia people like we all, Pushpa. Time come already for new thing. Now we feel we also can strong like Japanese. But Tuan cannot see. He don't believe we all clever, isn't it?'

He pulls away from the open window and stands, as upright as his hunching back will allow, and watches wood-pigeons that have flown into the courtyard and are pecking at the ground. 'Free as bird, Tuan like to say.' He sighs and glowers absorbedly at the birds. 'Not so free, you know, Pushpa. Bird have wing, that one is true. But they are like we also. They living inside body. Can feel pain, can get the red-red hole like Tuan have on his leg. Can die. You think is free?'

She folds her arms against her chest and glares at the floor as though she is thinking hard, or else dreaming of something unconnected to the corridor they are in, to Abu, to his words.

'Before when I taking opium, inside the opium is a free feeling. How I can tell you? Everything is stopping. I am sitting inside cloud. How I feel? In the cloud, nobody can touch Abu. Inside is safe. Like Mummy and baby. Cloud is Mummy. Abu is baby.'

She winces. 'If it was like that, then why did you stop?'

A wounded wave sinks his eyes. 'It causing more pain, that why. You see me that time, Pushpa. I going to die . . . What I know now is opium not true. It only pretend to be true. Actually, that free feeling is servant feeling. Free feeling? Abu don't think anyone can really feel it.'

'Isn't that what you think the Japanese are here for? To free your people from their feelings of inferiority?'

'You don't think so? Is your free feeling also. Maybe when we is free people, we feel more true—'

'My life does not depend on who is governing this place. That's where we're different, Abu. I don't put my worth in someone else's hands.' She clutches the fabric of her sari. 'I know why you're here. It's *your* fight, Abu. Not mine. I don't take sides.'

'You think you living on one tree, Pushpa?'

'A tree?'

'Up one tree. Big, big tree nobody can come up because is too high to climb. We all got poor feet. Up tree, can see everything nicely.' A smirk appears and stays on his lips.

'Your bad village blood still hasn't left you, has it, Abu? You can live, breathe and die for a British gentleman, but you'll always have that crude blood running through your veins.'

The smirk slowly changes into a smile. 'Is okay, Pushpa. God love you best, best. He bring you here, don't give you problem.'

Pushpa grabs the lamp and turns towards him. 'There *are* no problems in this world, Abu.'

She storms off towards the door of the cellar, slams it behind her and lingers there for a long time before she descends in slow, circumspect steps.

*

They walked around Yalpanam in silence, towards the jungle at the back of the house. Yalpanam's garden was still flowering and fruiting like mad, empty of people, but the birds were there as always, bees and the tiny insects that floated in the air in constellations close to the pumpkin patch, still doing their dance. It had only been three days. What did she expect would change?

She studied Hadi's back, his T-shirt clinging to his skin with sweat, his calf muscles tight, his walk almost rushed as though it was his purpose too.

He skipped round the corner of the fence and strode past, looking back once in a while, as if checking that she was still there. She wanted to fling a stone at him, get him to *get* it. Not your business. Not your business! She turned round the same corner and stopped opposite Yalpanam's well. It stood the same, its dark, brown stone rough, the blue dipper she'd used to bathe in its place on the grassy ground as though she still lived there. She looked up. Large grey-tinged clouds covered the sun. Eagles—or maybe hawks—flew in slow, graceful circles like ice-skaters going round and round a ring. On the ground, the four grey stones stood like little tombs in a row, by the edge of the jungle.

He looked behind again, checking. Even in the distance, she could see him expecting something. She saw it when he finished mending the veranda, when he brought her the charger, his first act as unwanted benefactor. She held her hand out and gestured for him to wait. Her other hand clutched the small pink plastic bag he'd materialized out of his pocket, just the right size for the journal and the phone Mother would never be able to call. She drifted towards him, the uncertainty on his face gradually changing into relief.

'Should I have worn sports shoes?' She stopped. Suddenly she seemed too close to him. His face soft, waxy with sweat. She took a step back.

'This jungle is okay. There's a path. Mainly flat.' He looked ahead at the jungle, his cheeks blushed.

'Let's go.'

'Max.'

'What?'

He shook his head and glared at the damp ground, more soil than grass. His toes tensed against the Japanese slippers he seemed to live in. 'There's nothing. I just wanted . . .'

She couldn't see his face, couldn't tell if the low tone of his voice was the one he used when he wanted to show her he was older, or the one that slid into his words so naturally when he wasn't sure about something.

'We better go now. Before it gets dark.'

As though that was what he wanted to hear, he stepped onto the path leading into the jungle, walked slowly, then more quickly in. Dead leaves littered the path, crunched on their heels, but the sound slipped back quietly into the jungle as if it belonged there, in the black gaps between trees, in the thick, suffocating foliage. The air was different, cooler, more compact with dark, earthy smells like when tree-bark is cut, or when leaves are crushed, or water mixes with soil. It was motionless air, hanging like God of the jungle, everywhere, forever.

He walked steadily ahead, so sure of this place, of himself. There was another kind of silence here, not like the silence in and around Yalpanam which was sweet, warm, almost perfumed. The jungle's silence was very still, eerie, the silence of caves where every sound eventually gets swallowed as though it never existed. She sped up, made sure her steps were in sync with his. But in the forefront of the silence, like an afterthought, or maybe because she was just noticing it, a soft insect-shrill lingered as if it had always been there and would always be a part of the silence that devoured everything the deeper they went in. She quickened her step and reached out for his shoulder but pulled her hand back and stuffed it into her pocket. Everywhere green, green, green. Black-green, lime-green, moss-green leaves, some as big as a human head. Mismatched vines and stalks, here and there, as though everything and anything could live here. He veered off the path.

'Follow the track!' She slapped an insect on her arm, glanced at the blotch of blood left by the mosquito, pulped and flattened on her palm, and wiped it off on her shorts.

He slowed down, stopped, turned around, a look of surprise on his face as if he'd suddenly realized she was behind him.

'There's another way this side.' He pointed to a dark collection of trees on his left.

'My father called you and told you, is it? You know where you're going?' She scratched the mosquito bite on her arm. She scratched and scratched until her skin singed with pain. No answer. No words. No reaction. A tall block of nothing. 'I don't even *know* what I'm . . .' she said.

The sharp, continuous insect-shrill filled the space between them. The trees seemed to be tilting forward, bending, forming a dark circle to trap them. Something cold and jittering heaved in her chest.

He looked up at the foliage and nudged his head at one of the average sized trees. 'That tree, you see it? It has white flowers but you cannot see it. Will only bloom at midnight.'

The cold, jittering something ripened, escaped in an explosive gasp, and another. 'Let's go. Let's *go*.' She turned back towards where they had come from and scrambled away from the slanting trees, away from their thick barks, their smell of earth and old, dark things decaying in the mud.

The leaves behind her crackled. He grabbed her hand and twirled her around. Their faces met. He looked into her eyes and her eyes rested on his. She felt him as a another set of eyes, like hers, the same kind of eyes, brown, drenched in feeling, in life that was still going; like her, searching. He held her hand, gently stroked a knuckle with his thumb, their eyes still on each other's, one big eye; one big eye pretending to be two pairs of eyes. She felt her face move closer to his, her heart a feral animal, his face blurring into her whole self, his breath like ammonia and spit. She pulled back. He removed his hand from hers. Slowly his face became clearer, his eyes his own again.

'Don't be afraid, Max. I'll guide you into the jungle.'

He held his hand out. She watched her hand move towards his. Their fingers intertwined. He turned around, she with him. They walked back, deeper into the jungle's interior.

*

The injured man lies flat on a wooden slat in the corner of the cellar. He is covered in blankets sewn by Savitri on days and nights when she feels the urge to 'manifest something out of nothing'. The light from the lamps surrounding the slat create a dusky orange glow around him. Savitri sits on a stool by his head and wipes his forehead with a cloth she periodically dips into a large ceramic bowl of water.

Pushpanayagi stands quietly in a corner across from the makeshift bed. She holds the lamp given by Abu, her hand's tremble disguised by the natural flickering of its healthy tangerine flame. Not that Savitri or the injured man are looking at her, or would even look at her had they been facing the other way. The man on the slat is staring intently at the ceiling, momentarily oblivious to everything else. And Savitri has forgotten the cellar, the house, her life. Ever since the man was carried into the kitchen by two panting Communists, she has not rested. Her eyes are fixed on the man before her, her face etched in an expression of perpetual ache.

'Mister, close your eyes,' she whispers feverishly.

But the man's eyes, filled with bewilderment, refuse to close. She slides the cloth smoothly across his brow and, expertly, as though she has been doing it for years, she dips the cloth in the bowl of water, wrings it out and brings it back to his forehead.

The man yowls. Pushpa jerks forward, but Savitri, used to the man's predicament, to the scene of his pain, rests the cloth on his forehead and gently holds on to his shoulders. 'It's ok, Mister,' she whispers, 'it will be like this for a while, but only for a while.' She leaves the cloth to lie on his forehead, then moves her stool near the centre of the bed and sits down to begin her work of cleaning and dressing the wound. She slowly lifts the blanket covering his torso. In the gleam of the lamps, the white cotton gauzes, stuck closely together over the wound, look brown as though they have been primed with mud.

'Bring the strips and iodine, Pushpa.'

The man screams. The scream is long, from the gut, dripping with torment, with animal terror. It dissipates when Savitri strokes the sides of his neck, but trumpets again, despite her increased kneading and massaging. Pushpanayagi, who is slowly stepping closer to Savitri's stool, breaks her journey, closes her eyes and takes a slow, deep breath.

When she opens her eyes, the cellar is quiet. She tiptoes towards Savitri, past her, and bends down to remove the metal medicine box from beneath the wooden slat. She unlocks it, her eyes unwavering from the box, avoiding the sight of the body recumbent in pain above her. But the acrid smell of medicine that persists in the cellar as though a chemical has been released into the air, is part of the injured man's insistence: I am sick, I am *dying*. For they all know—at least the three people in the cellar do—that the man on the wooden slat, his head propped up on Savitri's own pillow, does not have long to live.

Pushpa hands the medicine box to Savitri but before she can walk away, Savitri grabs her arm and looks at her. 'Stay,' the eyes say. Pushpa quickly looks away. Savitri places the medicine box by her feet, opens it, removes a small metal bowl and rests it on the floor. Then she begins unwrapping the blood-soaked gauzes. As the strips of gauze come apart, she drops them into the metal bowl. Pushpa stands behind the slat, behind the man, and gradually makes her way to the other side of the makeshift bed and kneels on the floor.

The man winces.

'Do what you do, Pushpa. Soothe him.'

Pushpanayagi looks in wonder at Savitri, as though the woman who, in a matter of hours, has grown so naturally into her role as nurse, is demanding the same of Pushpanayagi. Blood sisters, Savitri had said, blood sisters from different lands. A new bond formed after a voyage across the ocean, even though Savitri is young to Pushpanayagi, so much younger than Pushpanayagi, even though Savitri is from India, not Ceylon.

Savitri gently goes over the wound which is deep and still oozing blood with a piece of cotton soaked in iodine.

'No!' The man pleads through clenched teeth. 'Stop!'

Savitri pulls the cotton away from the wound, the yellow of the iodine now tinged with blood. She tenderly pats the man's knee. 'I know, I know,' she says, half-whispering, 'It is like that, I know.'

Pushpanayagi watches Savitri's lowered head, watches the hand that has not budged from the man's knee, watches the bloodied mass of shapeless cotton, and suddenly, as though she has become aware of the situation unfolding before her, averts her eyes and grips the edges of the wooden slat.

'I don't know what to do,' she whispers to herself, her voice lost in the man's groans.

'It's coming! It's coming!' The man shuts his eyes. 'Coming, coming!' He turns his head towards Pushpanayagi and opens his eyes. His hand fumbles the air, falls on her knee, clutches the fabric of her sari. She looks at him, puzzled by the sudden shift in his disposition, his face contorted.

'Leopard's eye is yellow,' he tells her, 'yellow like that'. He points at a dull yellow sphere that has formed on the wall from the light of the lamps' flames. 'It bit deep,' he says, almost with regret, 'it bit deep.'

'Close your eyes, Mister. Sleep nicely. You will dream good dreams.' Savitri drops the soaked piece of cotton into the metal bowl and gestures at Pushpanayagi to come away from the makeshift bed, to the other side of the cellar where the man will not hear them.

'Cheah Soon Bee. My name is Cheah Soon Bee! Tell them, tell them.'

'Mister Soon Bee, your name is very beautiful. Now you must rest. Goodnight, goodnight.' Savitri hurries to the entrance of the cellar, Pushpanayagi close behind. They stop by the door. Savitri catches Pushpanayagi's arm.

'He won't last the night,' she whispers, 'Pushpa, he's come to die here. In *your* house, darling. Welcome him. Give his soul rest.'

Pushpanayagi looks away from her. She glances at the body on the wooden slat, now still and silent, and joggles her arm free from Savitri's grasp.

'It wasn't my choice, Savi. I will help you, but stop acting like a saint.'

Savitri shakes her head. 'Not a saint, darling. Simple humanity.'

Pushpanayagi grips the edges of her sari blouse. 'I *know* humanity. Stop pretending like you're better than everyone else.'

*

Deeper in. The silence thickened. He marched ahead, but his steps had slowed down as though his feet remembered her, the silly girl, scared of the jungle, of leeches, of all the other million insects in this festering place, scared of this whole intertwined and jumbled mess. This dark, old-smelling maze. Her calf muscles stretched and ached. He wasn't here. Daddy wasn't here. They should stop. Go back. Still, she peered past every gap between trees, thinking she would see his nicely-pressed Gucci pants, his crocodile-leather shoes dirtied and tattered, the constant look of discomfort on his face.

'Slow down, Hadi, please.' He walked much faster when they weren't holding hands.

He grunted and muttered something about the night and the track. He turned around, checking.

'Do we even *know* where we're going?' She brushed her fingers against the cool damp bark of each tree they passed, some trunks as thin as her arm, others as wide as at least a dozen of her arms. Ferns everywhere, curling, braiding at the base of trees, sprouting out of reddish slime from slopes beside the path, fanning out their leaves dotted with spores.

'Walk only. We don't know where your father is. He could be somewhere—'

'But we don't *know*.'

He stopped by a large, looming tree, its trunk massive. Jumbo ants, some red, some black, crawled up the jagged bark, over dark green moss growing in patches around the trunk, growing over whitish, rubbery blobs pushing through the bark. Part of its lower trunk thrust out in a curve towards the soggy ground, creating a nook big enough for someone to sit in. The trunk went up, up, up into the sky.

He leaned against the tree. Trees have spirits, Kak Isma said. Never sit under a tree at night. Never lean against a tree without asking permission first. He casually folded his arms and rested his head against the mossy bark.

'This tree is called a Meranti tree,' he said.

'I'm not waiting around like this, Hadi.'

He glanced at her, at the ground, relaxed. 'We'll walk again soon,' he said softly, his voice buttery, like Auntie's.

'You went to see Auntie?' She regretted the question immediately.

He unfolded his arms and stretched them like someone waking up from sleep. 'I went the day you left . . . I didn't know . . . the reason why you left so quickly. Auntie didn't say anything.'

Heat flickered in her throat. 'The *reason*? You didn't know the reason? Are you trying to make a *joke*?'

'Sorry, no. That's not what I meant. I didn't know . . .' He started playing with the zip of the pouch around his waist, 'I didn't know that would happen. I only thought of what your mother . . . I mean, what your mother . . . I don't know. I didn't expect . . . all of this.' He pulled at the tab of the pouch zip, zoomed it back and forth.

'I don't want to talk about that now. I don't want to know about anyone, anymore, no one.'

'It's okay, Max. I'll take you where you need to go.'

Suddenly, the insect-shrill sounded louder in the expanding jungle-silence, louder still was her mad, beating heart. The mulch on the ground moved, alive, loud, the mulch, loud, the rustling leaves, loud, his breathing, loud, his eyes loud, his face . . .

'I want to go *back*!'

He stepped forward. 'It's okay, Max.' He took another step towards her. Her feet, paralysed. The jungle-darkness, the trees, the smell of old mud. Cold black void. A place to disappear, for animals to die. Ghosts. Lonely, dangerous, like death.

She allowed him come to her, to hold her hand, the warmth from his palm seeping into hers, his breath so close, a soothing breeze in the void. She closed her eyes, a warmer warmth, close, closer, closest, his body against hers, his arms around hers, over her back, chest warm against his, his pulse against hers, her face on his neck, his smell of sweat and leaves. His fingers moved up and down her back, slowly, stretching out of the long warmth of melting bodies, slowly, tenderly, he kissed the side of her neck.

Leaves rustled. She unlocked her body from his, checked his face for panic, but there was only concern. The leaves rustled again.

'What's that?' she whispered.

He shook his head and placed a finger on his lips. He gestured for her to stay put, then he darted around the tree. She followed him. In the distance, a dark figure, a child, scurried past the trees. It was a boy, ten or eleven years old. He ran on a separate track, up an incline, towards a steeper slope where the trees collected in black masses on either side of the track. Hadi moved quickly, she close behind. The boy did not look back but he proceeded as though he knew he was leading them somewhere. He scuttled up the path towards a row of three small wooden houses. Two of the houses were dark, the one on the far left faintly lit. The boy disappeared into the lit house. Hadi nodded at her, held her hand, and led her quickly up the slope, quickly onto the veranda of the house the boy had gone into. They stopped outside the door.

He clasped her hand and whispered, 'It's orang asli. Some still live in the jungle.'

She squeezed his hand in response, her heart hammering in her chest. The door slowly creaked open.

The boy stood at the door, his face calm as if he knew they were coming.

'Good evening,' Hadi said.

The boy nodded without a smile and pointed indoors. Hadi stooped forward, peeked in, and jerked back. Even in the dull light of the house, she could see his face had paled. Words swarmed through her mind but none stayed. Her mouth felt heavy as though there were stones on her tongue.

'He's here,' Hadi said, his voice flat.

*

What more could be said about these bones? Sometimes they were inert, yes, covered in soil, no longer distinguishable from animal bones, fused, quite early on in their first ever encounter with the earth, into the subterranean landscape, worked on by the underground life-stream, without prejudice. Yes, quite easefully, the worms and the termites and the cicadas navigated around or over the bones as though they had always been there. But the worms' ancestors had feasted on the dead flesh once attached to the bones, and the flesh gave the worms life and the worms after that, and the worms after that, as memories that survive in the cells. Could a proclamation be made that the flesh of the dead subsisted in the form of worm tissue? A clue, perhaps? Death is not what it is presumed to be? When human flesh lies in the ground, no longer animate, is that what a person is and has always been? The flesh, the bone, the blood, over and through which a beautiful fishtail palm tree grows and is nourished. The fishtail palm gives thanks to feet, to thighs, to necks. Feet, thighs, necks are in the roots and bark and leaves. There, somewhere, a person continues, somehow reborn into a tree.

In the early days, when Pushpanayagi strolled leisurely around the land, her eyes frequently fell on the tiniest details: pink wildflowers the size of a fingernail, sudden movements in the foliage, a single spinach-green caterpillar munching quietly on a leaf the colour of its body, a ladybug nestling between the petals of a flower. If her eyes had been properly open, she would have seen something, the clue often missed, century after century. Instead, she only gaped, and delighted in an ordinary natural beauty. It is the way a human being is when they gaze at the large red sun lowering on the horizon. With what eyes are they seeing? Eyes that have witnessed fifty setting suns and that know the sun through old words and old feelings? Or eyes that have forgotten the fifty suns? And with those eyes of forgetting, would they have seen, for the first time, the brandy-brown aura around the sun and allowed it to fill them to the core and get them drunk? And in that drunkenness, would they have seen the entire landscape wink and, in that moment, would they have understood the story? The story of their life and of the human lives before them, of the lives of the stones, the sky, the periwinkles, the python devouring the rat, and of the rat as it fades away inside the warm, moist throat of the python, and on, and on.

See the eagle soar and dip.

See the ants march towards a sugar cube.

The whole play is winking at the sun-gazing human, asking them to ask the question.

What does it mean to die?

Death followed the old woman like a shadow that did not want to end. So much flesh had crumbled around her. So many words had passed through her. So many eyes had looked into hers.

'Death is here,' she said as she woke up, 'death has been in me all this while.'

She looked at the walls of her bedroom, raised her hands, buried her head in them and wept. For a long time, she wept. If the words could have been said, they would have been, 'I have died to myself.' But the old lady was too unnerved by grief to speak again. She closed her eyes and returned to sleep.

The bones behind the house shifted slightly in the ground, not by the work of worms or termites or the patient cicadas, but by the invisible force that mushroomed through the earth, from a place unknown. The violet sphere of light around the house grew brighter and transformed, in a slow flicker, into pale gold. A gentle wind rose. Voices loud and soft, high and low, bloomed, one by one, in the wind and gradually blended into the dissonant symphony that emerged. Through the darkness of the night, to the robust yellow moon, they said, almost in unison, 'We wait, we wait, forever we wait.'

14

Morning light streamed into the front hall through the shut green-glass windows. Pushpanayagi stood in a corner of the hall, near the passageway by the rooms, and watched particles of dust dance in the diffused yellow light. All had been wiped out: people, furniture, paintings, the smell of Charles's minty talcum powder, Abu's spittoon, Savitri's pots and pans. Wiped out that year, before the Japanese left, not in time for Charles to die happy. *Happier*.

She took slow steps into the hall, her limbs stiff and painful as though there were knots in her hips, her legs. The sunlight felt open, like it was past eight in the morning. The vegetables would be waiting, but all of that felt futile, done with, over—weeding, plucking, watering, digging. No more earth. The toil was finished. A nervous, swampy feeling pushed through her throat and sludged down her chest. She sat on the chair bathed in soft glimmering light. She opened her mouth as if to drink the light and eat the dust. Heat filled her tongue. She licked the air, tasted the glow, and felt it feed her growling belly. For days, the belly-stone had simply sat there but this morning when she'd woken up and seen the shadows circle her bedroom, part of the stone fell away and the shadows disappeared into the walls.

She closed her eyes and listened to the sunbirds chattering from their nest on the veranda. They chirped so happily as though they had reached the peak of Samadhi. Blissful, at peace, in love with themselves. The eggs had hatched. The new generation had come. In a few weeks, the nest would be abandoned. Then slowly, over months, the nest would decay and disappear until the next cycle came and the veranda would have a nest again. As all that had decayed, turned back into the earth, Earth. Tears filled her eyes. Could it be true? Could it really have been like that? Her body loosened, felt like it was becoming the air around her. She'd lived with the panic of not knowing how. She lived anyway. But was it that which she'd thought it had been?

Could she have done something else? For an icy moment, she felt her heart stop. It fluttered back to life. No. What's done is done. The sweet young baby, that girl Maxim, she had to go to the home she'd been given. And Savitri didn't want more from her. No. Savitri had already decided she wanted to be an angel. Abu and Charles, they were not in her hands. Mary, there was nothing they could have done. No. People like Mary wanted to die in that way. Tragic. No. Yes, it is so. No, it could not have been otherwise. Yes, it is so. It is so, it is so.

She kept her eyes closed. The coldness grew through her body like a rising tide, higher, deeper, colder and colder, in the roaring blackness, colder and colder through the stars and past the dancing light, down into still, silent darkness.

She opens her eyes.

'Hence, the coming of the Age of Enlightenment was not—'

'Charlie, *please*!' Savitri spins the wheelchair around and charges towards the front door, pushing the chair as though she is about to drive it into a river or heave it off a cliff.

'Miss Savi, I take Tuan. Wait! I take Tuan.' Abu scurries towards the pair, spittoon in one hand, but his ageing legs cannot carry him quick enough and soon, he stops, catches his breath, and resigns to holding his hand out in protest.

Savitri wheels her husband down the ramp and onto the veranda, Pushpanayagi stands by the hall entrance, clutching the frame of the front door. Once in a while, her mouth opens as if she is about to say something, but each time, she promptly closes it, and continues watching Savitri whose face is reddened and damp with the exertion of fury as she pushes the chair carelessly towards the steps of the veranda.

'I've had it up to *here* with all of your rubbish,' she screams.

Outside, clouds the colour of a deep blue sea have gathered in the sky, blocking out the sun completely. It is only noon, yet it feels as though the structure of time has collapsed, and a new night has entered. The world is the blue of melancholy, of the darkest ocean and, suddenly, waves of silvery yellow light slice through the darkness and form beaming lines around the clouds. The sky closes in on the earth. It brings the trees, plants, birds, and people together into a large family of objects. Everything feels close together in this new noon-night, the strange muted light pricking the dark.

'*Cancel* the birthday? With this tragedy going on! All the killing and . . . the least we can do . . .' Savitri chokes on her tears. She looks up at the sky as though she has momentarily forgotten her plight. Then, abruptly, she thrusts the chair onto the first step of the veranda.

Abu leaps forward. 'Miss Savi! Stop!' The spittoon falls from his hand, crashes onto the veranda floor. Red liquid splatters like blood from a gunshot wound.

Pushpanayagi observes the scene. She observes Abu hobbling towards Savitri; she observes the thinning cotton-white hair on Charles's head, the jittering of Savitri's skeletal arm. Abu grabs the back of the wheelchair. Savitri moves aside and turns to her. She notes the tear-soaked eyes, pleading, begging for something—the bond of blood sisters perhaps.

Abu re-orients the wheelchair back in the direction of the entrance. Charles slump, arms limp on the hand-rests, eyes closed as if asleep. But Pushpanayagi knows he is pretending. She has seen him shut his eyes at the dinner table when silence permeates the air, and nobody says a word about the tapioca they have to eat so as to not die, as though all the food on the island had suddenly evaporated. She has seen Charles close his eyes in the courtyard when Abu and Savitri are arguing, but Pushpanayagi knows he is listening, as he is listening to the silence now, and to Abu's wild panting as he rolls the wheelchair away from the veranda steps, relieved that he has saved his master from the hands of the wretched, hysterical wife.

'Do you not *care*, Charlie?' Savitri screams. 'Do you not *care* how we live?'

Abu wheels his master, past Savitri, back up the ramp and into the hall. He parks the chair close to the entrance.

'Miss Savi, Tuan very tired. Why we want pretend with this war? Birthday not so important, Miss Savi.' Abu's voice is gruff, stern, all traces of pliability gone.

Pushpanayagi clutches the frame of the door and gradually steps away from the door and down onto the veranda, in front of Savitri. Charles opens his eyes and, together, he and Abu watch the two women.

'It's a trivial thing, Savi. I never wanted a birthday celebration. It's a joke, really. Trying to pretend we're young and that we deserve to cut birthday cakes. Charles is right, we don't need to prance around, celebrating—'

'Even if I bled to death in this house to make all of you happy, my blood would not be enough.'

'Didn't you say the poor man is dying in the cellar?'

'He's *dying*. Of course he is, Pushpa! He is our duty now. You think I don't know that? Who has been cleaning the wound and wrapping it and talking to him so he doesn't—'

'You, you, you. You've made this house your own, Savi. No one can say you haven't. With your pots and pans and tins.'

'And what would have happened if I hadn't done that? The three of you would be living in darkness, in dirt.'

'Because we didn't know how to live before you came.'

'Who *knows* what you did before I came.'

Silence soars and saturates the hall and leaks onto the veranda. Savitri bites her lip like a remorseful child, tears streaming down her face, arms hung by her sides as though she is waiting for something, or waiting to start walking, to start moving again. The sky darkens but the strong, silvery light still pierces through pockets of dark purple cloud. A deep bellow of thunder echoes through the hall.

'Sibyl,' Charles says softly, but loud enough to pique the women's interest and make him their new point of focus.

'Sibyl,' he continues, 'the Black Sibyl was before you came, my darling. Like a force from the heavens, she keeps me on this island. It was a frightful time, my darling. Before you were even born. I was young, of course, but all that has ever driven my life has been the desire to know. To know everything . . . the ways of the Malays, the ways of native life. Where is order amidst multifariousness? Alas, this land kept fooling me. Each time I thought I knew, something would annihilate my knowledge. It was as if the island was playing a big joke on me. Like I was trying to catch a shadow. I knew the colonials, or so I thought. I knew the natives, or so I thought. But the butterflies . . . the butterflies, I could know. They live in simple stages, stages clear even to a fool. *Seen,* observable, clean stages. Don't misunderstand me. I yearned for the mystery too. She has kept me here, my Black Sibyl. She has come not from Ceylon, but from deep in the Universe.'

Pushpanayagi's face sinks in embarrassment as if he has said too much or said something she cannot bear to hear, an exaggeration, an untruth. She lifts part of her sari and drapes it over her head. She catches Charles's glance and quickly looks away, at his liver-spotted feet, at the beige tiles of the hall, at the wooden planks of the veranda.

'It's a shame,' Charles says, his voice low, flecked with sadness, 'in all my years of rearing and studying butterflies, I have never witnessed a butterfly emerge from its cocoon.'

Pushpanayagi lifts her face hesitantly. She makes sure her sari-shield is firm around her head. Her eyes meet Charles' ice-blue eyes, now lustrous with the softness of regret, of a life missed, and as though they had both anticipated this moment, they peer into each other's eyes like two people trying to find an object or a clue. The deeper they peer, the darker the sky turns until, at last, lightning flashes through the sky and a loud groan of thunder fills the land and the first raindrops fall thick and big. Pushpanayagi takes her eyes off his, and steps back.

*

In a sarong, on the floor. In a sarong, on the floor, eating roasted broad beans from a free Fernleaf bowl. Daddy isn't Daddy. Not here. Not with the kind of light bulb that hangs from the ceiling without a lampshade. Daddy in an old Milo T-shirt, borrowed from the man of the house maybe (Mister A something. Aneh? Anyoh?), or it could just be an object from his Other World.

Daddy sat in a corner, on the floor, between two dark wooden walls, the bowl not far from his feet, quiet. Outside on the veranda, Hadi's head bobbed up and down in conversation with one of the five children of the house. Twice, he'd turned his head far enough to reveal his profile as if to tell her he was here, just a few metres away. They'd all left them alone, invented excuses to talk on the veranda, do work in the kitchen, this brand new family in the jungle.

'They've still got food if you have changed your mind, Maxi.' Daddy's voice was low, delicate. She felt his stare, smelled his desperation. Not the woody musk from the drawers but a vague smell of medicine used for wounds, floating around the bare front hall, spiced, prickly, desperate.

'I didn't come here to eat.' Her chest felt weighted down, tight. She had to suck hard for air. Even her throat was clotted with something but strangely, her heart was quiet.

'I know, girl. I didn't mean it like that . . .' He breathed heavily and sighed. 'I just wanted to make sure . . .' He reached for a bean from the bowl, popped it into his mouth and crunched hard. His teeth kept going, the crunch loud, louder, loudest.

'Can you please *stop* that?'

Daddy's mouth paused. She looked up at him. He searched her face.

'Sorry,' he said softly, 'I didn't realize . . .'

'Of course, you didn't.'

A light breeze blew into the room. It carried with it a gentle smell of leaves and mud. She breathed in the scent which momentarily loosened the tightness in her chest. From the room behind her came the sounds of pots and pans clashing, but no voices. The small wooden house, so naked and sparse, every inch and corner screaming poverty, this whole house had made space and time for her and Daddy as though they were the stars of the movie, suddenly so important. In the other corner of the room, an unzipped sleeping bag, dirty maroon, tired-looking, lay flat below the thinnest pillow she'd ever seen. Daddy's reading glasses sat on the pillow like the final piece of a jigsaw puzzle.

'Maxi . . . do you . . .' His voice trailed off into the breeze.

She glared at him, his hair no longer styled with the hair gel Mother bought from that boutique in KL, his face sagging, as though, somehow, it had grown longer, like an old mango.

'I want to explain something to you, girl.' He adjusted his ridiculous sarong, the shade of blue not his colour, the chequered pattern too unfamiliar on him.

'Is *that* where you've been sleeping?' She jerked her head at the sleeping bag.

His cheeks reddened. A shy smile briefly appeared on his face and as though to prevent the smile from happening again, he pursed his thin lips, slowly parted them and said, 'For a while only, girl. Only for a week so far. You understand? Mummy told you?'

'She told me *nothing*.'

Daddy's eyes softened. A light watery gleam spread across them, threatening to bring tears but none came.

'I see . . . I needed some time,' he said, his voice shaky all of a sudden, 'you were gone so I . . .'

'So you also abandoned ship—'

'Not like that, Maxi. I wasn't . . . I couldn't.' He sighed and pressed his fingers together, the palms too far apart to be in prayer. 'I didn't know how I . . .'

'Hadi sent the letter. So, you *knew!* You *knew* I was at Yalpanam, and yet you left.'

'Maxi, please listen. I wasn't abandoning you—'

'Then *what* do you call what you did? Holidaying in the jungle? Just hanging out with a random family? Trying out being poor for the heck of it?'

The watery gleam clouded his eyes. Two perfectly shaped teardrops, one from each eye, fell gracefully down his sunken cheeks.

'When I found out where you were . . .' More tears fell, fast this time, as though there was a whole well of tears inside him. He didn't bother to control them or wipe them away.

'When I found out that you were up there, something in me wasn't, I don't know how to explain it . . . something wasn't right, maybe that's how it was, I don't know, girl.'

She nodded and abruptly stopped. She hadn't meant to agree with him. But she knew, she knew that gnarled expression of grief etched everywhere on him. Even though she'd never seen it on his face.

'I came here . . . it's nothing, girl. I'm not trying to keep a secret. A few years ago, I found these houses. I made friends with Anyeh . . . and I come here . . . I come here sometimes to . . .'

'Breathe.' Her face fell.

'Yes.'

He leaned back against the wall. His arms dropped to his sides. Peace washed over his face.

'I don't have a reason, girl . . . I just feel drawn to this place, to this jungle . . .'

'Oh, *really*?'

He turned to look at her. His eyebrows lifted the way they did when he was disturbed.

'You've kept a lot from me.' Her voice sounded powerful, the tone strange, unfamiliar, not quite hers.

His eyebrows fell back in place. But the perpetual crease on his forehead kept the look of puzzlement and worry intact. Slowly, his eyes mellowed in that new layer of grief he seemed so comfortable in.

He cleared his throat and said, 'You left out of choice. When we found out you were with the old lady, and that we would have to bring you home, that's when . . . that's when I realized I couldn't face you. I couldn't see you. Not yet. I wasn't ready.'

'Ready for what?'

But his mouth closed, his lips tightened and, suddenly, even the hushed voices from outside seemed loud. She turned away from Daddy and looked ahead. Hadi turned around, looked into the room and smiled at her. She stared at his mouth, at the deep dimples that popped up beneath his cheeks, the smile like a sedative, and she felt a faint glimmer of the ball of silence slowly build around her. He smiled at her for a long while and as the silence between her and Daddy grew, the other silence, the better silence from the ball, filled her heart and it was easier to block out the silence rising in the room like an infection.

*

The man's face has changed into a colour Pushpanayagi cannot name. His eyelids flutter. She gently touches the edges of the bloodied gauze covering the wound on his upper thigh. He bites his lip and stifles a scream. She quickly pulls her fingers away and looks behind her. Darkness hangs like a stubborn, oppressive cloud.

Savitri has said no. She will not come to the cellar. Her job as nurse is done. There are plates to clean, uneaten food to put away; but first, she has to sit alone in the courtyard to wear out her anger.

The man has grown smaller, it seems. His face contorts and attempts to stabilize, but with each stab of pain from his leg, the face scrunches into a sea of creases.

'You are beyond the pain,' she says.

He groans, bites his lower lip, and writhes on the wooden slat.

'The pain is an illusion created by the body, which is also an illusion,' she says. Her voice this time is louder but the man does not to appear to be listening. He stares at the ceiling as though looking for an answer from the darkness above.

She grips his arm and squeezes it tenderly, the way Savitri did when she still believed in her role as nurse, as caretaker of injured freedom fighters.

The man turns his head towards Pushpanayagi. She leans to the side where he can see her better, and smiles at him. It is a long, tranquil smile that does not seem to register in the man's eyes. He blinks away and settles his vision on the shadows on the wall. All are motionless except hers, a wide, stumpy shadow that periodically bends and rises and shifts this way and that. He gazes at her shadow and slowly, his face relaxes, his mouth opens and a long sigh fills the quiet cellar.

'I died fighting,' he says in a faltering voice, 'Cheah Soon Bee died fighting, tell them that. Wong Ai Ling, my wife. Tell her I died fighting.'

Pushpanayagi strokes his arm. Softly, she says, 'And the leopard?'

He watches her shadow fixedly. The flames from the lamps on the floor waver. Her shadow suddenly dances again. He screams.

'The space behind the pain. Go to there. Behind the pain,' she says.

He tries to rise but quickly falls back on the slat. 'Take my life. I don't want it anymore. Not like this.'

'Be with your breath. Go to the breath. In the breath is the place without pain.'

'I can't! I can't!'

She grips his hand, holds it tight. 'You must, Soon Bee. There is no other way to go if you want to go properly.'

'Please. *Please.* Give me something. *Quick*'.

Pushpa jolts forward and places her head on his chest. His heart ticks fast, unevenly. His fevered body warms her ears. She listens intently to the sounds of the world inside him. Rumbling. Pounding. Hissing. Babbling. A river driven wild by a storm.

Gradually, his breath slows down. 'Lady,' he whispers, 'please don't let me die like this. I fought . . . I fought too hard to go like this. Can't die with this, this shame. Tell them . . . I died fighting . . . the Japs came too close . . . tell them that.'

Pushpa pulls away from him and reclines in her chair. She shakes her head. 'How can you die with a lie hanging over your spirit?'

His face crumples into a pained frown. 'A baby is coming. Ai Ling . . . is pregnant. I can't . . . please . . . I can't leave this for my son.'

'The truth will be better,' she says, her voice firm.

'To die from an animal's bite is . . . it's not how I wanted to die.'

'The way we exit this world is not our choice, Soon Bee,' she says curtly.

*

'They never found his body. Disappeared in the jungle. Just like that. Never had a father, never knew him—'

'You've *never* talked about him.'

The pink plastic bag at her feet made a swishing sound. She didn't dare take the journal out and smack it down on the floor. There! She could have said. There! All your sick words. All your small little *truths*. But he looked too soft, almost like a clay doll with two dark brown button eyes, too easily destroyed.

He shook his head slowly and stared at the wooden floor too dusty to sleep on and yet, for days, that's where he'd been, rejecting his wife's floral sheets and essential-oiled pillows.

'Maxi . . . I—'

'Daddy?'

'Your grandfather was a hero.' He studied the floor, refused to look at her. But she felt him, a nervous lukewarm ball beside her, not heavy, smelling a bit like medicine. It was okay, this other ball, not silent, but full of somersaulting stuff. She moved an inch or two towards him. He sat slumped against the wall, looking the way people did at funerals, opaque, faraway sadness all over the face, even in the body, somehow, as though it had gone into the bloodstream.

'Daddy . . .'

To the floor, he said, 'You know, he died seven months before I was born. Your grandmother kept a small picture of him in a corner of her bedroom. I watched her talk to him every night.' He shook his head in the regretful, anaemic way he seemed to have picked up in this house of strange men and women. 'Now that I think of it, she must have known I was standing there. Popo never closed the door, you see, it was always a bit open.'

He lifted his head, not to look at her, but at the old man of the house and Hadi, talking on the veranda, their words inaudible, perhaps polite, forced to keep going while she and Daddy did whatever it was they were doing.

'She talked to him like he was real, you know. Like he never died. She asked him questions a lot. What would she do with her son?' Daddy sighed. He shifted his eyes to the floor as though he was not really there but daydreaming of something she could never see.

'The son didn't have fighting spirit, she said. No passion, you know. Always counting marbles like a girl. Popo was always sad. The son was not brave like the father, she said. What to do?'

'Daddy . . . why are you telling me this?'

'I . . .' His lips began to tremble. She moved closer towards him, slid her hand inches away from his limp hand. Nervous, lukewarm ball. Her finger slowly touched his thumb. The ball softened, became a little smooth, and exploded into a flood of quivers. She moved her hand over his and squeezed, not yet ready to look directly at him.

He turned his quivering head towards her and the quivering slowly stopped. His dark brown eyes grew, vaster, vaster, as wide as a landscape, with pools and trees, roads, buildings, cloudy sky, birds, jungle. She looked away.

'I'm . . .' He pressed her hand. Through her side-vision, his head shook in the mournful, repentant way that had suddenly become a big part of this Daddy, the new broken Daddy. 'I'm . . . sorry, Maxi. Maxi, I'm so sorry. I should have . . . should have taken better care of you. I didn't . . . know how much . . . how to . . .'

'How to do it with Mummy around all the time?'

'Your Mummy, your Mummy. She's—'

'She *stole* my life!'

She pulled her hand away and glared at him. 'And you didn't *save* me!'

His lips twisted and curled, his cheeks lifted. The sob came quickly, unbelievably. 'I . . . never knew how to be a father.'

Her chest fell and a calm wave spread through her throat and arms. Her fingers felt warm, her toes too, her whole body was warm: the wave glided through softly, nicely. It filled her body. Filled out of her body, and grew into an old-new ball of silence.

'What's finished is finished,' he said softly, the words almost swallowed. 'I can't go back in time and do anything, you know.' He took her hand and held it cautiously in his. 'You are born with one mother and one father. Whatever it is, those are the people who brought you here . . . to this . . . to this place. Mummy . . . she . . . you don't know, girl . . .'

The breeze ushered in a sudden pungent smell of soil. Auntie appeared outside the window by the veranda, and disappeared. She looked again, and again, but there was only a dimly lit empty space where Auntie had stood, in front of Hadi and the old man. The pulse on her neck throbbed. She turned towards Daddy.

'Your Mummy,' he said, his voice full of an unnameable feeling, 'Mummy . . . she has problems, girl. I didn't know this when I married her . . . her family . . . well, you know, well they lied to us. They never indicated that she had . . . she had, well, all those mental problems, and that . . .' Then, quickly, as though he regretted what he had said, he whispered, 'But don't think about that.'

Auntie re-emerged in front of Hadi and the old man. She looked at Maxim with kind eyes, a small, mysterious smile carved on her face as if it had always been there and would be there forever. She fizzled out into the air.

'Sometimes, girl, Mummy's head goes off somewhere. She gets . . . what do they call it? Mental attacks. She has to take—'

'Pills.'

He raised his eyebrows in surprise. 'Yes, girl, I, we, didn't . . . There was no need, you know, we wanted—'

'Mummy to live her nice little lie.' Her heart pounded. The black empty feeling from Daddy's study suddenly formed and threatened to suck her in but she pushed it away.

'Not like that, girl—'

'It's exactly like that. I've seen Mummy taking pills but they're just for headaches, you both said. *Lying* to me—'

'Not like that, girl—'

'And you didn't think for one second that I might have needed to know. *I* could be sick like her—did you ever, even once, *think* that it might be important for me to know?'

'I'm sorry, girl, so sorry—'

'To *know* my inheritance, my *history*. You didn't think it was important? That I have a right to belong, to belong . . .

somewhere . . . to *something*. But you go about forgetting me, as though, as though I'm a ghost, not even *here*—'

'Not like that, girl—'

'It's like that, Daddy. You don't think I deserve to be a part of this family.'

'That's not true.'

'Like it's not true that your money is dirty, like Mummy says? That you've been getting dirty money from dirty land deals? It's not true that all the nice, shiny things in our house actually stink of garbage? Not true that you've built so many ugly buildings on the island, you've actually ruined it?'

'I've done some terrible things, Maxi. But I can tell you now, you know, I failed you . . . I'm sorry, I'm sorry. I thought all of that . . . I thought . . . Well, I don't know. The truth is . . . I failed myself.' He sighed. 'When I came to Anyeh's house, I realized. I could never be a fighter like my father. I don't have his courage. I couldn't die fighting for something I believed in. I just . . . don't have it in me . . . his spirit. But I am whatever I am.'

Auntie appeared by the window, her face immersed in sorrow. She watched Maxim as though nothing else in the world existed. The more she watched, the more Maxim felt as though she wasn't really in the room with Daddy, as though she was drifting further and further away, out through the window, into Auntie's body, and through her new body by the window, she watched her old body sitting beside her father. She saw a young girl, her face overflowing with grief, struggling to move closer and closer towards an old balding man who looked as if he was trapped in his own body. The old man was very sad and very frightened. He looked like the loneliest man in the world. And the young girl, her skin pale and clear and almost beautiful, appeared to be waiting for something, the way a person waits for important news or for the sound of a car engine that signals the arrival of someone special. For a moment, as she watched these two people with her new-old eyes, she felt the darkest, heaviest sadness fill her throat, and as it slowly wedged itself down into the depths of her chest and broke her heart, the young girl in the room collapsed into the old man's arms. He held her in his embrace for a long while. It felt to the girl, to Maxim, as she floated back into the room, slowly, finally, into her own body, like a happening with no happening, a moment with no moment, like something that had been going on forever. Time didn't exist. Body didn't exist. It alone did.

*

The old woman opened her eyes and rose from the mat she had been using as a bed for at least three decades because, on a whim one afternoon, she threw out the bed frame and mattress she had inherited from Charles, 'for the good of everything,' she'd said to the house, 'we don't need trouble.' She grew used to the hardness of the floor, and to the serrations in the locally woven mat. She did not need luxury, she confessed to her plants, nor objects to collect, or any distractions to divorce her from her simple life. For that, she believed, was what her life had become. A simple road, onwards and up, undisturbed by overgrown vines, scattered leaves, mud, animals crossing here and there, messy roots accidentally growing beneath the road, people walking up and down—no, her road was clear, beautifully tarred, insect-free even.

Really, if someone gazed at her road—it began right outside the gates of the house at the point where the banyan tree had once stood (before she caused its destruction at the end of the nineteenth century), and stretched all through the island, through a bridge over the Straits of Malacca, up the West Coast of Peninsular Malaysia, across Thailand, Burma, through a phantom bridge on the Indian Ocean, and up the length of Sri Lanka, until it finally ended in the original Yalpanam, land of her ancestors, Jaffna—they wouldn't have seen much, some pebbles now and again, certainly no potholes, perhaps some flowers fallen from trees that lined the road for shade. It simply went on and on and followed the natural rises and bends of the land.

But, of course, as with all roads, and more so with buildings, the earth is disturbed by their existence. Such activity isn't evil—it wouldn't be fair to misuse hyperbole—but as roads are built and the foundations for buildings are set, and when more roads are built and more and more buildings rise, so many that there aren't enough people to inhabit them, it isn't only the indwelling spirits of the soil and roots that rage, insects and worms and wildlife displaced from the annihilated jungles rage, and eventually wither too. So it was and so it is with the old woman's road. It wasn't an actual road, we know, but it also caused rage and produced the withering of things.

She waddled to the windows, shut to keep out the rain. She looked at her reflection in the green-glass window. She saw the sagging cheeks, the dark rings beneath the eyes, the mouth partly open, and finally, the eyes gazing back at her with awe and revulsion. She covered her mouth with a hand and suppressed a gasp. She stared at the eyes that stared at her, unbelievingly, as though they were not her own eyes but the eyes of another. She removed the hand from her mouth and screamed, the scream piercing, echoing through the house, the surrounding land, the Universe.

She rushed—as quickly as her bulk would allow—out of the bedroom, into the hall, out the front door, into the garden, past the front gate, round the corner, to the back of the house. She stopped at the edge of the jungle. It was night, but she was not thinking of practicalities like torch lights and lamps, and, somehow, as if this night was known by the moon, it shone a powerful silver light on the land, and on the four stones that stood in a neat row like a small ritualistic ground where offerings are given and prayers are said, sacrifices made. She genuflected before the stones.

A cool, mild breeze blew gently over the land. It brought with it a fragrance of flowers. The old lady placed her hands on the damp earth. 'To the departed,' she whispered, 'Soon Bee. I never did. Never went. Never cried. Never breathed. Never, never. Never listened. Never saw. Never touched. Never, never. Never felt. Never held. Never listened. Never saw. Never touched. Never, never.'

She staggered up, took in the darkness around her, undisturbed by its depths, disturbed only by the eyes she had seen glaring back at her on the window, and following the scent of flowers, inspired by the strong hint of jasmine that had risen so unassumingly, she lifted her hands to the sky, closed her eyes and smelled the cool fragrance as if that was all she needed to do at that point, in that moment, as if every breath taken in her one hundred and eighty-five years had been leading up to that—jasmine-rose air brushing against her nostrils.

15

'So, I waited for him to come out of the sea. Then, I strangled him.' The ruddy-faced man stares at the snaking branches of the banyan tree. The branches have grown long, they nearly reach the ground. Within, behind the trunk and the branches and the parasitic vines, in the dark cavity of the tree, spirits congregate and watch. The man's eyes have latched on to the largest branch. He loses himself in its long wrinkles through which a procession of flame-red ants moves at a fast, steady pace.

Pushpanayagi sits on a low wooden seat, almost the shape, size and length of a large brick, in front of the tree, at the exact spot that marks its centre. The hot, dazzlingly bright day has only just turned grey-mauve. Swallows roam the skies, announcing the coming rain. She closes her eyes, relaxes whatever tension there is in her face, and nods. She knows they like the special 'floating face' she wears for them, the knowing, enigmatic look she has mastered for these sessions her customers have branded as mystical. She also knows they like the turban she wears faithfully at every session, fashioned out of glittering coral red fabric from an old sari. They come because there is nothing else they can do, because there is nothing left to be done.

'Did the man die?' she finally asks.

'Maybe,' he says in a half-whisper, 'I just let him fall and I ran away.'

The tree breathes its warmth into her ears, into her eyes and heart. She feels its tingling presence as though the tree and its breath are not separate from her. She opens her eyes and looks into the man's eyes. She has gazed like this into so many eyes that, by now, at her hundredth-something customer, she knows how to lock her eyes into a stare loaded with implications, connotations, mystery, purpose, meaning, resolution. The stare, the turban, the 'floating face'—these only came later, after she stopped depending on the tree for its life-source, after she discovered what she meant to these men. This man's eyes, light brown from his Portuguese heritage but dark enough to reveal his Chinese blood, fall very easily into hers as though they have been waiting to be consumed by hers.

She knows what the eye-lock does to them. Somehow, as the myths and stories swirl around the island, particularly in shut rooms where men are free, and as those myths and stories whirl up the hill and through the land where she sits beneath the banyan tree, the words add power to the obligatory stare that comes at the end of each session. *The Banyan Woman's Magic Stare. If Sibyl's eyes fall on yours, you have been touched by the gods. Don't be afraid to reveal everything; for once you have, her eyes will take everything away.*

Pushpanayagi feels her power rise. The longer the eye-lock, the bigger she feels, as big as Hanuman when he steps across the ocean and onto Lanka.

More rainclouds appear in the sky. Two or three groups of swallows have come and gone. At last, Pushpanayagi looks away. 'I am renewed,' he gasps, 'renewed!'

She nods and rises. She picks up her small wooden stool, takes the shillings from the man's open palm, and saunters away from the tree, onto the muddy path, into the compound of the house where her lover is sitting on the veranda, waiting for her return. She lifts the turban from her head and clamps it beneath her armpit. A cold, foggy feeling fills her heart. Her legs are heavy, her steps laboured. She sees him on the veranda, a drink in his hand. He waves at her but she is too tired, all of a sudden, too full of lethargy to lift her hand and wave back. She drags her feet along the gritty path, past rows of red and white roses planted by his hand and nurtured by him each day. She pushes forward, the heaviness in her legs corresponding with the heaviness in her chest, and makes her way up the steps of the veranda.

'Darling,' he says, his green eyes glassy and warm like two wet gems. He settles his drink on the white rattan table between the veranda chairs, gets up from his chair and opens his arms wide as if to welcome her into his whole self, but she ignores the gesture and sits in one of the chairs.

'It's going to rain,' she smiles.

'I dare say, my love. It looks like quite a storm is brewing.' He sits back in his chair and, slowly, as though there is nothing else to do, he resumes sipping his drink.

'You're not going to the club, then?'

'I said I was never going back there.'

'But do you want to, Richard?'

'I don't want to do anything of the sort. We've spoken about this. Darling, are you listening?'

'I've been listening for a long time, Richard. I don't want you to—'

'Every love story that matters includes sacrifice. Anthony and Cleopatra. Tristan and Isolde. Romeo and Juliet. Why would love be easy?' He places his drink on the table and fidgets with his ample ginger hair.

'Oh, so that is what love is about. I never knew, Richard. You will stop going to the club that will not allow a brown woman from Ceylon to enter its very special doors. And I . . .' She grips the armrests of her chair.

'We'll marry. You won't need *those* shillings. My love, why can't you see the picture? We'll be happy in this house. I have enough money for us both and . . . children if you so wish to have them. You needn't—'

'Be a filthy coolie woman underneath a tree—'

'That's not what I am saying, darling. You *know* you're not like them. You didn't come here to work on plantations. You can read, for God's sake. Coolies wear soiled loincloths and look out of sly, suspicious eyes. And, really, my love, I don't want you sitting with those misdirected men. I want you to *myself*.' He snatches his glass of dark brown liquid from the table beside him, takes a large gulp, and another, and another, until the drink is finished. '*My* Penelope. Mine. Mine alone,' he whispers.

They turn toward each other. Little blood vessels like tiny, heavily-twigged branches grow in the whites of his eyes.

'Richard,' she says gently, almost kindly, 'would you tell me the truth? Love is warm and loves to love, but isn't it also honest?'

His face sinks. 'The truth, Penelope . . . Pushpa, is that I love you. In you, I feel myself. It is like being in my village parish at dawn, when no one is there, only the warm silence of God. That is the truth.'

She searches his eyes and as though he gauges she isn't finding what she is looking for, he reaches for her hand and envelops it in his. 'We come from different places,' he says, 'that's true as well. But love burns those differences. Love doesn't see the walls that people in the Club see. Love doesn't know anything about skin and accents, habits and cultures. Love only knows how to unite. It simply does not fathom separation.'

'Love,' he continues, 'takes everything into its arms.'

'Even my life underneath the Banyan tree?'

'You don't belong on a stool—'

'It's what was chosen for me—'

'Chosen by *whom*?'

'I don't know . . . but it was chosen—'

'*You* chose it—'

'I did not!'

'You feel something when you're with those men—'

'Something you'll never understand.'

'My God, what is there to understand?'

'That I am . . . I am . . .'

'They look at you, their filthy eyes; that's what you enjoy—'

'Don't be crude.'

'Then, why would you insist? Why would you choose them over me?'

'You're denying me—'

'*Denying?* My God, Penelope, I am *affirming* you. I am telling you that you should be on a *throne*, not a stool.'

Pushpanayagi pulls her hand out of his grip. 'It's going to rain hard,' she says, getting up, 'and there will be mud everywhere. Make sure you wear your strong leather shoes when you go out. The canvas ones give hardly any protection in this weather. I don't think I'll be eating tonight, so you'd better dine at the club. Your Cookie can take the evening off. After all, everyone needs a break from time to time.'

*

Mummy sat on a bench on the porch, hands folded, partially hidden by the BMW. It's possible that the hands were elsewhere when Daddy clicked the gate open. Perhaps, when she heard the humming gate, she knew what was coming and got into a sulking pose. But the face, low, dull, even sorrowful, looked real, not a part of the pose.

'Mummy.'

Maxim stood by the side mirror of the BMW, Daddy behind her. She didn't bother to turn around, to see what was on his face, now that they were finally home after what felt like an eternal journey back from a dark, cavernous place.

Mummy slowly raised her un-permed head, the hair flat, shockingly straight. A feeble smile attempted to ease the despair spread so finely and completely across her face, reaching even the green tattooed eyebrows. They looked so small and wretched now like two little worms that had accidentally died above her eyes.

'Come, come,' Mummy said, the tone of her voice as cheerless and as low as her unchanged face. She lifted her body as though she didn't really want to, and turned in the direction of the front door where Kak Isma magically appeared with a tray of drinks. Mummy looked back as if to check with them. Did they want drinks? And as though she knew, Mummy said, 'It's ok, Isma. Take drinks back.'

They walked into the house, through the hall, into the dining area, Kak Isma leading, Mummy behind her, Daddy trailing last. The quiet here was round and chilly, a new ball that had just been born. Kak Isma stood by the kitchen entrance. She smiled at no one in particular, at all of them. The smile wasn't asking for a smile in return. It felt more like a smile that needed to express itself, just because. The smile finished, Kak Isma turned into the kitchen and disappeared beyond the enormous fridge.

On the dining table, no cups stood. No plates, no bowls of noodles, no Chinese coffee shop bread, no boxes of cornflakes, and Koko Krunch. No sweating carton of orange juice (not from concentrate). The plastic sheet was gone, the mango-print cover beneath the sheet also gone. The table was dark teak. Empty. Naked. A little frightening. Like someone had stripped the table of what made it it. The table was only a table. It looked lonely, useless, no longer needed. Strange, a bit old, like Mummy.

'Mummy, can I have something to eat? Nothing much, just a small thing.'

Daddy pulled out a chair and sat down. He unstrapped the backpack from his back and placed it on the floor. He threw Mummy a look, smiled, and as though it was their secret code, she nodded, somehow knowing what she had to do. She shuffled off into the kitchen.

Maxim sat next to her father and rested her elbows on the table. The wood felt good on her skin. No plastic to stick to her, no droplets of water to irritate.

'I was thinking, girl . . . maybe we should go to KL for a break. Go see Auntie Bonnie.' His voice sounded healthy, traces of excitement here and there.

'But Mummy—I mean, doesn't she not really like her sister?'

Daddy laughed, his laugh jarring in the rising quiet of the house, but suiting his face, his mouth almost pretty when it stretched.

'She's okay with her, lah. Just sometimes, they clash. Auntie Bonnie . . . she likes to have fun, that's all.'

'Of course. I'd love to go.'

'Good, good. I was thinking . . .' He turned to her and smiled, his teeth not quite white but white enough. Shining, square. She hadn't seen them in a while. Chewing gum, she used to think, chewing gum squares. 'I was thinking, girl . . . sometimes, after you left, these days, what a man like your grandfather would think of us now. He never got to see independence. He didn't know whether the people became free. What happened to his country. Adopted country . . . but some of these Chinese never saw it like that, you know, they loved it like it was their own. When I really think about him dying in the jungle . . . fighting, you know, *really* fighting, believing in something, I don't think he will be happy here now . . . not with me, not with how we do things . . . I don't know how he believed like that, where the passion came from.'

'Daddy . . .'

'Hold on, girl, let me finish. He seemed to love it, this island. This country . . . where does that love come from, you think? I also don't know. I have been thinking, girl, what would it be like to . . . to be ok here. To just be okay.'

Shadows played on the fridge in the kitchen. Mummy walked out alone, a saucer with a hardboiled egg in each hand. She placed one saucer in front of Maxim, the other in front of Daddy, and sat on a chair opposite them.

'If you want, girl. Don't want, is okay. Mummy eat for you.'

The egg glistened on the plate, a perfectly cooked, perfectly white egg, cooked not by Kak Isma, but by Mummy herself, like she had done years ago when they used to come back from the club after the tennis-squash-tennis routine she and Daddy did, Mummy watching at the sides, a perpetually amused squint on her face.

Daddy popped the egg into his mouth and chewed, his mouth open, as though he wasn't tasting the egg but still thinking.

'Kong ah,' Mummy said, 'better chew nicely ah.'

Daddy smiled. 'Next week, we go to KL, okay or not?'

Mummy touched her hair. 'Can also.'

And, as if they understood each other perfectly, no more needed to be said.

Maxim bit the top half of her egg and stared at her mother. Suspecting a pair of eyes on her, she looked back, and they smiled at each other, suddenly, unprepared for the tender exchange. As she bit into the egg again, a pond slowly formed within her. It grew larger and deeper, its dark green waters very still. No fish, no water snakes, no waterlilies. Only deep, still waters. Dark. So deep it was depthless; Mummy's pond, filling her to the brim on the inside. She smiled sadly at Mummy, and as though Mummy knew the smile, knew where it was coming from—that deep dark pond they now shared—she smiled back. Almost proud, no, not proud, more a smile of something else, a smile with some happiness, no, more than that, another thing, a more mature thing, a thing that came later, *afterwards*, much later than all the things that had to come first, trudging through a jungle, lost, lonely, scared, then seeing the lights of a house and finding the thing you had been looking for—that moment of *finding*, and after that, all the happenings and all the people who had brought you there are suddenly so sweet to you, and you are so thrilled that they are there and have been there with you all along, and you had only misunderstood everything before the moment of *finding*, when actually, these people are not mistakes you have to put up with but *actual* people with *actual* lives and beating hearts just like you, troubles just like you, struggles just like you, and they, like you, also only want to live and see it through till the end. Gratitude, that was what it was. The thing growing on Mummy's lips, a smile of giving thanks.

*

The young girl thumps her feet in the mud.

'Why are you doing that, silly Kalyani?' Pushpanayagi asks. The girl has two strings of flowers in her hair. She jumps up and down, splashing mud on her dress. Around them, the trees are wet and birds, swallows, fly low and rise again.

'It is to play, that's why.'

'We must go back to the house, or Amma will think we have been kidnapped.'

'Let her think what she wants. I am going to play in this mud.'

Pushpanayagi pinches the girl's ear and drags her through the mud, across a small field of weeds, past the thatched-roof huts.

'Oh ay, Pushpanayagi Rasalingam!' a lady shouts from her hut, 'teaching the girl a lesson again, I see! Ya, ya, you have to do it like this. Otherwise, she will grow up not knowing the difference between a pot and a ladle.'

A group of children straggle behind Pushpanayagi and her sister. They throw marigold flowers at them.

'Shoo! Shoo! Go back home. You are real trouble, you children. Can't you see I have to take Kalyani home? I can't take you home as well!'

Pushpanayagi stops to collect a few limes that have fallen on the ground. 'At least, I bring home something for Amma. What have you got? A dirty dress and dirty feet. Make sure you use the well water before you go inside'.

'Why should I?'

'Because I said so. Amma will beat you if not. Do you want to get whipped?'

'No, no. Don't say that, Akka. I was only playing'.

'This is not a time for playing. I am not so young anymore, but what do I have to do? You see me going to our farm every morning, don't you? What do you think I do there? Play?'

'Maybe. How do I know? Maybe you dance around the trees with the dancers from the other day.'

'Those dancers can only dance sometimes. Not every day. Not like what I have to do, working hard every day. So, you must listen to me and not get your dress dirty.'

They pass more huts and a few people, squatting on the steps of their homes. One man spits out little red blobs onto the ground. 'Hey, hey, Pushpanayagi Rasalingam, our woman has a mango for your mother. Wait a while. She will bring it out for you.'

Pushpanayagi grips her sister's hand while they wait, but the girl labours to wriggle herself free.

'Here is your mango. Make sure all three of you have some. It is not so sweet, but it will do,' the old lady of the house says. Pushpanayagi takes the mango and off they go again, past the wood apple and the jacaranda trees, a field of lime trees, two temples, and a Shiva shrine until they arrive at a narrow bend in the path and they are almost home. A white man on a horse nods at them.

'Give me a sweet!' her sister instructs the man.

'Don't do that, Kalyani! He's not here to give you sweets.' She tightens her grip of Kalyani's hand.

The man gallops away and the horse neighs.

'Don't do things like that anymore. Are you listening? These people don't understand what you want. You cannot make them give you a simple sweet. Only *they* can force people to do things. That is why my back aches and Amma tells me that I will never have children because all that farm work has broken my body. You want to end up like me? Better be careful then.' She pulls the girl's plaits as they walk and the girl whines like a goat. Bleehhh. Bleehhh. Bleehh. Two goats wait for them at their hut. Their mother is getting ready to go to the river to wash clothes.

'Oh ay, naughty girls! Where have you been? You will get kidnapped if you are not careful. We have nothing here and you can still do all these things. What will happen if I die? Will you know how to take care of yourselves?' Their mother pushes the goats out of her way and leaves with a bundle of clothes in her basket.

'I am hungry,' Kalyani says.

'Eat the mango.'

'I don't want the mango. I want something salty.' Kalyani folds her arms and pouts.

'There's nothing else for you. Eat the mango,' Pushpanayagi says, shaking her head.

'Cut the mango for me, please.' Her pout stiffens in place.

'You are old enough. You can do it. Here, take this knife. I will watch you as you cut.' Pushpanayagi gently holds out the knife.

The girl moans as she takes the knife. 'Why do you have to go out every morning? I thought only chickens get up that early.'

'I told you. If I do not work, then we will have nothing. Amma is not so young anymore, so she can't work as much.'

'But I thought we have nothing.'

'That is true. But we have a little bit more than nothing. One or two more ants, something like that.'

'Why do you steal books from Mr. Popper's house?'

'Chaik! You naughty girl. Have you been spying on me?'

'I was bored, so I followed you the other day, when you went there to clean. I saw you putting three–four books into your bag. What are those books?'

'I will show you when you are older. That's not stealing. That's borrowing.'

'Then when you put the books inside your bag, why did you look like when you pull the cat's tail?'

'Don't ask too many questions, child. I am seeing how I can help this family in my own way. If I work on this barren land for too long, we will never get anything more.'

'When will you get married?'

'What is wrong with you?'

'Amma said that nobody will marry you because you are so old already. Amma said that maybe one day, if we are lucky, you will marry when the time is right. So, I want to know, is the time right?"

'Chaik! Don't say such things. I will not get married. Can't you see I am already thirty-four years? From now on, I will take care of you and Amma. That's all I will do.'

'Like old maid Saraswathi.'

'Better than her! I will read all the books in Mr. Popper's library. You like reading, don't you?'

'I hate it. My head aches when I read. This mango is sour. That old woman must hate us.'

'Why do you say that?'

'She gives us sour fruit.'

'That is not her fault.'

'Then whose fault is it?'

'Why must it be anybody's fault?'

'It is God's fault.'

Pushpanayagi slaps the girl.

The moon appears in the dark, clear night, then the sun beams in the sky, and later, the moon comes again and goes, and the sun, two more moons, two more suns. Pushpanayagi cannot, will not sleep.

'Akka!' 'Akka!' The dead child screams all night and all day, screaming, pleading for help, but Pushpanayagi cannot save the drowning child. 'Akka! Akka!' The gasping, the small eyes squeezing shut, the pure, absolute fear on the young face. 'Akka! Akka!' But Pushpanayagi is motionless on the banks of the river. She cannot swim, does not know what to do, what she must do.

'Help!' she shouts, 'Help!' But there is no one there. They are alone, by the river in the forest. She closes her eyes, walks into the water, and prays that, somehow, her feet will know what to do, but the water gets deeper and deeper, and her body sinks, her eyes meet the water, her arms go everywhere, and she pushes herself back, somehow, she pushes herself safely back to the shore, and gasps. Kalyani! Kalyani! But the water has taken the child. Kalyani! There is only silence now, and the drowsy song of a river-bird.

'There is nothing more for you to do here, Pushpanayagi,' her mother says, 'even your sister is dead.'

'The farm is not doing well. You are hearing?' Kanagalingam Mama says.

But Pushpanayagi cannot speak. She glances at her mother and at her mother's brother with a fallen, faraway look.

'When you are in that other land,' her mother says, 'you and Mama can send back money. You cannot stay here anymore, Pushpanayagi, doing nothing.'

'Tell me, Pushpanayagi. Which man is going to marry you? You are so old now, not even a cripple will want you as his wife'.

'Yes, Pushpanayagi,' her mother says, 'listen to your Mama. No one in this village or the next village wants to marry you. Listen to your Mama.'

'I am a kind man. I am willing to marry you and take you to the other land.'

'How is this other land, Thambi?'

'There are houses there, Akka. Real houses. Not huts. The white man prefers that place to Ceylon. He lets them build proper houses. There is no mud there.'

'How can there be no mud?'

'It is a good land, Akka. Some are calling it Malaya.'

'But I have not heard of anybody else going to Malaya, Thambi.'

'The Indians are already going. There are many plantations there. It is a rich place. People here don't know yet. We will be among the first ones from Ceylon to go. We are lucky. I have made friends with the British. They will take care of us when we get there.'

'It is settled. Pushpanayagi will marry you and you will take care of her in the other land.'

'What will you give me, Akka?'

'You can take two cows. I have a necklace too. It has one or two pearls on it.'

'Very well. We don't have money for a big ceremony. We will do it quietly and quickly. And then we will go. On the big ship.'

Ship! Ship! The ship is breathing so loudly. One hundred, two hundred people. Waiting, like her. Waiting, walking, talking, goodbye, write to me, come back later on another ship, goodbye, goodbye!

Where is he? Where is he? Ship, the big ship!

A woman beats a drum and sings.

Take me to my mother's land. Ai oh, Ma Durga, Take me to my mother's land, The time has come for me to go home. Ai oh, Ma Durga . . . Ma Durga, Ma Durga, I have been waiting for too long . . .

'Lady, are you going on this ship or not?' a white man asks Pushpanayagi.

'Yes, yes. But let us wait until this woman has stopped drumming.'

'You silly people. You either get on or not. We can't be waiting around for you to finish listening to asinine songs.' He walks away and the woman stops playing her drums. Now, she only sings in low, mournful tones.

Take me to my mother's land. Ai oh, Ma Durga. Take me to my mother's land, I have cried too many tears. Ai oh, Ma Durga . . . Ma Durga, Ma Durga, I have gone too far from home . . .

A whistle blows. Where is he? Where is he?

Loud sounds are coming out of the ship. The poor ship is trying to *breathe*.

'So are you getting on, lady?' the white man asks again.

'Yes, in a short while. I am waiting for someone.'

'The ship will start moving in a few minutes.'

'Okay. Thank you.'

Tall people, short people, fat people, thin people. They are all going on the ship. The big ship like a rakshasa. Hide! Hide! In between two fat women. The big men will not see. Bend the whole body, make the body small so they won't see.

'Thank you.'

'Thank you.'

'Thank you.'

Inside the ship, are they looking? Can they see no ticket in her hand? Move, move! Where is he? Is he that man? That man? That man? That man? No, no, no. He is not coming, he is not coming.

She goes out onto the deck. The ship starts to move. At the harbour were crowds, and him.

There he is. Standing and looking. Looking and smiling. Smiling and waving. *At her.* At her, seeing her go on the ship, away from the village, from the land, from the farm, from Amma, from Kalyani in the water.

Days and days. Cold, salty nights. Stars, so many stars. Big moon, thin moon. Wind colder than early morning well water. Water, water, big waves, no waves, Kalyani's face. Akka, Akka, will you see *tigers* there? People there will be like us? Akka, Akka, where are you *going*? Don't leave me, Akka. Come into the water with me. The water is too cold. I cannot *breathe.* Come for me, come for me. I am scared. The water is *black.* Take me also. I want to go also. Akka, I want to go! I am so sleepy, so sleepy, I cannot open my eyes.

A horn blows. Her feet touch the ground, her mouth tastes the hot salty air. The trees look like the trees in the village. But there is something else here, something strange. The air smells of another kind of soil. Yellow men, light brown, dark brown men, pale-skinned women, women darker than her, stand around, laugh, talk, eat, stare and stare at the new people coming off the ship. A rooster crows. She picks up her cloth bag, grips it tightly, looks at no one, and walks into the crowd.

*

Once in a while, when the business of university life had momentarily ceased and there was little left to do in the city, Maxim returned to the island. On her first day back, she could be seen—and, indeed, her fellow islanders *did* see her—hiking up the hill to Yalpanam, outfitted in flowing printed skirts and blouses with animal faces, dangling feather earrings, bright-coloured leather shoes, a strange new creature, the islanders felt, a *city person*. She'd stand before the freshly painted gate of Yalpanam, eye the garden indulgently, a small, contented smile on her face, unlock the gate with a key Hadi had cut for her, and enter the grounds like the university student she was, returning home. She ran up the dirt path, an action somehow incongruous with her outfit and, usually, would not go further than the veranda, for the old woman had taken to sitting in a large armchair on the veranda, drinking milky tea, reading the newspapers with an expression of deep satisfaction as though she had found out a secret about something important.

'Do you *know*, Max,' she'd say when Maxim had sat down to her own cup of milky tea, 'the Americans were thinking of Mara, the Demon when they voted? They wanted to face him so they voted for him.'

'And, Max, we *must* send some money to the Middle East. Go and find out where. Then, tell Hadi to transfer the money.'

'Today they reported about one family with *nothing* for Hari Raya. We must give them something.'

'Go and find out about those refugees who have come from Burma. See if we can send them some pencils and books. Of course, food, also.'

Maxim would listen, nod, sometimes kiss the old lady's forehead, and say, 'We can't be giving everyone something, Auntie.

You don't have much anyway. Pick one thing that is meaningful for you.'

It was part of their routine, this passionate discovery of the world by the old woman, kept in check by the vigilant wisdom of the university student. But even in such routines, a kernel of something true and possible exists. Deep in the altruistic awakening of the old woman, the non-identical twin of her epic yearnings to help was waiting to reveal itself on a day both unremarkable and significant.

Perhaps struck, finally, by Maxim's words, or perhaps by the stirrings of her own heart, on a day unremarkable and significant, the sun not blazing, not benign, just nice, Pushpanayagi set the newspapers down, unlocked the front gate, left it wide open—a dramatic gesture, some might say—and announced to Hadi and Maxim, to the birds she felt were listening, that she would be offering her garden and her teaching services to anyone who wished to learn the art of planting vegetables and flowers, free of charge. Flyers were promptly printed and stuck on lampposts and bus stops around the island and, soon, two, then three people appeared at Yalpanam. They walked in casually, easily, for the gate was still wide open, and weeks later, these three people—a middle-aged bachelor, a retired headmistress, and a deaf teenager—sat with their teacher on the veranda after a day of studying seeds and soil, and between sips of milky tea, they planned their flower show. Heliconias, anthuriums, roses, lilies, orchids, they said, in pots here, curling around a post there, near the pumpkin patch.

Need it be said what the earth did? Well, the earth, by itself, did not do much. But the underground spirits rose and the spirit of the flowers soared from the ground and flooded the garden with unimaginable fragrance. Flowers, flowers, everywhere. The show itself was grand, poorly attended, but grand. The handful of people—Hadi, Maxim, her father, the mother of the deaf teenager, the curious ex-colonel who lived down the road and, it must also be said, the various ghosts dwelling on the land—each one of these people, and the ghosts, looked at the flowers with a steady peace in their hearts, and they smiled as if they had unleashed the secret joy stashed away in their bodies. No, it wasn't a time for secrets, for anything hidden. No, there were too many orchids and roses to delight their eyes and noses, to reveal the untouched cavities in their unseen selves. And when they walked onto the veranda and saw the opulent spread of food—purple jellies, bowls of noodles, a mound of curry puffs, catered from a friend of Hadi's at Market Square—Maxim's father exclaimed, 'It's like the garden of Eden.'

'Eden,' the old woman said as she walked back indoors, the show over. 'It is like Eden also, maybe,' she said to no one in particular, and, really, to nothing in particular, for there were no longer shadows sleeping in the walls and darting around the house, and the old lady had stopped talking to the ants and the lizards. She munched on a curry puff and laughed. 'Eden,' she said, 'Eden? No lah. There's no such thing as Eden. These flowers also will be dying. Of course there will be new roses but it won't be *exactly* the same, and anyway . . .' She took another bite of the curry puff, chewed thoughtfully, and swallowed. 'Anyway, why would anyone want the exact same roses again, put in a pot the exact same way? Carbon copy, they used to say. Replica. Ha! Ha! Ha!' She took another curry puff from the plate Maxim had prepared for her before she left, a habit she still kept after all these years. 'Not replica,' she said, sniffing the curry puff, '*honour*, maybe. All the things that had been there before this one, *honoured*. All the flowers that had died so the new flowers could come, *honoured*. Eden . . . yes, I think so. That's the real Eden. Actually, the big fat rose everyone liked today had all the dead roses in it. That's why the boy's mother liked it so much. Two tears nicely came down her face.' She bit into the curry puff, ate it with relish, and rose to prepare for bed.

The old lady will sleep deeply tonight, and for many nights to come. Her days will be long, her nights deep. Such is the way she has inherited from the land, from her own memories, from the objects in the sky she faithfully observed each day and night—the sun, the clouds, the moon, the stars, the birds, the butterflies, and the flying insects. She will deepen and open, more and more as the years pass, to the inevitable darkness and the inevitable light that waxes and wanes and creates time. She will have forgotten much of space and sense, only that there is earth beneath her feet and solid walls around her, but she will know that she too is something in space, an actual thing rich with risings and fallings, but also a non-thing existing nowhere and everywhere.

Thirteen years from now, at the ripe age of two hundred, when she looks up from her bed and sees the matured, lightly painted face of the girl who had, one day, dared to enter her home, Pushpanayagi will shed those final tears that often come when death looms and, before her last breath is released, she will say to the young woman, 'The walls need paint.'

A permit will be requested by Hadi to bury the old woman at the back of the house, close to the bones now resting quietly in the soil, and when enough time has passed, Maxim will look carefully at Yalpanam, inspect it for holes and fractures, rotting wood, and broken windows, and supervise the restoration of the house. It will take two years after the old woman's death for a moment thick with muggy afternoon air and loud chirping from the veranda sunbirds when Maxim will say to Hadi, 'I feel it's time for a change. We need to do something with this house. Let more people see it.'

No, Yalpanam today isn't a museum. There would be nothing to show—not really. Nothing, in any case, that the eyes can see. Who would see air-beings and water-beings and beings of the soil? Islanders drive their cars up the hill not to commune with them, but to feast their eyes on the paintings and the handicrafts created by local youth. Something in these islanders is touched when they walk through the front doors, now painted lime-green. They lift a tiny kampong house made of matchsticks (*Aishah Mahmud, 12 years old, Sekolah Rendah Pulau Arang*); they look at

Market Square bustling with life across from the still blue waters of the sea (*Darshini Lingam, 15 years old, Sekolah Tinggi Pantai Timarara, oil on canvas)*; they smile at an old Malay man standing beneath the clock tower in town (*Paul Gomez, 14 years old, Sekolah Tinggi Pantai Timarara, acrylic on board*). Afterwards, they scout out the owner of the gallery, who often sits at a desk beside a series of paintings of the house itself, and they say, 'Thank you, Miss Cheah. Who knew children could be so clever?'

Afterwards, when they have seen and openly marvelled at representations of their island, the ones who have heard the whisperings of the wind will pause at the gate, turn around, and marvel at the house. One or two will point at the stained-glass window of the topmost room and their hearts will be filled with an ineffable sensation. Now, all at once, they recognize something they have always known, but have not been able to see. As they slowly walk away, they, like the old woman before them, will feel the earth, indescribably real beneath their shoes, as if for the first time. They will feel the weight of their feet, the breeze upon their skin, the light upon their faces as strange new homes made of indestructible unblemished love, as sensations no longer dormant in the fields of their bodies, but stupendously real; as if all prior sensations had been rehearsals. Yes, a voice within will say, yes, it cannot be any other way.

But—this is to come. More arguments and tears, lonely nights and tremendous laughter, and divorces and deaths must be given their chance to soar and ebb before a light enters and they remember that time exists differently in each heart. Then, perhaps on a quiet day, perhaps on a day filled with the sounds of life, but in a most ordinary way—as ordinary as a set of eyes glancing at a setting sun—they may see what has always, already been, that which is.

Acknowledgement

I would like to extend a big thank you to Sivagurunathan Rasiah and Carina Hart for reading the manuscript and offering their insightful suggestions and perspectives. Thank you to Thatchaayanie Renganathan for her astute editorial eye.

My deep appreciation also goes to my dearest colleagues at the University of Nottingham Malaysia who supported me during the sabbatical I took to complete this novel.

I am grateful to Nora Nazerene Abu Bakar for believing in this book, and to the team at Penguin Random House Southeast Asia who worked on getting *Yalpanam* ready for publication.

To my dear friend and editor, Chuah Guat Eng: the time we spent together on this novel was priceless, deep and life-changing. Thank you for being a wonderful mentor and friend.